I0681886

Denali
A Dylan Baker Thriller

This is a work of fiction. Names, characters, places businesses and incidents either are the product of the authors' imaginations or are used fictionally. Any resemblance to actual persons, living or dead, locations, businesses and events is entirely coincidental.

Published by Mt. Hood Press
Portland, Oregon

Manufactured in the United States of America

ISBN 978-0-9772608-3-6

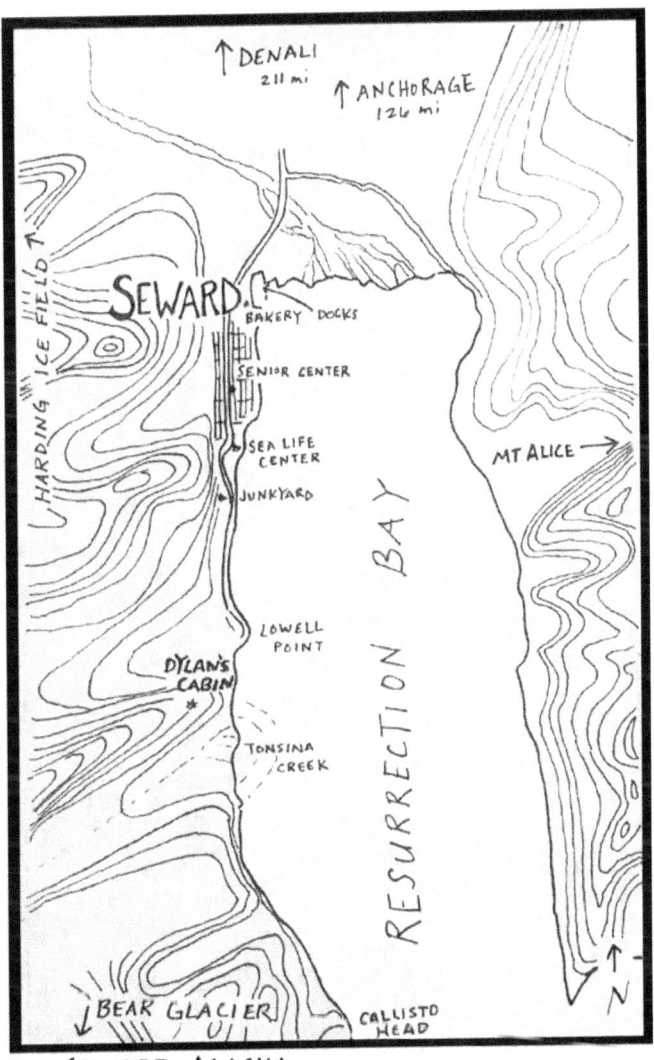

↑ DENALI
211 mi

↑ ANCHORAGE
126 mi

HARDING ICE FIELD ↑

SEWARD

BAKERY   DOCKS

SENIOR CENTER

SEA LIFE
CENTER

JUNKYARD

MT ALICE →

RESURRECTION BAY

LOWELL
POINT

DYLAN'S
CABIN

TONSINA
CREEK

↑ N

↓ BEAR GLACIER   CALLISTO
HEAD

SEWARD, ALASKA   EACH INCH EQUALS APPROXIMATELY 2 MILES

Denali

Tyler Blackthorne

A Dylan Baker Thriller

1

. . . .

PETER IVANOV HAD NEVER KILLED a person. He looked down at the familiar revolver in his hand and tried to imagine what it would be like to fire a bullet into his best friend.

He would make it quick. That would be a kindness. He returned his gaze to his target: the shadow of Dylan Baker inside a jewel-box of a log cabin nestled among huge moss-covered spruce trees.

Nearby, Sergeant Rolf looked down at his personal defense weapon. "Can't keep shit clean here. This Alaska mud is worse than my first boot camp in Georgia."

Rolf smeared his spit around the grip with his sleeve, diluting the dirt into a runny brown sheen.

With his two counterparts, Sergeant Rolf stood at the edge of the clearing. Against the backdrop of a Sitka spruce forest and the distant view of the snow-capped fjord, Rolf's black uniform, body-builder bulk, and extravagant gun were clearly out of place.

"Sergeant, your bodily fluids should not sully that noble weapon," snapped Captain Zwart. He always delivered his reprimands with a biting grace. The comment was not lost on his inferior. Zwart, too, appeared out of place, like a palm tree in the pines. Without taking his eyes off Rolf's weapon, Zwart drew a pressed handkerchief out of the crisp, starched pocket of his uniform and handed it to his man. The sergeant went to work on the muddy grip, applying his enormous strength awkwardly from their squatting lookout.

To an onlooker, Peter may have appeared to be a local guide. It would have been a good guess. Peter's jacket looked as if it had spent years in temperate Alaskan rainforests. Behind his blank expression and watery eyes dwelled a veiled disdain for his companions. While Zwart and Rolf engaged with each other, Peter's gaze remained focused on the shadows of Dylan's movements.

Zwart refused his handkerchief back with his posture, and Sgt. Rolf tossed it on the trail and drawled, "Let's get this done. I want to see if the tail in Alaska is better than Alabama."

"Mr. Ivanov?" Zwart turned his attention to Peter.

Peter didn't take his eyes off Dylan's shadow, but could feel the captain staring at him.

"Mr. Ivanov, I assure you that despite his diction, Sergeant Rolf is highly capable. You needn't carry out these orders on your own. In fact, I prefer you don't. Had my client not indulged your sentimentality, I would have forbid the interference."

Peter looked ahead, expressionless.

Rolf, uncomfortable with the silence, glanced around at the view of the mountains jutting out into the ocean.

Zwart squatted from their hideout with the poise of a dignitary at a dinner party. "For example, on our last mission, Mr. Rolf expertly left seven men and their wives dead with clean head shots. Only one silenced bullet necessary per target. He can also take his time when necessary.

"My intel says that today's target is a good friend of yours."

Rolf shifted his ox-like bulk and grunted.

Zwart changed his message. "Mr. Ivanov, these mountains, what do you call them?"

As the shadow in the cabin moved about, Peter tracked the target. "When the mountains go into the sea like that, we call them drowning mountains." He paused. "I'm the right man for this job. Dylan will give me the Bible because he trusts me. I'll kill him with honor."

"There's nothing dishonorable in an honest day's work for Mr. Rolf, either, Mr. Ivanov. And trust isn't the only way to get what you want." Zwart calmly smiled, as though amused. He ran his thumb over his own immaculate Sig Sauer 553.

Peter turned to face Zwart and Rolf. "I'll get the Bible and kill Dylan." He rose with determination that didn't quite mask his fear, checked his well-worn pistol, and walked into the clearing.

2

. . . .

HE HADN'T TRIMMED his beard for 10 years. In an hour, he would chop it back to Alaska normal, and the whole world would turn inside out.

If he could have looked ahead to the next 30 minutes, he would have left everything and just melted back into the wilderness.

Dylan Baker could not see into the future, except to know this would be a great day to take the dogs hunting near Bear Lake.

As he set the fire in his chilly hand-made cabin, he noticed his routine proceeded without conscious thought. Let the new flames consume the kindling and heat the bigger pieces, watch the flickering light reflect off the buttery log walls, and smell the sizzling moose sausages.

Dylan knew that by the time the coffee was ready, the sun would crest the mountains and send golden light through the windows to reflect off the tools that allowed Dylan to live in the wilderness: everything from fishing and hunting equipment to climbing apparatus and a small engine repair kit. Ever since the accident, Dylan had lived off the land and become more Alaskan than anyone else within rifle shot of Seward.

Outside, Bergen whined at the doggie door. Dylan smiled. Would he ever be able to teach that dog anything?

As he approached the door, it clicked, and Bergen burst into the room, knocking over anything within reach of his busy tail. Old Doolie, his dog who had undoubtedly unlocked the doggie door, quietly entered with a "look what I must bear" expression on his noble canine face.

While Bergen would push his curious nose into any situation, Doolie would hang back, analyze the variables, and wait for Dylan to give him a command. Every fiber of Doolie's German shepherd body longed to do what Dylan suggested.

Sadly, Dylan thought, Doolie's getting too old for some of the tasks I need. Dylan moved past Bergen's wild enthusiasm to offer old Doolie some love. Ten years is a long time in a dog's life —even longer for a man escaping his past.

Dylan attempted to enter the dawn outside his cabin without tripping over Bergen's Golden Labrador Retriever antics. As he pumped his water, the handle squeak disturbed the peace lingering in cottony mists clinging to the dark trees and pewter-colored bay. As soon as the metallic clatter of squeaking pump stopped, stillness rushed in to fill the void.

Looking around the tree-ringed bay from the cabin's cliff-top perch, Dylan listened to the ordinary outside noises that anyone could hear, but he also took in the subtle sounds that only a long-time resident, intimate with this part of the wilderness, would know. Living off the land took an exceptional set of skills that Dylan had honed out of necessity.

Locals whispered that he lived like he was born to the life, or that he must have had some kind of supernatural native master to show him everything. Dylan laughed at this. He sure had a master all right, but his master, a climbing wonder named Sid Green, had never returned from a mountain climbing disaster of Dylan's making. Memories of Sid and the other dead on that climb haunted Dylan whenever the darkness became too much.

As two resident ravens quarreled out of habit, Bergen chased a butterfly, and Dylan planned how he'd cut his magnificent beard without scissors. Sometimes Dylan felt that everything he did was to the "it would work" standard. Living away from civilization required he jury-rig nearly everything that gave him essentials or comfort. Outsiders who knew him, saw him as a man of supreme wilderness grace, but Dylan knew he too often made do.

Bergen tipped over a stack of skin-stretchers in his wild pursuit of a vole. The slow progress on Bergen's training made Dylan wonder just how good a woodsman he really was. Doolie burned to please his master and had responded perfectly to Dylan's training regimen since he was a pup. So far, big Bergen lacked the discipline.

Anyone walking into the carefully built cabin would notice right away that Dylan had a place for everything, from the tools of a woodsman to the latest outdoor sports and gun magazines. A non-Alaskan would wonder at the amazing skill set of this man. His home was so beautifully crafted for the wilderness; people would say Dylan was a master outdoorsman, designer-builder and engineer.

His breakfast ready, Dylan sat at his hand-hewn table with a sense of peace enveloping him. His coffee steamed fragrantly, the sausages and rice waited for him. Fingers of golden light glowed in the lake mists. While it never really gets dark during summer, the high sharp mountains framing the Kenai Fjords keep the actual sunbeams from the cabin until sixish.

Doolie rested his head on his master's knee as Dylan munched and reread the application papers he'd signed the week before. It had been so long since he'd signed anything, but his friend Peter had assured him the new job would not pull Dylan out of the woods.

Imagine, becoming an animal surveyor for the Department of Fish and Game. Years ago Dylan had moved to the forest outside Seward to disappear from everything. Seward, about 100 miles south of Anchorage near the Kenai Fjords, offered everything Dylan needed to purge himself of the guilt over the deaths of so many on Denali.

Since moving, survival occupied his entire existence, but now Dylan found he was beginning to care again. He was caring enough to dip his toe into the waters of civilization. Dylan found himself concerned about the sustainable harvest of the bear populations. Peter, being the head of the Seward field office for Alaska Fish and Game, needed someone to supply the data that would allow the Anchorage boys to set the bear quota.

How often the two men had spent an evening together, planning a hunt, reloading rifle cartridges and arguing about the bear population!

Peter, looking like a sad limp string bean, would press his point of view with his gloomy, pale eyes. Dylan thought Peter looked sad even when he landed a trophy salmon two seasons ago. If Dylan were an actual employee of Fish and Game, his surveys and reports would carry real weight.

Now to cut the beard. The only mirror Dylan could find was hidden in an emergency kit in his collection of mountaineering gear. It was a thin, credit card sized piece of polished steel used for signaling. Propping the tiny mirror on a shelf with some bow-hunting gear, Dylan looked at who he was.

What he saw was an ordinary man in so many ways: slender and wiry from living off his hunting and fishing, and dressed in the fleece/Gore-Tex outdoor clothing that he bought by bartering his guiding and handyman skills. His skin appeared older than his near forty years, but his chestnut beard and hair were unstreaked with gray. People told him his pale eyes made him appear wise, but Dylan didn't think he had made the best choices in his life. He picked up the crescent-shaped ulu knife.

Peter had explained to him that his shovel-sized beard should be trimmed down to an inch or two for his ID photograph. If he looked too wild, Peter might have trouble with his picky, born-in-the-lower-48 supervisor. The Alaska Department of Fish and Game does not employ cavemen.

Inches of multi-hued beard fell onto the bench below the mirror. Dylan was admiring his new short beard when Bergen spotted a squirrel and crashed against a window barking furiously. Dylan contemplated locking the dog-door he had designed to keep the critters out, but allow his dogs access the outdoors. He didn't want Bergen running off, but knew that Doolie would keep him under control. Dylan was going to hike the five miles into town for his ID picture.

Dylan pulled up the trap door leading to his ice cellar. Grooming done, it was time to put away the uncooked sausage and do a little reorganizing while down here. In the winter, Dylan would put tubs of water out to freeze and dump the blocks down the outside trap door. This ice would last nearly the whole summer and keep Dylan's food cold. The melt water would follow a crevice under the cabin and run down the nearby cliff face.

At this point in the summer, there was not much ice left, but not much meat either. The fall hunts and freezes would fill this cellar in a month. Although he seldom needed money, Dylan had a can full of gold coins buried by his outhouse. A man down at the docks traded Dylan a quarter-ounce Chinese bullion coin, called a Panda, for every kilo of bear gall bladders he brought in.

Dylan never hunted a bear unless it was for his own cellar or a client, and he knew it was illegal to sell the bear parts, but it seemed wasteful to just throw out valuable gall bladders.

Doolie shadowed Dylan downstairs and solemnly watched as Dylan moved the cured bear and moose meat closer to the remaining ice. Dylan moved the smoked salmon to the warmer areas of the ice cellar. Upstairs, Dylan heard a crash and frantic barking as Bergen undoubtedly spied another squirrel scampering by the window.

Dylan wondered if he should take one of these moose shanks down to Peter. They might not last until this ice melted, and Peter loved the way Dylan cured his meat.

At the next crash upstairs, Doolie did his arthritic lope up the stairs and added his deep bark to Bergen's.

Who could that be? Dylan wondered. His only visitors were Peter and Shorty. Peter wouldn't hike in if he expected Dylan to meet him at the office. Shorty had a bad hip and only came out when he needed Dylan to fix his boat. That boat was purring last week.

"Dylan?" Peter's voice floated down the stairs.

"Hey Peter. What's up? I thought I was coming to you." Dylan mounted the stairs to see Peter looking out his window and down at the bay while Bergen tried to climb into Peter's non-existent lap.

Dylan smiled, waiting to see what Peter would say about his neatly trimmed beard.

Later, Dylan would remember that when Peter turned to face him, if possible, his eyes looked sadder than ever.

The pistol Peter held, a Smith & Wesson .357 revolver, looked oddly out of place pointed at Dylan's face.

3

Ten Years Earlier

. . . .

THE VAST MASSIF expanse called Denali, known to some as Mt. McKinley, lay cloaked in pristine winter snow, sparkling in the morning sunshine. With a summit at over 20,000 feet and a vertical rise of 18,000, it's the tallest mountain in the world from base to top.

In the harsh environment above 12,000 feet, the winter temperatures often hit -100° F. Every winter attempt at climbing Denali ended in death until 1967. Since then over 100 lives have been taken by the mountain. It is said that only heroes or mad men climb this mountain in winter, but most think it's only the latter.

Yet, looking closely at an ice-protected winter base camp perched at 19,000 feet, it would become clear that four orange tents trembled in the frigid wind. One trembled more than the others.

A couple finished breathless lovemaking under the fluffy warmth of a pair of zipped-together Arctic sleeping bags. Heather's skin glowed as she caught her breath. She kissed Dylan and playfully bit his ear. A slender green necklace graced her throat framed by her short-cropped blondish hair. Dylan, a man working unsuccessfully to put selfish athletic ambition second to his feelings for Heather, gently stroked her cheek.

Heather rested her head on Dylan's shoulder. "Where do you get your energy and how do you catch your breath at this altitude? You carried Boris's pack the last two hours yesterday."

Dylan smiled. "He must be bringing some bricks up here. His pack weighed a ton. You give me energy. You are so beautiful and together we set the love-making altitude record." Dylan smiled at his perfect fiancée.

"Everything has gone so well with this winter ascent." She carefully drew symmetrical circles on his chest with her finger until her smile changed and several shivers began distorting the circles.

Dylan noticed the difference as he pushed back a wayward strand of her hair, "You worry too much. I've planned for any foreseeable disaster. It's why we have all that gear cached at lower elevations. It's why I've climbed Denali so many times finding the perfect route and way points."

Heather snuggled into his chest, "You're right. I shouldn't worry." Unnoticed, Heather's necklace slid off her neck and into the folds of the sleeping bag.

"I've planned for any foreseeable disaster." Dylan spoke a little more slowly for emphasis.

Heather looked into Dylan's eyes. "Tell me again why you want to marry me."

Dylan pulled Heather close savoring the touch of her skin. Soon she'd be dressed in more layers than a giant onion. "Because I want you forever. I can't live without you."

Outside the tent a jovial Russian voice roared. "Dylan, time to move fast. We summit today."

The special moment was lost. It was time to abandon the warmth of their sleeping bags and begin the task of suiting up for climbing.

This trip was all about getting Boris to the summit and documenting his accomplishment with photographs and GPS data. Dylan inhaled deeply as he remembered last night's discussion. Huddled in their wildly flapping tent, Boris had wanted to abbreviate their rest time and reach the summit immediately, now that they were so close.

Sid, an expert climber, suggested resting overnight to give the weather a chance to moderate now that wind chills were approaching -60 and predicted to go much lower.

As always, Dylan sided with Sid. One usually sides with one's coach. Anyway, the summit was impossible to see, and the screaming Arctic winds nearly deafened them.

The men had pushed raisins into their ears to muffle the noise. "Boris, from here we have hundreds of meters of very steep, icy terrain left to go. If the weather was good, it would take us less than five hours.

Bad weather would mean it would take us 12 hours. We'll leave at dawn as we planned. You can wait until then."

LATER, AS THE SKY BRIGHTENED, the five climbers gathered around Dylan wearing only their daypacks and Arctic space suits.

Boris was a rounded archetype of a Slavic rich guy. Had his face been visible, his bushy eyebrows and mutton chop sideburns would have identified him as a coarse Russian tycoon.

Boris and the tall, longhaired Svetlana simmered at the delays. Boris had brought his wife so she could witness his glorious accomplishment. As a result, Boris had urged Dylan to bring Heather and Sid to bring Julie to keep Svetlana company, and had offered a staggering amount of money if the women came along.

Julie checked Sid's daypack. Sid, with his olive-colored skin, looked more like he belonged in the Caribbean than Alaska. He worked as a freelance photographer who mainly contributed to outdoor magazines and catalog photo shoots. Although Dylan was widely regarded as a world-class climber, he knew Sid was the far better alpinist.

Sid and Julie had just honeymooned in the Andes climbing and photographing a peak called Aconcagua. Outgoing and friendly, she was the perfect opposite of quiet and calm Sid. The only time Dylan had ever seen Sid animated was when he was talking about Julie. Dylan would laugh and say, "You guys are like the ice and rock, together you form a beautiful mountain peak."

Dylan took a moment to enjoy the view of the cloud-filled continent stretching to the horizon. Perhaps it was the golden sparkle of the sunrise or maybe it was the deceptive peacefulness of the scene, but somehow Dylan could sense an icy fierceness approaching this rare world.

After checking his radio for the latest weather broadcast and getting some very bad news, Dylan had to decide how to share the information with his indomitable client.

Dylan reluctantly returned to the situation at hand. He wasn't looking forward to the next few minutes. Through his protective gear Dylan shouted to be heard. "I just received an emergency alert on the radio. High winds and extreme low temperatures are expected. It should be here later today."

"We better get going then." It was clear Boris meant to summit.

"We are climbing on the leeward side of the mountain. The benefit of that is we have calmer winds. However, we also lose a visual check of the incoming weather. Boris, you can't tell how bad it's going to be. We'll have no better warning."

"We better get going then." Boris's tone indicated that he was unaccustomed to delays.

Heather leaned towards Julie, "Is it my imagination or do men frequently repeat themselves?"

Julie looked perplexed and then smiled. "Sometimes I find it difficult to differentiate the effects of reduced oxygen from what's normal for a guy."

Dylan took a deep breath, "I know this will disappoint you, but we need to start down to a lower altitude right now. It will take us several hours to summit and 30 minutes to get back to this sheltered area. The storm will be here by then. The lower camp is much safer."

"Nyet. We summit. I paid you, Mr. Best-Denali-Guide-in-the-World, to get me and my Svetlana to the summit in winter."

Heather tried to defuse the escalating situation. "He's the best guide because he knows how to keep his clients safe. I say we go down."

Dylan felt his love for Heather as she provided support. Julie may have been the best thing that ever happened to Sid, but she also introduced Heather to Dylan on an Italian photo shoot a year earlier. Despite her cheerleader good looks, Heather was rugged and smart. As the art director for a major climbing gear company, she had been all over the world and knew her way around a climbing site.

Sid glanced at the sky then towards the summit and then his photography equipment. Sid set down his camera gear pack. By this action, Dylan knew Sid didn't think a summit attempt would work. "Dylan's right,"

Sid said. "We need to get to a lower altitude as quickly as possible."

"Sid's agrees. We need to get to a lower altitude as quickly as possible. This is not a vote." An ominous sharp gust of wind swirled ice pellets around the party and added an emphasis to Dylan's words. Distant clouds hid the far off forests that grew below the permafrost.

Boris' look hardened.

4

· · · · · · · · · ·

"PETER? WHAT'S WITH THE GUN?"

Dylan's mind leaped into overdrive as he reviewed his training. If he is stuck clinging to a sheer rock face and there's no way down, go up. When a grizzly charges, a city dweller will run, but an experienced woodsman stands his ground.

But what do you do when your best friend points a gun at you? There was nothing in Dylan's experience to help him here. Suddenly the beard trim and moose shank were forgotten.

Dylan automatically changed his breathing pattern; a survival skill he had learned many years ago. Without conscious input, his breathing pattern became even and balanced.

Ten feet across the room, the powerful revolver came up to Dylan's face. From Dylan's perspective, the gun barrel looked big enough to fit a walnut down the muzzle. It was Peter's halibut gun. He used it to kill monster fish before they could knock someone out of the boat.

Peter was a good shot, and Dylan saw Peter's adam's apple bob like it did when he was about to squeeze off a shot. *My God! He's going to shoot!*

"Peter! Wait. What's wrong?"

"Dylan. Blood is . . ." Peter sobbed, but his aim was as unwavering as granite.

Bergen, unaware of the emotional hurricane in the room, continued to beg for attention from Peter, who, in the past, always had time to roughhouse.

"Peter, what blood? Put the gun down, and we'll solve this problem." *I need a weapon.*

Dylan eyed his gun closet. Locked. The bows were up on the wall to the right of Peter. The nearest knife was over in the utility area with the clean dishes. The crescent-shaped ulu is worthless as a throwing weapon.

He had a five-pound shank of cured moose in his left hand, but by the time he threw it, Peter could get off several shots from the trusty .357 caliber cannon in his hand. Dylan knew the revolver held 5 rounds. Peter usually kept low powder rounds in the revolver so if fired into a big fish, the bullet would not exit the fish's skull and punch a hole in his boat.

If Peter had loaded his gun with high-power hollow points, each hit could blow golf-ball sized chucks of his body away.

"Peter, what about blood?" *I've got to keep him talking.*

"It's thicker . . ."

"Peter? What are you trying to say? Blood is thicker than water?"

Peter sobbed again. His long face and watery eyes a caricature of gloom. "Dylan I don't want to do this, but what kind of man would I be if I let someone else take care of it?"

Bergen again stretched up to get some love from Peter.

"First, where's your Bible? I'm supposed to ask." Peter brushed away the enthusiastic Bergen.

"My . . ." Dylan's voice trailed off in confusion.

Bergen's left front paw suddenly caught on Peter's sleeve bending the dog's toe back. Bergen shrieked in sudden pain.

The big gun went down then fired. A huge crater opened up on the floor scattering gold-hewed wood slivers into the slanting sunshine: high power hollow points.

Dylan didn't recall throwing the moose shank. He remembered the sounds. The sound of meat and bone connecting with meat and bone. The sound of Bergen crying and the crash as Peter went down.

Dylan didn't remember pinning the revolver to the floor with his foot and sliding it away.

Peter was out. Finding himself unconsciously stroking his short beard, Dylan examined the knot swelling on Peter's head and wondered what he should do. *I should get him some ice, but maybe tie him up first.*

Peter Ivanov headed the Seward Satellite Office of Alaska Fish and Game.

He was a steady and reliable worker, but this best friend and hunting pal just tried to kill him.

Looking down at Peter, Dylan exhaled. Bergen whined and nudged his snout at Peter's unconscious form.

"Don't worry, Berg. He's alive, just knocked out." Dylan picked up the moose shank and admired the make-shift weapon, certain that it saved his life.

Unable to stop his own worrying, Dylan ran through what just happened. He wondered what could have made his friend, Peter Ivanov, a sympathetic man who's slow to action, wake up one morning and decide to kill. *Why was he talking about blood?*

Dylan couldn't think of a reason. The very day before, Peter and he had shared an afternoon beer at Yukon Dave's Pub to go over their plans for the year to come. Peter's droopy eyes had come to life as he detailed their work together.

Dylan would be making use of his knowledge of local geography and wildlife to survey. Peter, representing fish and game, would be Dylan's new boss.

Peter was a loyal friend, a trait Dylan assumed he picked up from his big Russian-American family. Peter was also fairly religious, a subject Dylan didn't care to fathom, but still he had always respected his friend's devotion. *I thought God-fearing men didn't murder.* It wasn't as if Dylan and Peter didn't quarrel. Dylan used to get irritated when Peter pestered him to "join society." And just yesterday they had argued over whether Dylan needed to trim his beard. But deep down Dylan had always believed that Peter wanted the best for him.

Why would anyone want to kill him—Dylan Baker? Dylan had few friends, and no enemies. Living in obscurity you don't expect conflict. Dylan avoided attention.

Although his lifestyle was unique, he didn't brag about his exploits. By now, his tenth year living in the woods, his life actually felt boring sometimes. Wake up, walk the dogs, prepare food, hunt and trade when necessary, get a beer with Shorty or Peter, do freelance mechanics for pocket change.

Dylan's days of fierce competition were over. In fact, few in Seward even knew about his days of athletic rivalries. He led a quiet life that in no way invited spontaneous murder.

A drop of meat juice left Dylan's hand and hit the floor. *Why did you pull a gun on me, Peter?*

A trained mountaineer and survivalist can think on his feet in high stress situations. Dylan was well trained. *You're self-reliant, but go for help.* He hoped Shorty would be in the store. Maybe Dylan should go right to the hospital. Realizing that Peter must be off his rocker, he should get him help as soon as possible.

If he took the well-worn trail down the hill to Seward, he could be there in a thirty minutes. He would meet no one on the trail since it led only to Dylan's cabin. There were countless ways down, but today, the regular path to the main hiking trails would be the wisest.

The dogs were chewing on the moose shank while Dylan pulled on a light yellow coat and slipped the revolver into his pocket. Dylan checked that his own guns were securely locked in his safe, and hurried out the back door of the cabin. The dogs would keep the unconscious and tied-up would-be murderer company.

He got as far as the end of the clearing. Two men blocked the trail. The first stranger's army fatigues were crisp. His beret balanced at a mean angle atop a tall, athletic body. The other stranger, thick-necked and built like an ox, wore all-black combat military fatigues. As if on cue, they brought up the barrels of their assault rifles.

Without thinking, Dylan's oval breathing focused his thoughts. *Why were military-type guys, carrying guns that looked like they came out of some science fiction movie, positioned here? Were they waiting for Peter to finish his deadly job? Did these men put Peter up to killing his best friend?*

His breathing steady and utterly calm, Dylan directly approached the men. If they had a description, they'd be expecting a shaggy-faced Dylan-the-mountain man, not a normal guy in a yellow jacket.

Speaking urgently Dylan closed the distance. "You're here. Good. Peter needs your help in there. He's holding down some kind of wild hairy man. Here, take this."

Dylan awkwardly held out Peter's halibut gun handle first. The tall guy let the barrel of his machine pistol drop as he collected Peter's gun.

"Wait here. Don't leave." Tall guy ordered. Then he and his ox-like comrade jogged over to the cabin.

Dylan stood there dumbly while the men followed standard military assault procedure to gain entry to the cabin. Dylan whistled to signal the dogs to leave through the doggy door and hoped that Bergen would abandon the moose shank and follow Doolie. Dylan did not doubt that these soldiers would shoot his dogs.

The moment the soldiers were inside, Dylan sprinted toward the cliff face on the lakeside of the cabin. It meant he would cross the view of Tall Guy and Oxman—if they happened to look out the cabin window. He wanted to crawl off the cliff and shimmy down to a protected ledge.

Doolie saw Dylan headed for the cliff, a short cut down to the lake unavailable to dogs. Doolie trotted left to the bay path. Bergen gracelessly. but joyfully dragging the moose shank, followed Dylan to the cliff face.

"Bergen, go with Doolie," Dylan commanded. Bergen, weighed down by the bone, attempted to leap near Dylan nearly tripping him, as they crossed the front of the house.

The ground near Dylan exploded as a series of four bullets hit the dirt in front of him. Dylan heard the tinkle of glass break where the bullets had shattered his window. A bumblebee stung his right shoulder. *Am I shot?*

Dylan cut toward the cabin where some shrubs gave cover and rolled onto his stomach just as the path behind him erupted with four fist-sized craters. More broken glass. Those guys had silencers on their weapons.

As Dylan rolled, he knew they would need to leave the house to get a good shot off now. With amazing speed, he sprinted over the last yards to the cliff edge and leaped off. The rock face seemed to detonate as if an explosive charge had been planted while the twang of ricocheting fully-jacketed bullets disturbed the morning.

Bergen, completely unaware of the dangers, had sharply cut back toward the bay path and ran in joyful pursuit of Doolie dragging the moose bone.

Dylan dropped to a small ledge two feet below the lip. He would be safe here for at least 45 seconds.

Tall Guy and Oxman would take that long to leave the cabin and cross the space to the cliff.

5

Ten Years Earlier

· · · · · · · · · · ·

ON THE NORTH side of the mountain, the climbing party was sheltered from the fierce southern winds, but also from the vision of the terrifying dark storm rushing at them.

With the dire predictions Dylan received over his weather band radio, he was afraid for himself as well as his party. Had he been able to actually see what was coming, he would know what it's like to see Death itself rushing forth on his swift black stallion.

Wind-driven ice pellets scoured the climbers' goggles, but Boris turned his head toward the summit and bellowed. "We are just hours from the top. I'm going with or without you." Boris motioned to Svetlana, and started up the final part of their doomed climb.

"No you're not. You signed an agreement." The urgency of the wind plus the intensity of his emotions challenged Dylan's calm as he yelled at Boris's back.

Boris rotated his entire body to look back, "I'm unsigning it."

Svetlana obediently started following Boris. Until she showed she could hold her own on a training hike, Dylan and Sid had resisted approving Svetlana for the Denali climb. Skinny and pale, Svetlana could wear a 50-pound pack and doggedly pull a sled up a 1,000 foot snow trail. Watching her stumble after Boris, Dylan regretted taking her on this trip. He regretted taking anyone up this mountain of death.

Heather stepped toward the departing pair and yelled into the screaming wind. "Boris! Svetlana! Come back. You'll get hurt."

Dylan echoed Heather's concerns. "Boris! Wait. We need to rope up."

Boris didn't indicate he'd heard them.

Stunned, Heather looked to Dylan. "What are you going to do?"

Dylan looked down as he weighed his options. "He'll probably get himself and Svetlana killed. I'd better stay with them. It will be easier than a rescue."

Sid surprised Dylan with unsolicited advice, "Let them go. You can't save them from themselves, and you can't prevent them from attempting to summit."

"Sid, they are my clients. I have to attempt to help them. Plus, since I should follow them up, I wouldn't mind bagging the rare winter ascent of Denali myself."

Sid stared back at Dylan. Dylan knew Sid would not explain his position or argue. He had said his piece.

Heather changed the subject. "Dylan, if you go, I'm coming with you."

"No! It's too dangerous. Stay here. You and Julie stay. You guys can shelter under that cornice where we slept last night. Build us a new base camp. We need water, how about if you melt some more snow?"

Sid picked up his pack. Dylan knew he would help with the Russians despite his misgivings.

"OK, but radio us about every hour if you can." Julie looked through her layers and face protection at Sid.

Despite all the clothing, Sid could imagine her curly dark hair and dimpled round face and longed to kiss her.

Sid just held up his radio and nodded.

With Heather's and Julie's acknowledgement, Dylan motioned to Sid, who hoisted his photography pack, and they started after the Russians.

After about an hour of trudging upwards, Dylan and Sid had caught up to the Russians. Denali was like a frozen marble and attempting to stay on their crampon-clad feet took a great deal of effort in the wind. Despite the amazing protective gear he wore, Dylan felt cold creeping in: cold to the point where he wondered if he and the others could make it back. He knew the Russians must also be cold.

Sid tried to radio Julie. For some reason, there was no answer with the base camp. Both Boris and Dylan had radios, both of which they tried, but the women didn't answer, or if they did, it was impossible to hear in the howling winds.

Dylan felt a sense of dread creeping up his back.

Again, Sid wanted to abort the climb and check on the lower camp. Boris wanted to summit, in good weather, they were only a few hours from the top. After reaching the peak, the men could do a night decent and reach the base camp in good time. Dylan knew he would probably never get another chance at a winter Denali climb. There were dozens of ordinary reasons why the women's radios weren't working. Dylan began to doubt the wisdom of overruling Sid's unsolicited advice.

Even as he resumed the assent, Dylan felt an unaccustomed heaviness to his steps. It was far more than the physical strain of the altitude and exertion. He kept telling himself that the reason was Sid. He respected Sid's wisdom more than his own, and he had never questioned any call made by the quiet man. Sid seemed to be an unemotional robot as he climbed. His mind dwelt elsewhere. Despite their ice-gripping crampons, nearly every step required an ice axe. This was going to take longer than they expected. The final climb turned into eight hours of crawling, resting, crawling.

Icy dread seemed to envelop Sid and Dylan. They had to work hard to pull in enough oxygen to keep alert and mentally sharp. Once on top, only the nearly exhausted Boris and Svetlana felt the exhilaration from a successful winter climb of North America's highest mountain. But it wouldn't be a success unless they made it off the mountain. The winds slammed against them with the force of a locomotive and the shrieking of a jet engine.

Sid was more intent on surviving the elements than photography. He would not remove his outer gloves in this intense cold to manipulate the camera despite Boris's gestures to take a picture. The view was nothing but horizontal golf-ball sized ice pieces hurling at 70 miles per hour against their multiple layers. Dylan signaled that they should leave. He knew they would get colder on the descent. No photos. GPS data would have to do to prove their accomplishment.

Cold and fatigued beyond caring, Boris and Svetlana allowed themselves to be roped up with Dylan leading and Sid at the rear. As Dylan picked a way down in thin, cold air, the sky began to darken even more.

Besides the weather, Dylan had to lead his party around some dangerous ice crevasses that could swallow a bus. He knew if he could get everyone down to 19,000 feet, they could stand up and walk the next 1,000 feet to base camp.

Dylan felt an urgent tugging on his rope. Looking back he could see it was just the wind snapping it crisply. Boris and Svetlana crawled blindly down the steep slope depending on the rope for guidance. This wasn't working since the wind was pulling the rope in the wrong direction. Sid was constantly redirecting them as their movements became sluggish, and they responded ever slower to directions.

A burst of wind and airborne ice knocked Boris onto his back. This immediately started him sliding down the steep, icy slope. Suddenly Svetlana was jerked off her feet and slammed into a rock. Her inert body tumbled after Boris who looked like an upended turtle, arms flailing in the air.

"Falling!" Dylan heard himself shout the word into his facemask. The self-arrest term that signaled the others to throw themselves belly-down and bury their ice axes in the ice, could barely be heard above the howling wind. Sid and Dylan attempted to deploy their ice axes hoping the rope tying them together would arrest the slide.

Suddenly, Dylan felt himself jerked from the ice by the parties in an uncontrolled slide. Hitting a pillow-sized chunk of ice knocked the wind out of Dylan and dislodged his goggles sending -100 degree wind-chilled air to burn his face and eyes. Blind, Dylan felt himself pulled down and northwest. *Where was Sid? Couldn't he stop this slide?*

Miraculously, Dylan's goggles righted themselves, and he could make out the insentient figures of the Russians' bodies, slamming brutally against ice humps and sliding ahead of he and Sid. Like Dylan, Sid slid on his belly, his ice axe sending up a spray of powdered crystals as it was dragged over the iron-gray surface.

Suddenly the Russian's bodies disappeared as they went over a lip in the ice. Was it a crevasse? Dylan hoped it was just an ice lip that would protect them.

As Sid slid toward the black opening, he lifted his axe and forced it down into the concrete-hardened ice. Like sparks flying from a grinder, the axe dragged and miraculously dug in. Sid stopped just before the blackness.

Dylan was able to stop his own slide about two meters above Sid. Adrenalin pumping, Dylan transitioned into oval breathing by relaxing his shoulders and breathing in through his nose, pausing and out through his mouth.

If you've been trained by the best, you instinctively transition to oval breathing during times of physical or mental stress. You feel the cold air sting your nostrils as the air slowly and deeply circulates in, and you feel it tingle in a slow, controlled exhale. It's the alternative to halted breaths that cut off oxygen to your brain and muscles, a substitute for shallow huffs and puffs that send you into hyperventilation at high altitude.

He and Sid looked at each other across the wire-tight climbing rope. Sid, in obvious distress, could not hold on for long with the weight of the Russians' bodies held only by a quarter-inch of steel ice axe, and Sid's oxygen-deprived muscles.

If Sid were pulled into the crevasse, Dylan would go down too. The only thing to do was to cut the line: a cut that would mean the certain death of Boris and Svetlana, but survival for Sid and Dylan.

Dylan could see that the only rope within reach of Sid's axe was the one that, if cut, would separate Dylan from the rest of the party. If line were severed, Dylan would be free from the dead weight of the Russians' bodies dangling in the crevasse, but Sid, unable to hold the weight by himself, would be pulled to his death.

There was only one thing for Sid to do. He seemed to nod at Dylan.

"NO!" Dylan screamed.

Sid moved his axe, chopped at the line and disappeared.

Dylan, suddenly free from the weight of the line felt his body buck. The weightless rope snapped in the wind, the cut end fraying into dust with amazing speed.

Dylan worked his way carefully to the crevasse to see how deep it was and whether it might be possible for anyone to survive a fall into it. All he could see was a hellish blue-black emptiness. Overhead, demon rivers of rushing wind screamed harshly, angry at only killing three, while a fourth clung to the edge devastated at what just happened.

BACK AT BASE CAMP, Julie looked up at the protection of the icy cornice above them, "Think this will fall on us?"

Heather regarded it, "If Dylan says it's safe, it's safe. Let's get this camp in order and melt some snow for the gang. They should be back soon."

"I don't know. That looks unstable."

"Geeze, you worry too much. It's probably looked like that for the last 100 years. And it's the only place on this whole mountain where the wind isn't ready to knock you off your feet."

The women worked to make the base came homey by setting up the big tent in the calmest place and anchoring the gear against the rocks in the windy area.

Heather knew she should feel safe, but couldn't keep back a feeling of dread. Was her subconscious trying to tell her something? Was Dylan in danger? Would the cornice fall as Julie wondered? "I'm just a worry wart." Heather told herself as she busied herself with domestic chores.

Julie climbed into the big tent to melt some more snow while Heather stood under the cornice ready to receive a call from Dylan. A massive gust of wind and an eerie groan from the mountain started Heather.

"What was that?" Julie's voice floated from the tent.

Another groan, this time from above, was followed by a loud snapping sound.

"Julie! Get away from the tent!" Heather screamed.

"What? I can't hear you. Who turned up the wind?"

Heather pulled at the tent opening, her heart pounding and adrenaline surging through her body. "Julie! Let's go!"

This time, the snapping was followed by a roar. Heather watched as the massive cornice cracked and began sliding toward the tent. Heather fell away from the avalanche just as tons of ice buried the tent. Screaming, Heather attempted to stand only to find her leg pinned under the ice. Where the tent had stood was a house-sized pile of blue-white ice.

"Julie!" Heather screamed into the uncaring wind.

6

· · · · · · · · · · ·

THE APPROACHING FOOT falls of Oxman and Tall Guy added urgency to Dylan's predicament. Quickly, and breathing in his controlled rhythm, Dylan's boots found the tiny holds he knew from hundreds of climbs up and down this face. It was the other way to town, and he could do it blind-folded. This time he was doing it under fire and wearing clumsy boots instead of climbing shoes.

Dylan knew that as soon as he was 30 feet down the face, an overhanging ledge would offer protection from bullets fired from above. It would be nearly an impossible decent for an inexperienced rock climber. *Could these guys climb?*

One of the reasons Dylan had earned a reputation as a brilliant hunter was that he had the ability to ignore any distractions: cold, hunger, fear and emotions, in order to get a good shot off at the perfect moment.

There was one thing that Dylan could not ignore, the ghosts from ten years ago. This was a time when he let his breathing vary from the oval process he knew so well and fear forced him to veer from success. He prayed the spirits would stay away now.

Dylan knew he could not stop right now to wonder why these men were after him: he had to survive. He had honed survival skills over the last 10 years of constant wilderness living. Dylan had learned that pouring all his attention into survival seemed to pacify the ghosts.

If these men could climb, he would need a weapon. Dressed to go to town, Dylan had not taken even a pocketknife with him when he left the house. Peter's gun was now with his enemies, but they might not have dismissed him as harmless if he hadn't given the revolver to Tall Guy.

There was one ghost that might be able to help him: his old mentor. *Sid, what should I do?* Dylan looked around the ledge for an idea.

Years ago, some climber had pounded an 8-inch steel piton, which was basically a metal spike with an eye-ring, into a crack in the stone face. Dylan didn't use these metal spikes when he climbed. They widened cracks and made the climbing line cluttered with junk. Using a stone, Dylan pounded on the piton until he could get it to shift a few inches.

From above, a shower of rock fragments told him the two men were testing the rock face for a decent.

Dylan worked at the piton soundlessly in case the men didn't know he was on this ledge. Maybe they would believe he had made it all the way down to the bay and away.

Just then his red nylon climbing rope splashed down over the slab of rock above his head. These guys were going to belay down and shoot him on this ledge.

Without a change in breathing, Dylan was able to remove the piton and his yellow jacket. He arranged the jacket and his sock hat on the floor of the ledge around a rock so it might look like a man at first glance. If a soldier came down fast, he would have one hand on his belaying line and one on his gun. Since only one line was down, Dylan figured only one man would descend.

Dylan dropped into hunting mode. He wedged himself up near the roof of the overhanging rock and waited inches from the shaking red nylon line. He would be invisible until the belaying man cleared the overhang.

Dylan's arm remained cocked—the 8-inch piton held in striking position. He would aim for the neck. The morning sun in his eyes, the near freezing air on his exposed torso, the shock of his best friend trying to kill him: none of these caused even a flicker of tremble in his thrusting arm.

A brilliant red dot reflected off the outcropping in front of Dylan. Rock fragments blasted all around the ledge as one of the two men above poured cover fire downwards.

Dylan waited with utter focus and calm.

The red climbing line waved as something heavy moved down. Suddenly his jacket turned into yellow shreds as Oxman's boots appeared at Dylan's eye level and the Sig let loose a burst.

Dylan shivered in the cold morning as he waited.

Oxman's body presented itself to Dylan as it came over the rock ledge. Still, Dylan did not strike. He waited for a chance at a killing stroke.

Oxman's eyes were suddenly a foot from Dylan. The machine pistol quickly abandoned the yellow shirt target and came up toward Dylan. Like lightning, Dylan's arm shot forward.

The piton disappeared into the Oxman's neck, was ripped out followed by an amazing rush of blood then instantly thrust into the other side of his neck rupturing both branches of Oxman's carotid arteries.

The thrusts happened so fast, Oxman did not realize he had been mortally wounded. The arc of blood spurted over the cliff face, and Oxman fell wetly onto the ledge, his body displaying small spasms as it drained of blood.

Without a second's hesitation, Dylan unhooked the belaying bracket from the dying ox and jerked the climbing rope so it lost its hold above and came raveling down to his ledge. Now Tall Guy would have to go back to the cabin to get another rope.

When the next attack came, Dylan would have Oxman's gear.

First: get warm. Dylan stripped the dead man's blood-soaked jacket and found a dry, tent-sized fleece. Good equipment. Once covered, Dylan began to methodically mine Oxman's body for survival gear.

As he worked, he heard fragments of radio chatter come from Oxman's earpiece. " . . . this is an obvious malfunction. . ." Then a strong voice rang in the crisp Alaskan morning.

"Mr. Baker. You are under arrest. Come out with your hands up." Tall Guy's authoritative voice broke the momentary morning stillness as it rolled down the rock face.

Dylan searched Oxman's body while he ignored the voice.

"Mr. Baker. If you come out now, you will be safe. I can't guarantee your safety if you hesitate. Come out now!" That voice had the unmistakable ring of authority. It was an effective weapon. This man was good.

Dylan, finding no identification on the body, decided to probe Tall Guy for information. "Who are you?" Dylan yelled up the rock face.

"Ah, Mr. Baker. So you aren't dead. I thought maybe Sergeant Rolf was able to subdue you. He's never failed before. You surprise me."

"You want me to give up. First tell me who you are and why you are trying to kill me."

"Mr. Baker, as a threat to national security, it should be no surprise why we are after you. You've been a very bad boy. Besides, we will soon collect your Bible. However, my orders are to bring you in, if possible."

Threat to national security? Evidence? My Bible? Dylan could not make sense out of Tall Guy's words.

Dylan had nearly every useful object from Oxman tucked into a huge belt pack he had found around Oxman's waist. Dylan slung the belt over one shoulder.

He sat down to extract the gun from under Oxman. As he worked, he called up the hill. "There's been a mistake. I have nothing to do with national security. I'm a handyman and a guide."

"Oh, if there's been a mistake, I promise you we'll make it right." Tall Gay soothed.

"How do I know I can trust you?" Dylan worked the radio from Oxman's jacket pocket and finally pulled the dead man's gun from beneath the massive arm.

"Mr. Baker, I give you my word as a government employee."

What a gun! Dylan had read about these but never seen one. This Sig Sauer 553 was a Swiss-made short-barreled rifle chambered in 5.56 X 45 NATO with a 30-round magazine of armor-piercing copper-plated solid steel bullets, a noise suppressor and a laser sight. Advanced military weaponry, but with the serial number freshly ground off. *What kind of military removes serial numbers?*

Dylan fitted a fresh magazine into the gun and called up, "But what is your name?"

"Mr. Baker, call me Captain Zwart. If you come out now, you will not be hurt."

Dylan pulled up his shirt to examine his shoulder where he had moments earlier felt the bumblebee sting. A small trickle of blood congealed where a bullet or rock fragment had pierced his shirt. There didn't seem to be any shrapnel in the wound.

"Captain Zwart, I'm going to need some help getting up this rock face. I'm wounded." Dylan examined the climbing line for damage and secured it to a rock. He put what was left of his yellow jacket on the arm of Oxman and hung it out over the ledge.

A red dot appeared on the dead man's wrist as a burst of bullets shredded the Oxman's lifeless hand. Dylan cupped his hands to his mouth and shrieked as if in pain. "I'm hit. I'm hit, you bastard. Now you did it."

Ready to make the descent to the bay, Dylan knew he needed to be sure he remained under the overhanging rock so Zwart couldn't see him. "Send down a first aid kit. I'm bleeding. Oh God, I'm bleeding." Dylan called up.

"Sorry about that Mr. Baker. I had to make sure you didn't try to go anywhere until I could get a team in position. Don't worry. Help is on the way as we speak."

"Zwart!" Dylan prepared to slither over a lip and down the wall. "Go to my cabin. There's another climbing rope. You can lower the first aid kit in the kitchen. I need to stop this bleeding."

Dylan couldn't hear Captain Zwart's response as he repelled the last 50 feet to the dark forest surrounding the bay.

Putting me in these woods is like throwing a rabbit into the briar patch. I'm free. I'm free, except for another ghost to haunt me: an ox-sized one added to the group.

With a last look up the cliff face where the dead Oxman lay, Dylan untied after his repel. A 10-foot rivulet of blood meandered down the rocks below the dead man's location. Dylan tried to control his violent emotions with a deep breath before vanishing into the forest.

Dylan didn't have to run very far to feel safe enough to lean his back against a scaly Sitka spruce and let the quick replay of the morning's events wash over him like the tide, or like a tsunami. Less than an hour before he had been thinking about his moose shank. He couldn't believe that that very meat was used as a defense against his best friend's gun.

In his mind, a mix of images fought each other for attention. Dylan needed to determine which of these were of immediate importance for his survival: Peter unconscious on his floor, the bullets striking all around him, the Oxman dead with an old climbing piton through his neck. This last one would mean another ghost to haunt him, as if the others he had killed weren't enough.

Dylan shook his head as if he was trying to fling the images from his brain. Like the successful survivalist he was, he quickly focused on the immediate problem: a man in army fatigues just a few trees and cliff-face away. Those who underestimate the Alaskan wilderness tend to find themselves dead, and Dylan figured that in this jungle, he might as well be a needle in a life-threatening haystack. No one could find him here. If Zwart followed, Dylan could go deeper. He'd done it before.

A decade ago when he retreated into these trees and this world, no one had been chasing him. He had been escaping his guilt, a mocking enemy closer to him than his shadow.

Who is after me? He had patted down the body of the Oxman, but found no ID. No dog tags for the fallen soldier.

The pack Dylan had taken off the body suddenly weighed on his shoulders. He opened it and began taking careful inventory, hoping for a clue. Besides a sour-man-smell, Dylan noticed the radio. This tiny radio definitely looked military-grade. Dylan popped off the back panel, revealing a mini tapestry of wires and computer chips. Nano-technology. No obvious ID here.

But who was Oxman? Dylan reattached the panel and pulled a small knife from the pack. Once a gear snob, Dylan examined the blade.

The slumbering elitist within him stirred when he turned over this Swiss-made beauty in his hand. It could slice through ropes, pierce skin at a touch and its blade was in excellent condition. It was a precision tool and a deadly weapon. There was also an ugly big knife not much use in the woods. This one was for show: razor sharp and custom made, but too big for a hunting knife and too small for a machete.

From the belt pack he also emptied an additional cord of rope, leather gloves, and a 7.5 topo map of the Seward area. Nearly all of these things clung to a strong body-odor from its previous owner.

Then there was the rifle. Dylan ran his hand over the silky steel barrel. The silencer appeared to be slightly bent from where the Oxman had crashed against the rocks when his heavy lifeless body collapsed over it. This possibility of a bent barrel rendered the expensive weapon utterly useless. Armor-piercing shells? According to their gear, these men were well funded and lethal. The thought of Peter and his halibut gun suddenly seemed trivial after looking at this gear.

Zwart had said he was with the government. Yet Dylan being a threat to national security sounded stranger than a winter swim in the bay. Zwart and his lackey were not Alaskans. They were far too high-strung, took themselves too seriously. The forty-ninth state humbles people. If they weren't from the state, from which had they been sent? Zwart spoke with a light southern accent, which made him sound well educated and reasonable.

Dylan allowed himself to crouch next to the tree, a comfortable position for the hunter. He quickly surveyed the forest. A deer path wound up the hill off to the left while stream sounds echoed from the right.

Maybe they won't pursue me here, Dylan hoped.

7

. . . .

DYLAN SHOULDERED Oxman's pack and weapons and moved quietly up along the deer path. At the top of a small hill, he paused and absorbed the view of Mt. Alice through the trees and a commanding view of the hillside. A downed tree provided an excellent spot to sort out what just happened. *People are trying to kill me. Peter tried to kill me. Peter? It doesn't make sense.*

This kind of self-talk was not helping. Dylan straightened his back, relaxed his shoulders and found his mind clearing as oval breathing filled his brain and muscles with oxygen his stress levels lowered.

After a few moments of focusing and connecting with the energy of the forest, Dylan listened to his internal dialogue.

I have two choices: Go to the police, resolve this mystery and reestablish my life, or retreat into the forest to heal from the loss of my best friend, Peter.

Forest life offered bittersweet rewards: the savage beauty and the peace replenished the soul, while the solitude came with its terrible price. A hunting cabin near Lowell Point and a friend's vacation home in town could provide the equipment he needed to disappear. But Dylan considered that retreating to the woods would not be to heal, but to hide.

It would mean he'd be abandoning Peter at a time when his best friend so obviously needed help. Peter wasn't dead and shouldn't be abandoned.

If he remained in Seward, he knew he could straighten out this obvious misunderstanding. That is if his life-learned skills would allow him to survive long enough to make his case.

I guess it boils down to who I am. Am I a man who abandons my friends when they need me most? Am I a man who cannot face physical danger?

The mountain scene expanding before Dylan summarized his choices: Seward with all the ties to people and opportunities for growth stretched to the north. The forest and mountains, a pathway that avoided conflict but embraced emptiness, stretched to the south.

A small bunny popped its head around the trunk of a tree and peered at Dylan. After a moment, it turned and scampered in the direction of Seward. *Yeah, you're right, little guy. And, maybe I'll finally be able to rebuild my life to what I had before Heather died.* Dylan turned, retraced his steps and retrieved Oxman's gear.

Committed to staying in Seward and helping Peter, Dylan was unsure what to do next. Should he try to convince Peter to get help? Something had obviously happened to Peter. Could something beside mental illness turn his best friend against him? Dylan was personally familiar with mental distress, and if Peter was sick, he needed his friends' help.

Perhaps Peter was not ill. Did someone convince Peter that Dylan was an enemy and needed killing? That didn't make any sense. Peter wasn't a killer.

Anyway, who would want to persuade Peter that Dylan should die? Maybe a family member of one of the Denali ghosts was after him? They surely must hate him, but how would a family member ever find him?

Maybe Sid had somehow survived the Denali disaster and is out for revenge after Dylan's poor leadership resulted in Julie's death. Perhaps Heather's wealthy family wanted revenge. It could be that Boris's rich family or business associates wanted to kill Dylan, but why would Peter help any of these people? How could anyone even talk Peter into trying to hurt Dylan without discussion?

When he vanished into the woods, Dylan's intent had never been to hide from any living person or to avoid danger, but to recover from his losses. This craziness made no sense.

Also, why would Peter and Zwart ask him about his Bible? He didn't own one. That didn't fit into any possible reason for this mess, since the only books in Dylan's personal library were repair and maintenance manuals. Zwart and Peter must be looking for someone who has a valuable Bible.

Dylan felt a jolt of euphoria when he realized his course was clear. His focus would be razor sharp. He would not try to hustle Peter to a doctor. He would help his friend by finding out why Zwart and Peter attacked. Knowing Peter's motivation would allow Dylan to help his friend back to sanity.

Dylan let Oxman's worthless gun fall to the forest floor. Dylan would learn the truth. He would find out why big men in crisp fatigues were trying to kill him. He would discover why his best friend attempted to shoot him with his halibut revolver. Dylan knew there must be people who wouldn't mind seeing him at the bottom of a deep crevasse, and maybe they were after him. But it might just be a problem due to mistaken identity.

A rustle in the undergrowth to his left brought Dylan back to the forest. A rank smell told Dylan it was probably a porcupine. A crackle on the radio sent him right back to his immediate problem: survival.

"Advancing to quadrant 842, Captain Zwart. Our team is on him."

A few hundred yards from Dylan, a noisy flock of crows took to the sky with indignant cries.

Dylan's eyes followed the crows. Every part of his body became still except his eyes, which thoroughly scanned the direction the crows had come from. This neck of the woods had been frequented by mostly just Dylan and his dogs for the last ten years. Dylan knew his territory, and understood he couldn't be tracked from the direction his eyes scanned.

How are these guys finding me? Dylan realized he'd have to retreat deeper to the dark of the forest before he could go for help.

Dylan silently slipped the belt pack over his shoulder and across his chest. Ten years ago, Dylan Baker had taken to the woods to heal from an onslaught of internal demons in the dark of the Alaskan woods. This time the attack was from his best friend and an unknown, well-equipped army. Dylan was known as the best hunter west of Juneau. He felt confident he could track down the answers to this mystery.

A PERSON WHO has never been to a Northern rainforest might think it is a place of silent and peaceful tranquility. Dylan knew better. He could not yet hear the team that was after him because of the magpies, ravens, varied thrushes and bald eagles chirping in the forest canopy.

The wind ran its unpredictable hand through the treetops, sending pollen clouds to the forest floor. Of course, the pollen doesn't hit the bare dirt. Far too much underbrush obscures the mix of soil and rock, evidence of a geologic history tougher than the pioneers who walked upon it.

Dylan wove his way around wild blueberry bushes and devil's club to a cold path few non-natives would want to travel: the icy stream of glacial runoff from the mountains. There weren't many options for which road to take to town. Only a few worn pathways actually get a person to where civilization clings to a wild landscape. The question for Dylan was where on the road to emerge, and how to get there.

He knew following this creek bed would take him right by one outlet to pavement: the junkyard.

Static punched through on the radio every few minutes, but Dylan couldn't make out anything substantial about the pursuers' positions. He tried again to imagine how they had tracked him only a few moments after descending from the cliff.

Finding no better rationale, he finally decided that Zwart must have figured out an approximate quadrant in relation to the cabin and relayed it to his team. Now that Dylan was making good time down the creek bed, they'd probably run into a bear before they found him.

Always a few steps ahead, Dylan thought about what he'd do when he reached the road. He wanted to sort this out. No matter what he had done in his past, he knew the government had no reason to be after him.

"A threat to national security," Zwart had said. His worst federal offense was not filing an income tax statement over the last ten years. He had no bank account, credit cards or association with the government. Dylan knew he was innocent of threatening the nation. Who could help him convince these killers?

His two best friends in Seward were Shorty, over at the local tackle shop, and Peter, with Fish and Game. The only other townie with whom Dylan felt close was Mitch, a national park ranger.

Years earlier, Mitch had taught Dylan how to see game in the crazy woods near Seward. So many hunters looked for moose and never saw them. Mitch had taught Dylan to have "soft eyes"—to notice what he was seeing. Hunters trained this way could see just a hoof, a tail swish or an eye through the prism of trees common to this part of Alaska. It's a way of seeing that Dylan became locally famous for in Seward.

Mitch, as a national park ranger, might have information on federal law enforcement activities. He would probably know why these military-style hunters had come all the way out here to kill Dylan Baker.

To talk to Mitch, Dylan would need to hike out of his woods and into Mitch's office. This would be like presenting himself to the police and asking for mercy.

Still, he knew he could trust his friend. *But, thirty minutes ago I thought I could trust Peter. Mitch can help me solve this, and he can talk sense to Peter.*

Then he could clear the air with Peter, who was clearly operating under false pretenses, and go back to his life with his woods and his dogs.

Water started to seep through to Dylan's feet. *Why hadn't he worn his waterproof boots?* His wool socks had just begun to soak up the turquoise creek water when he heard an unsilenced gunshot.

Dylan froze and crouched mid creek. The shot was too far out of range to hit him, but close enough to know he had not lost his pursuers.

Water crept its way from the soul of his shoe to his ankle as he listened for a clue to his predators' position. Finally the radio came on.

"Foxtrot, what was that shooting?" crackled Zwart's voice. "Why isn't your silencer deployed? Is the target hit?"

"Ah Captain, I just shot a baby moose. You should see how these damn things bleed."

"Return to duty, Foxtrot. We're not out here to have fun. We talked about this, no killing for fun." snapped Zwart's voice.

"Captain, you should see this moose. It's crying for its mama, stupid animal just won't die."

Two more unsilenced shots rang out. It sounded like the soldiers were shooting side arms now.

Killed a moose calf! Few things are more dangerous than an angry moose cow. Nothing enrages a mother moose like hurting her calf. If these guys don't also kill the cow, the woods will be dangerous for weeks.

Dylan wiggled his toes to prevent them from going numb, still unmoving in his crouch. These guys were too close. They must be expert trackers. Maybe they figured he'd take to the stream. He quietly pulled the topo-map out of Oxman's belt pack.

As he suspected, this way was not even on the map. *They can't have assumed I took to this stream. They didn't know exists.*

Sliding the map back into the belt pack, Dylan consulted the more detailed map of these woods he had in his head.

If the trackers had come across the stream and now knew he was walking it, he could leave the water to take a path to the junkyard on firm ground. He had the advantage of speed and a head start, although a dry land path was easier to track.

His other option was to continue the creek walk at a faster pace, hoping to get to the junkyard right before his pursuers. Dylan looked behind him as a gust of wind blew by, pushing bits of leaves into the air.

Bits of leaves? Damn these silencers! I'm being shot at!

8
Ten Years Earlier
. . . .

THE SEVERED SAFETY line snapped out horizontally, pointing in the direction where Sid, Boris and Svetlana were blown. The rope seemed to beckon Dylan to join his lost friends. *Am I losing my mind?*

The wind beat at Dylan as if it would not permit any humans to thwart its will. Dylan shouted his anger, but the thin words were lost in the storm.

"Hey Dylan," Sid's familiar voice glided just above the hollowing wind. Looking up, Dylan wondered if he could make out Sid's shadowy image in the swirling snow. *How could this be? I just saw Sid blown into the crevasse.*

"Sid? Am I hallucinating?" Dylan attempted to remove frost from his goggles.

"Now's not the time for emotion. We need to think clearly and mourn later." Sid's voice sounded oddly untroubled and reasonable, like they were having lunch together in a quiet room and not clinging to life in a Denali-sized storm.

Dylan uneasily allowed himself to feel better in the presence of his mentor. Boris had insisted that Dylan Baker lead the expedition due to Dylan's fame as a climber.

The funny thing was, Dylan had achieved fame for amazing technical climbs all over the world, but approaching the summit of Denali along the West Buttress route was considered non-technical. All a mountaineer needed was winter hiking equipment and a great deal of luck.

The wind abated and Dylan searched the dark swirls for the lost climbers: nothing but endless black and the mocking screams of the wind. Sid was nowhere to be seen. *Had he gone back? Did I just imagine him?*

Dylan edged toward the darkness embedded in the grey swirls. Maybe he would be able to see Boris and Svetlana.

A great black maw opened before him with the outer edges glowing an eerie blue. He moved to a moose-sized rock and clung for a while. Looking over his shoulder, Dylan thought he could see Sid's retreat towards their summit camp. Dylan turned to follow Sid hoping his mind was not down the crevasse as well as his friend and clients.

Beaten by hundreds of ice chunks, grieving the loss of his clients, unsure if Sid was alive or some kind of friendly phantom, dehydrated, and close to hypothermia, Dylan felt himself crumbling. He needed water, food, warmth and the emotional support Heather would give him. He needed closure regarding Sid.

Hours later he stumbled into camp utterly defeated and close to exhaustion. Finally the high altitude seemed to cause him to gasp for each breath.

It wasn't right.

There was no cornice offering shelter to Julie and Heather. He could see the packs all lined up on the far side of the clearing but neglected and nearly covered in snow and ice pellets. Where were Julie and Heather? Why was there no cornice, just a pile of ancient ice where the campsite had been?

Walking around the pile of ice, he saw Heather, feebly chipping away at an icefall with a spoon.

The fall had obviously trapped her leg and bent it into an unnatural shape.

"Heather!" Dylan yelled, but his voice sounded weak.

She turned slowly toward him showing blue lips on a shockingly pale face. "Dylan, I need help! Julie is under this pile and my leg is trapped." She slumped in relief at seeing him. She looked defeated and ready to let Dylan take over the rescue.

As he watched, a huge section of icy debris suspended above the cornice slid down about a foot and stopped. Instead of the beautifully sheltered platform Dylan had picked out, a huge mound of ice, snow and avalanche debris lay coldly in the swirling silent frigid dark. Above Heather's position, it looked like tons of ice and frozen rock suspended malevolently were about to crush her into oblivion. While Dylan found the reserves to scramble over to her, a growling sound emanated from the potential avalanche above.

"Heather, you're going to be OK. I just need to move some of this ice." He assessed her breathing, pupils and consciousness.

"This hurts. Hurry." Heather paused trying to regain focus. "Where's Sid? Where are Boris and Svetlana? They can help. Help Julie and me."

"Honey, they are gone." Dylan forced himself to ignore the painful feelings welling up inside of him. This all was his fault. He quickly suppressed the thoughts that centered on Sid and Julie. *I need to be in this moment!*

"Gone?" Heather's face reflected her disbelief before she winced in pain.

Damn! Her leg looks broken. "Girl, you get a sled and piggyback ride down the mountain." Dylan forced lightness into his voice. He sprinted back through the thin air to the gear and threw the packs out into the open—madly pulling items out. He found a light climbing axe and returned quickly to start chopping at the ice near Heather's foot. The ice was like concrete, and Dylan could only remove tiny slivers with each hack.

Heather cried out again. A rumble from above sent several feet of ice and snow particles down on them. "Hurry. I want that piggyback ride."

"I'm going to get Boris's spare axe. He has a heavier one." As Dylan moved toward the backpacks, he heard another rumble. In shock he watched more ice and rock fall on Heather. Only her head and one shoulder were now visible above the ice mass. She looked oddly crooked. The tiny axe would be little better than a teaspoon at removing a mountainous sand dune. Another piece of cornice, the size of a house, seemed poised to slide down. Then, with an eerie subsonic rumble, the cornice slipped another few feet.

"Heather!" Dylan grabbed Boris' heavier axe.

Heather's face looked strained. "Dylan? Does this mean no piggyback ride?"

"God Damn!" Dylan chopped at the ice like a mad man, but it became clear he couldn't possibly chop through it in a day or even a week.

Heather's face focused with determination. "I need to tell you something."

"Save it for your piggyback ride." It was as if Dylan was a puppet with someone else operating his hands and arms as they removed thin layer after thin layer of ice.

"I love you. And I want you to know that my love for you will always connect us whether in this life or another."

Dylan paused and looked at the tears pooling in her goggles. "Dylan, something happened last year when we were apart. We need to talk."

With a roar of falling ice, more debris thundered down upon the scene.

Hours later, Dylan awoke to find himself stunned and buried to the shoulders in soft snow and ice pellets. He thought he heard Sid's voice in the wind.

Heather's gone. Julie's gone. There's nothing you can do. Since you are wearing the right gear and covered with light, insulating snow, it's time for you to rest. The snow will protect you from the worst cold. Sleep.

Dylan felt the blackness pull him away from consciousness. He slept.

Hours later he started to crawl out inch by inch. Behind him, where Heather had been, there was a massive pile of ice. No trace of Heather was visible. The entire camp was unrecognizable.

"Sid! I need your help!" Picking up his ice axe, Dylan climbed the pile and started chopping ineffectually at the ice. *This is all my fault. My fault!*

9

. . . .

THE BUSHES AND shrubs lay shredded by bullets. Dylan didn't have to think too hard to abandon his creek walk. Crawling bearlike under the tall undergrowth, Dylan made his way toward another feature not mentioned by the topo-map, a fresh cliff made by a landslide a few months earlier.

Not hearing the gunshots offered no comfort to Dylan. He preferred to see his end coming. Every breeze was potential death. Every little bird cry was Zwart cackling.

Many nights Dylan had dreamed that he might meet his end in the wild. A perfect death perhaps, yet he had never expected that it might be from a mysterious army avenging some unknown crime.

Dylan had experienced angry bears, fierce rutting moose, cold fronts, and rogue waves, but he had no idea how to beat an army. He crawled because he didn't want to be discovered, but he felt like some helpless animal. Movement erupted all around him, but this was no time to stop and analyze. He knew he was almost to his cliff when the radio crackled.

"Nice shot, did you get him?"

"We're closing in" a female voice responded.

Dylan figured they must see the bushes around him moving, but standing up wouldn't help. He could climb a tree, but these guys wouldn't just give up. His skills were out of place, a message abruptly reinforced by the sudden appearance of bullets slamming into the wide mountain hemlock in front of him.

He heard the hunters now, so close, there must be four or five men shouting. No use for the radio now, he could hear them. What a shame he was so close, a quick dash away to a cliff only Dylan Baker could scale. If he stood up and ran, he felt sure bullets would mow him down in an instant. He crawled around the big hemlock and used it as a shield.

What am I doing? Waiting for them to walk around the tree?

Dylan knew the thick trunk could only protect him until the army closed in. He fished in the pack for the knife. Maybe he could die trying.

Suddenly, he felt the ground tremble. Another landslide?

Then he smiled. He knew that sound. Moose.

As the first screams erupted behind him, he made his dash for the cliff sloping steeply downward. Leaping gracefully over a shallow embankment, Dylan gained his first handhold. No shredded leaves floated down after him and he silently thanked that charging cow. Moose killed more people in Alaska than bears.

Dylan knew as soon as he was under the lip of the cliff and on the wall of rock he was safe. The minutes he had gained with his climbing advantage felt like hours compared to the seconds standing between him and death moments earlier.

The climb was difficult, but Dylan felt at home clinging to a cliff side the way most people feel sitting on their couch. As the wet leather of his boots searched the wall for toeholds, he kept glancing up, waiting for ropes and combat boots to find their way down to him. He was halfway down when he heard a slide of rocks off to his left.

Was another climber on this cliff already?

The radio sputtered. "Charlie, what's your position?" Silence.

"Anyone know Charlie's 10-20?"

"He may have fallen off this cliff. You can't see it until you are right on it," the female voice reported.

"Able to Captain Zwart."

"Go ahead, Able. I hope you have good news for me"

So Zwart isn't with them.

"Yes, uh, Captain Zwart, we have some injured men. And Charlie is gone. I think he fell off a cliff."

"Did the subject return fire?" Zwart's tone sounded unconcerned with injuries. It was as if he was scolding them before he knew what happened.

Able responded after a pause. "No, Captain, there was a moose that charged us. The subject has not been sighted."

"I see. In what condition are the wounded?"

"Bobby took a hoof to the chest, I don't think he'll make it out. A-Rod isn't conscious."

"Yes?" Zwart waited a beat. "Well, Able, if there is a cliff, I assure you Baker did not fall off. He's clinging his cowardly hands to it right now. We'll have him within the hour—you can bet on that."

No plan to evacuate the wounded, no directions for his men, just a cool warning. The message's intended recipient: Dylan Baker. Zwart knew he was tuning in on the radio. The captain was trying to get Dylan to panic with that voice.

Through each steady step and hold of his descent, Dylan wondered about Zwart's message. Clearly Zwart had background on Dylan, that's how he had made the reference to Denali earlier.

With very little research, any interested party could know about Dylan's climbing capability before his retreat to Alaska. *That's how he knows I wouldn't have fallen off a cliff.*

Zwart's words echoed in his head, "his cowardly hands." Dylan knew of only a few people who had reason to call him a coward. *How does Zwart know about this?*

The part of the creek that Dylan brought with him in his boots was turning lukewarm from the action. As he touched down at the base of the cliff, he flexed and relaxed his shoulders and forearms.

Dylan looked at his throbbing fingers. The scratches from the rock oozed blood. Looking down at his dirty pants, he wondered where to wipe the blood off his hands.

Zwart's warning prevented Dylan from resting too long. "We'll have him within the hour—you can bet on that."

Sheltered by the cliff, Dylan took off his boots and wrung the creek water out of his thick wool socks. Outdoorsmen are fastidious about their footwear. Dylan wished he hadn't worn his town boots today, instead of the waterproof wonders he had under his bed.

I'm in the same position I was a half hour ago, Dylan thought. Yet Dylan was aware of a key difference from the last time he touched horizontal ground after a climb: now Dylan entertained no illusions that he was safe in his woods. These ruthless fighters wouldn't stop tracking him down or give up just because it was his turf.

As he roughly pulled the damp wool over his feet, he replayed his crawl through the undergrowth. How clumsy it was! How ashamed he felt that he could be so awkward and ignorant in his own backyard.

He thought back to his school days, and what he had learned about war. Wasn't this the perfect situation for guerilla warfare? An out of town army with no stake in the land fighting fewer numbers who had all the rich history and secrets of the landscape?

Dylan wondered what he could do to escape these guys. He just wanted to get to the road and down to his friend Mitch at the park service, but he imagined Zwart bringing what was left of his team from some surprise direction with machine guns to shred his forest some more. Dylan knew he couldn't count on being saved by a moose now.

When traveling through these woods, Dylan liked to tuck in his laces so they didn't catch on any plants. He wondered if Zwart's men had a similar footwear strategy.

This is ridiculous. I'm the hunter! It's time I did something active to protect myself.

When a grizzly bear charges, you never run. You stand your ground. Dylan wouldn't run now. He'd stand his ground, pursue the grizzly for a bit, and then back away to Seward and Mitch for help.

Where to go to make a stand? Dylan figured they'd start looking for him near water. A river about a quarter mile from his resting spot collected the stream he had creek-walked earlier. He'd start there. He stood up, tucked the laces into his boots and took off.

His pace picked up, and unnoticed by Dylan, his concentration and breathing had fallen into the oval pattern. Distractions faded and goals became as clear as the pure streams he crossed. He knew how to impede a pursuing predator.

The first trap was nothing fancy, just some willow branches pulled back with sharp, chest-high stakes quickly attached to a trip-line trigger. He set these so anyone hitting the line would get stakes coming from two different angles.

The next was a rock with his muddy footprint on it. As soon as Zwart's man stepped on it, the rock would tip and throw the hunter's leg into some sharpened, deadly looking stakes on which Dylan had rubbed some white hellebore.

Dylan knew this plant was highly toxic when ingested. Maybe it would sicken a hunter carrying a silenced machine pistol.

Dylan did not expect the simple traps to kill his pursuers, but to maybe slow them. If his hunters were as good as Dylan thought, the traps would only amuse.

Just as Dylan prepared a false trail that would lead a tracker into a wild beehive that would be ripped open when a trip line was pulled. He heard a scream about a half-mile away. Someone had found the first trap.

From the northeast a burst of radio static abruptly cut off, but it told Dylan the soldiers were still getting closer. Dylan knew he could track nearly any animal through these woods, and he knew how to leave no trace behind him. How did these hunters know his position?

Thirty minutes later the woods filled with a squad of black-suited soldiers spraying machine pistol bullets everywhere. These guys aren't into conserving ammo. Dylan always kept two steps ahead. As he finished carefully rolling some devil's club in an exploding bunch, he heard a commotion of groans and curses. The unit had walked into another trap, but hadn't lost his trail.

Dylan worked his way around a pond a half-mile from the junkyard. The route wove wide and indirectly to this inlet to civilization, but Dylan knew where he was going.

He planned on meeting up with an unmarked hiking trail that the junkyard employees use to get into the woods to toke up during their breaks. Until he caught this path, he continued to stay under the tree canopy and leave no tracks so he could not be followed by air or land.

Just before he came out into an open area, next to the lake, he let his vision go soft. He saw a black sock hat near some bushes and a black-suited soldier approaching him from the direction of town. *Jesus! How did they know he was here?* Even he could not have tracked himself to this place. And these soldiers are coming from the opposite direction from where he last left them.

These must be from a different squad. How did they know he was here? His radio squawked quietly then hissed. The radio! It must have some kind of GPS device in it.

Sock Hat hasn't noticed me yet. Not wanting to disassemble the radio in firing range of the enemy, Dylan slipped silently to his secret path to the junkyard, and jogged to the sagging gate that guarded Seward's junk.

Learning the unit followed him based on a GPS device in the radio had consequences for Dylan. In the first place, he felt vulnerable in a way he never had before.

Secondly, he felt paranoid that although his running path got him to the junkyard faster than any unit could bushwhack through the forest, uniformed men might be lurking behind a discarded refrigerator or busted tires in the junkyard piles.

Dylan found himself an uneasy hiding spot between a trashed wheelhouse of a boat and scrap metal he assumed came from the cannery. He took a hard look at the GPS/radio and knew what he had to do.

Dylan looked around, this time not trying to find his hunters. He saw what he was looking for and slowly stood up. Seeing a piece of fishing line and some weights on his way to his target, he approached Gerard, the junkyard eagle.

For years, Gerard had preyed nobly on Seward's garbage. While his brothers soared over the Kenai Fjords eating carrion, fish and small mammals, this symbol of the nation hung out at the dump. He was what anyone would imagine for a junkyard eagle: disheveled, dirty and grumpy.

In spite of this, Gerard was the most photographed eagle in town. Visitors, recognizable by their ubiquitous Alaska sweatshirts and caps, would usually be sent to the junkyard to be sure to get an eagle photograph.

As long as Dylan feigned holding a camera, Gerard would let him get fairly close. Holding an improvised bola, made of the GPS and a fishing weight separated by 18 inches of fishing line, Dylan crept within easy throwing range of Gerard.

For years South American gauchos used bolas to capture prey by tangling up their feet, Dylan hoped that his would attach the GPS to Gerard at least long enough to throw off his pursuers.

While the scruffy eagle expertly dug his majestic talons into a plastic bag, Dylan started swinging the bola over his head. He would have only one chance to change Gerard into a lure for the relentless trackers out there.

Dylan released his bola and watched it spin toward Gerard. The eagle hopped back, but too late. The bola wrapped itself around his legs.

Issuing a an angry chirp, Gerard ponderously took flight and headed off to the south, hopefully to Lowell Point to look for fish guts left by beach fishermen.

Gerard's razor sharp beak would easily snip off the fishing line, but Dylan hoped that would occur miles from Seward. He had to talk to Mitch.

10

. . . .

BECOMING PART OF Small-Town, Alaska is a different skill than fitting into the forest. As he entered Seward, Dylan made the change from Alaskan rainforest survivalist to a typical relaxed but muddy resident. With little event, Dylan found himself at the door of Mitch's Seward Ranger Station.

For the first time in many hours, a calm came over Dylan as late afternoon shadows announced the beginning of the long Alaskan twilight and the outside door to the ranger station office glowed with the reflected evening light.

As he stood mute before the door, Dylan began to feel the calm replaced with anxiety as he hoped Mitch would be in his office and have some answers.

For tiny Seward, all the USFS would provide Mitch and his fellow rangers was a small, pale-green three-room building attached to a garage. The rangers performed most of their duties in the field. Mitch spent days at a time on national forest land. He enforced park regulations, but often his job consisted of saving hapless tourists and wannabe mountaineers from hurting themselves in the wilderness. Dylan and Mitch's shared competency as outdoorsmen formed a basis for mutual respect.

Dylan remained grateful for Mitch's acceptance of him when he showed up in Seward ten years earlier.

Mitch, who resembled a beefy-blond Robin Williams, had a blustery but kind nature. This was perfect for a ranger, and also made him the right companion for Dylan in those dark days.

Mitch shared his hunting and tracking knowledge and Dylan taught Mitch survival skills, sea kayaking, and basic hunting.

In their time as friends, they had kayaked to remote beaches to camp and fish, hunted moose on lengthy expeditions, and shared nights staring silently and contentedly into the campfire.

Mitch respected Dylan's privacy, and never asked why Dylan refused to socialize much with others. Dylan felt he could rely on Mitch.

The lobby of the Ranger Station appeared professional with a touch of quaint. Government-printed pamphlets of park rules and maps sat displayed on top of a glossy oak table. A messy bulletin board advertised an Ultimate Frisbee game at the elementary school. Plastered on the wall were several unapproved signs with slogans like *Gut Salmon? Save the Ales*, and *I died and went to Seward*.

Dylan ignored the sign on Mitch's office door *I'm at the bakery, be back soon*, and slipped inside, closing the door behind him.

Mitch wasn't at the bakery. Although based on the ranger's startled expression at the sight of him, Dylan might as well have been a big loaf of bread. He remembered his trimmed beard and altered appearance.

"Dylan! What are you doing here?" Mitch stood up behind his file cabinet-inspired desk. He did not approach Dylan.

"Mitch. Listen. I'm in trouble. There are people after me. Some mistake. Have you heard of a Captain Zwart here in Seward? Or a military unit? I just now got away. They're shooting at me. I need help."

Mitch seemed to have regained his composure despite Dylan's nonsensical verbal barrage. Dylan was not a man who normally spoke in exclamations. "What did you do?"

"I ran away! What was I supposed to do? And Peter! His halibut gun! He said something about blood."

Dylan realized he was so relieved to be with a friendly person, he was just letting it all rush out.

Mitch made a sound somewhere between an "uh-huh" and a grunt. He had always been a man of few words.

Dylan continued, "Peter tried to kill me. I got off lucky, but a unit shot at me and tracked me through the forest. They're nasty."

Mitch glanced at his phone and back to Dylan. He touched his own belt pack. They were both still standing with the desk between them. "No, Dylan. What did you do to make them come for you?" He paused. "I want to hear it from you. Think about something you did ten years ago."

Dylan stuttered. He did not stand in the presence of a friend. Zwart must have gotten to Mitch first and told him something. "Mitch, what did they tell you? I haven't done anything. You know me."

Mitch took a step to the left around his government-issue desk. His foot brushed against the metal side. It rattled. "Zwart told me about your past, Dylan. You led us on. I know what you're capable of, and it makes sense now. How could you do it?"

Dylan instinctively took a step back. He ran into the closed door. Mitch's burly body made Dylan look like a skinny freshman next to the strapping senior.

When the ranger lunged at his friend, Dylan instinctually jumped to the side. Now Mitch loomed between him and the door. "Mitch, Stop! I don't know what's going on!"

But Mitch had made up his mind. One swing had Dylan on the floor clutching his jaw. Before the second punch, Dylan rolled to the side and used both feet to kick his powerful aggressor's ankles.

Mitch's muscular body toppled awkwardly forward. Before gravity got him to the ground, the side of his head slammed into the corner of the steel desk, bending him so his hip hit the floor first, then his torso and heavy shoulders rolled down to follow.

His head smacked the concrete with a sickening sound like that of a melon breaking open.

The phone rang.

Mitch lay there. He didn't stir. Head wounds bleed so much. A pool of blood began forming around his head, fed by the fountain above his left ear.

"Mitch?"

Second ring.

Dylan let go of his jaw. He crawled toward his friend. "No . . . No . . . Mitch?" Dylan gently rolled Mitch onto his back, grabbed the towel that hung on the water cooler and applied pressure to the wound.

Third ring.

Dylan checked Mitch's mouth. The airway was clear. Steady breathing. He tilted the head back to further clear the airway.

"Mitch . . ."

Fourth ring.

Dylan's right hand was red with blood soaking through the towel. His left hand found the neck, and a strong pulse. He reached for Mitch's arm, searching for more confirmation of life in his wrist.

The answering machine kicked in. "This is Mitch Handel with the Kenai Fjord Parks . . ."

Dylan desperately checked the airway, breathing, and circulation, again. Gently probing, Dylan learned that his neck showed no abnormalities.

He knew that the brain is a fragile organ, and that the corner of Mitch's desk could produce profound damage in a freak accident. He put his ear to Mitch's mouth and nose, reconfirming a breath.

The answering machine let out a long beep. "Hey Mitch, Tim here. I just saw Captain Zwart at the small boat harbor. He seemed mad. That guy is scary as hell. Anyway, a couple of big black SUVs are heading to your office, I don't know what he wants, but thought I'd give you the heads up."

Dylan could barely recognize his friend's face under the coat of blood. He didn't have time to grieve, or ponder how this could happen. He forced his ghosts out of his vision.

Zwart was on his way. Probably Zwart had more medical training that Dylan, and Dylan had one basic need: survive.

Dylan knew Zwart's men were getting out of their vehicle and approaching Mitch's office. He needed to escape, fast. Who would help Mitch? Would these soldiers help Mitch? I *can't believe Mitch is so badly injured. I've got to get out of here, and get Mitch some help.*

Dylan peeked out the front window to see two black-clad soldiers approaching the front door and two at attention outside the gleaming black SUVs. He silently turned the lock on the front door and padded through the tiny kitchen/utility room in the back of Mitch's small building.

A door opened in a garage filled with winter equipment and Mitch's green forest-service pickup.

He heard the front door knob rattle and a powerful knock. Dylan heard the muffled order from one of the soldiers, "Sergeant, see if he's in the garage."

Dylan stepped into the garage and quickly ducked behind a pile of dusty snowplowing apparatus.

When he heard the sergeant knock, then enter the utility room, Dylan slipped out of the garage and crossed the street keeping the garage between himself and the soldiers.

Once on a sidewalk, Dylan set off past homes and brown yards towards the nearby hospital. It had a free phone for the families of patients. Dylan needed to call in Mitch's injury even though Zwart's men were in Mitch's office. Dylan had to be certain the emergency call went through. Just then Dylan heard two muffled pistol shots. They appeared to come from Mitch's office.

Once at the hospital he saw the volunteer ambulance crew running over to their truck. A competent-looking middle-aged black man, one of very few blacks in Seward, pulled on his jacket as Dylan walked in.

"What's up?" called Dylan.

"Someone shot a forest ranger over at the office. This might be a body pickup based on the description of the injuries."

Holy shit! Those guys killed Mitch? Why? He was no threat. He was on their side. It was too much for Dylan to process. He turned back to town and walked aimlessly.

Dylan saw a trail disappearing between a tire store and an old camping trailer. Just as he passed some bushes, he heard shouts from the forest service office.

Once in the shadows and invisible from the street, Dylan took stock. He had been shot at, chased and attacked by two of his best friends. He hadn't eaten all day despite hours of laborious running.

Fatigue tormented his body. He knew he needed bread and a bed. Returning home would be walking into a trap. Dylan thought fleetingly of the dogs. Doolie would lead Bergen to safety. But where could he hide out? To take the only road out of town would require going in the direction of the boat harbor, the place Tim, on the voice mail, said Zwart's men were coming from.

And what of Peter and Mitch? Were they both dead? How could things have changed so much in such a short a period of time?

If Dylan took a path away from town and deep into the woods, he could live off the land until winter. Maybe his pursuers would be gone by then. Maybe not. Dylan knew he needed to find out what these men wanted and why, and the only way he could learn that was to stay near town. That decision made, where to go?

Reaching into his pocket, Dylan found his wallet with some cash in it. He could go to the bakery and get some fuel for his tired body.

What he didn't know then was he would also pick up some information that would change everything.

ZWART STEPPED AWAY from Mitch's office and pulled out a cheap cell phone. He'd never made a call on it before, and he knew it would be thrown away as soon as this job was done.

Zwart looked at the crappy phone and swore. One bar. Damn this little hick town with its Alaska idiots and slippery mountain men. Who the hell would ever come to this place if he weren't paid to do it?

His call to a throwaway cell phone in the lower 48 sounded like amplified static.

"Did you get the Bible?" a commanding voice answered.

"No, Sir. We did a thorough search of his cabin. It's not there." Zwart hated the way his voice sounded when he spoke to this client.

He wanted to sound professional and competent like he normally did, but noticed a shake in his words. Maybe the static would hide it.

"Find it." The order rang in Zwart's ears.

"Yes Sir. I need to tell you. He's not dead." Zwart found himself biting his lip.

"What? You're shitting me. Zwart, are you screwing with me? I hired you because you are the best. Just kill him. Do it now. I can't believe you haven't done this little thing. It's costing me enough.

"Look," the powerful voice continued. "I said you get the other half of the payment when the job is done. Do it! Do it, or I will withdraw my support for you and let you answer for any damage you've done in that backwater piece-of-shit town."

"Yes Sir. We're almost on him, but he's extremely competent in the woods. We have a GPS on him now so it won't be long."

"The Bible is probably hidden where he lives. If you can't find it, torch the cabin."

"Yes Sir. We're already prepping the cabin with incendiary devices."

"Next time you call me, it's to tell me the Bible is in your possession or it's destroyed, and that asshole terrorist is dead. Do you read me?"

"Yes Sir," Zwart said, but realized he was talking to a disconnected phone.

Zwart thought about this job. As a former Navy Seal candidate, Zwart knew how to carry out lethal missions. He hadn't made the final cut to the Seals due to some pesky psychological tests, but he had been able to weather 12 years in the Navy.

Afterwards, years of running militia-for-hire teams in foreign places had given him a reputation for getting things done. He had wanted this mission for the buckets of money he would make, but also because it allowed him to kill a terrorist.

This had to be the most intimidating client Zwart had ever worked for. Zwart knew he was the best mercenary money could buy. Zwart understood that no one could claim his record of success, and he was determined that this little job would not tarnish that record.

11
Ten Years Earlier
. . . .

A HUGE MOUND of ice now covered the spot where Heather had stood. Exhausted, Dylan could not admit she was dead. He craved past bliss. He ached to hold Heather and surrender to the blissful slumber of a man in the arms of his sweet lover. He longed to know what she was trying to tell him before being buried by ice and rock.

Looking down at the pitiful progress he had made against the tons of ice and rock, some part of him he knew he had to face it that Heather and Julie were indeed gone.

Like a sleepwalker, Dylan moved to survive. First shelter, then food and water.

Dylan found and uncovered the packs now hidden by blown snow and ice. He pawed through them, and found what he was looking for. He set up an orange tent and dragged in his sleeping bag, food and hydration packs.

Svetlana's stove, with her name in Russian characters, hissed as it warmed the air and melted ice for water.

Any pressure on his fingers delivered sharp pain. No wonder. Pulling off his mostly shredded gloves, he gazed dumbly at bloody hands that had been abused by digging.

Another trip to the packs, and he had the group's medical duffle. He watched himself treat his injuries, utterly detached and unresponsive to the pain.

Stoically, and with a full belly, Dylan lit a candle lantern and crawled into his sleeping bag. His descent into sleep was diverted by an awareness of something sharp under his hip. Digging around, he discovered Heather's necklace. He held it in the weak yellow light and stared unblinking at its sparkle. Wave upon wave of bitter loss washed over him.

Sleep eluded Dylan. In the noisy mountain darkness he could hear the moaning of Heather, Sid and the others. They blamed him for their early deaths. All night ghostly sounds tortured his already fragile mind and brought him to heights of anxiety and depths of depression. He was sure he could hear them calling his name, begging for rescue while he was unable to act.

He awoke to a relatively still morning. The storm had passed. The voices had stopped, but he felt more alone and miserable than ever. As if on autopilot, Dylan prepared for his lonely and dangerous solo descent.

Moving mechanically around the camp, Boris's red backpack caught his eye. Dylan reached for the pack and pulled out food packs and a brown paper-wrapped package. He ripped the paper open and saw a Bible with a large symmetrical cross expertly carved into the wooden cover.

Dylan placed the food, Bible, the stove and some fuel into his pack. He searched Julie's pack for something to take back, and found her small journal and a pencil stub. All the radios and personal locator beacons were gone, smashed or buried with their users. Dylan would need to make his way to the lower moun-tain to get replacements from a cache.

Later, Dylan would be unable to remember his ten-day trip down the mountain to the staging site. He seemed to awaken in an open area near the base of Denali.

This space was obviously a bivouac site with room to land a helicopter. He approached a crudely built hut, took out a package of batteries, put a set into his radio and made a call.

At least the park rangers would know the sad outcome of this pitiful winter ascent. Now it was a matter of waiting for the weather to clear before a helicopter could complete his trip.

Dylan trudged toward one of the wooden huts. A small fire in the hearth did its best to temper the cold as Dylan sat before Heather's necklace, Julie's pocket knife, Boris's Bible, the Svetlana's stove and Sid's climbing glove. His candle, removed from the candle lantern, burned in front of the objects.

Dylan mourned without tears, and considered his losses. He focused on his breathing and, for a few moments, only Dylan and the spirits of the climbing party were present.

Dylan stepped outside the hut, grabbed several small rocks, and approached the cliff edge. For a moment he was motionless. *I'm sorry I failed you as a guide, Boris and Svetlana.* Dylan threw a rock into the wind and the cloudy depths.

My love, Heather. You opened my eyes to the beauty of life. Anger and loss propelled Dylan's second rock into the abyss.

Sid and Julie, my mistakes ended your precious lives. A third rock launched after the others. As Dylan watched the rocks disappear into the mountain rubble, he wondered why he couldn't seem to cry. *Shouldn't I be crying? What kind of man am I?*

Back inside the hut, Dylan stared into the candle-light and the shadows on the hut walls. Memories rose to flood Dylan's mind: his feelings for Heather as they laughed in the soft glow of the lantern light and the times Sid had coached him on a difficult climb.

Dylan had read once that the rope was more than a safety device, it was a real and symbolic commitment to a partner. The safety rope and this Denali disaster had forged an uncanny link between Dylan and the lost climbers.

Dylan mind filled with a dark and frightening dread when he thought about hearing Sid's voice in his mind. A good friend would go back up and confirm Sid's death.

While the candle burned, Dylan placed the objects from each person reverently into a red dry bag and closed it. He hugged the bag to his chest as he stared into the candle flame.

THE TALKEETNA RANGER STATION appeared like a tiny island of civilization located near the base of Denali. Dylan approached the station dehydrated, hungry, dirty and crumpled. But none of that even faintly alluded to the emptiness within the shell that was Dylan.

The responsibility for the loss of life on the mountain was his. It was his vanity that made him side against Sid on the summit day. Heather, gone. Julie, gone. How Sid must loathe him! Boris and Svetlana depended on him, but he failed. It didn't matter now. Nothing mattered. No one could hate Dylan more than he hated himself. This whole Denali disaster was his fault.

In stunning contrast to the wild and bitter mountaintop, the warmth and quiet in the wood-paneled office screamed its tame silence and comfort. Weatherravaged, Dylan sat emotionally vacant in a sturdy government-issue wooden chair.

An older, fit-looking ranger peered over his glasses looking like a high school principal. "So the bodies are mostly near Pig Hill at about 18,000 feet?" The ranger waited for a response.

At Dylan's nod, he continued, "They'll have to wait to May for recovery. I'll inform the families and keep you in the loop about this matter."

Dylan shrugged.

The ranger assessed Dylan's apparent lack of emotion, and then with a flash of understanding and empathy, sensed the toll Denali had taken. "Dylan, this was not your fault. You received the Emergency Alert. You followed procedures." He paused searching for the right words. "You would be the only guide I would follow for a winter ascent up the West Ridge route."

Dylan shrugged, his gaze unfocused.

"That's all I need from you. Take care of yourself, Dylan." Another pause. "Do you want to talk to the chaplain?"

No response.

"Well if you change your mind, I'm here for you. You've certainly helped me through more rough spots than I care to enumerate when we had problems on the mountain."

The desk phone chimed, and the ranger turned to answer it. Dylan stood, gathered his wallet and keys from his pocket, tossed them in the trash, and walked out the door. "Yes I spoke to him . . . No, he was unable to bring their packs down. What? . . . Did you say a Bible?"

The ranger turned to speak to Dylan, but only the empty wooden chair remained.

The closing door isolated the ranger's words from Dylan. Unnoticed by the ranger, Dylan walked toward the edge of the forest. He removed his climbing equipment and tools and walked into the winter Alaska forest, naked except for his clothing and a red dry bag in his hand. The wilderness would only grant survival to the worthy.

Weeks later and after hundreds of miles of wandering, Dylan made another winter climb that season: a solo climb up Mt. Alice to find a place to inter the Denali mementos.

At the same time, he buried his past. Dylan abruptly cut off contact to all his former friends and family, abandoned his old life, bank accounts and his ego. Never again would he attempt to gain fame and recognition by being the first to climb a certain route, record an impressive summit or solo-climb an exotic locale.

Dylan would go from his rock-star status as an expert climber to a self-imposed obscurity. He would survive, or not, based on what the Alaskan woods could offer him. If he was worthy, he would make it.

12

. . . .

WALKING TOWARD the bakery seemed like such a normal thing to do on such an abnormal day. Dylan craved normal like a drowning man craves air.

He forced himself to run through the choices he expected to have upon arrival, and was comforted by wondering if he should get a whole-wheat roll or a cranberry scone. But the feeling of ease didn't last long. Other thoughts kept intruding.

Mitch. Mitch was dead. It didn't make any sense. Dylan knew that Mitch would have been able to explain to him the official law enforcement take on his situation. Mitch would know how Dylan suddenly became a threat to national security. And why had Mitch attacked him? Two of his friends had gone rogue.

The only other law enforcement in town was the local police. Dylan rarely had contact with local law enforcement, but once he had helped Officer Burl rescue some tourists who had managed to get their raft stuck on an island near Bear Creek.

Dylan knew that as nice as Officer Burl was, he would be all business if he thought Dylan had broken serious laws and needed to be brought in.

Dylan knew Officer Burl was a man of habit. At this time of the day, Burl would probably be heading to the bakery for some afternoon coffee and a chocolate glazed donut.

Burl's radio would squawk and garble cop talk the whole time he would nurse his coffee and wolf down his donut. Perhaps Dylan could pick up some useful information as well as something to eat just by hanging out near the bakery.

Balancing a cranberry scone and coffee, Dylan found a table crowded with tourist fishermen, but with an empty chair just outside the bakery. The tourists, who were back from a fishing trip, were happy to let Dylan take the empty white plastic chair and ignored him while Dylan hid behind a newspaper.

IT WASN'T LONG before Burl showed up looking like a mellow youth pastor with his hair just a bit too long and a smile a bit too benign.

He went inside to collect his "usual", which was all ready for him on the counter. As Burl traversed the bakery Dylan noticed he paused to speak with a tall, fit-looking young woman waiting in line to give her order.

"Hey Suzie. Any investigative blog posts I need to know about before my voicemail fills up?" Officer Burl's voice boomed through the bakery.

"Hi Burl, are there any departmental snafus I can reveal to the public?" Suzie's gray-green eyes flashed with just a hint of humor.

For a moment, they both acknowledged their friendship. "By the way, thanks for your help on the

Fourth Avenue project. Many folks appreciated how you and the department really stepped up to the plate."

"No problem." Burl carefully balanced his coffee and donut. "How are you doing these days? That guy was a jerk!"

"I'm better. I'm moving on." Suzie worked to refocus. "In fact, I have an important news interview tomorrow. Wish me luck!"

"I remember the Suzie who dominated the state volleyball tournament. Talk about the ability to be direct and precise! You will always come out on top." Suzie's grateful expression summed up her feelings. She stepped away from Burl with a wave as the barista prepared to take her order.

Once outside, Burl sat down at the table right next to Dylan's, but facing the harbor, away from Dylan and his fishermen tablemates.

Moments later, Burl's radio made some unintelligible sounds then rang. It was a cell phone ring. Burl's cell phone. Burl put down his coffee, turned down his radio, and dug his phone out of his pants pocket.

"Hi Jack," Burl took a huge bite of his donut smearing chocolate on his cheek while he listened. Dylan did not have to strain to hear Burl's side of the conversation.

"Then you tell that Zwart guy that he does not own this town. I don't care who he has connections with." Burl wiped the chocolate from his cheek onto his finger and then licked it clean.

"I don't care if God himself gave Zwart his orders, that jerk is not running things. Mitch was my friend, too." Another bite of the donut, smeared more chocolate on his cheek.

"Did you talk to Peter about this? I bet Peter would know why Baker went crazy and killed Mitch.

"You mean Peter's in Anchorage for the whole day? Dylan must have hit him pretty hard."

Dylan saw Burl lick the paper plate. Betsy, in the bakery, always put too much chocolate on the donuts, just like her customers preferred.

"When will he be back?

"Tomorrow? You're sure?

"OK. When Peter returns, I want a statement from him." Burl pulled off the lid to his coffee cup and poured a sugar packet into it.

"What do you mean a Bible verse?

"What does that have to do with this investigation?" After tasting the coffee, Burl added another sugar packet, stirring the coffee by swirling it around.

"Well, figure it out." Burl used his finger to pick up some crumbs on the plastic tabletop near his paper plate.

Just then the fishermen made as if leaving, so Dylan left too, and turned toward a fish house restaurant.

From the conversation he noticed animosity between Zwart's forces and the locals. Alaskans are easygoing and likeable, but they don't tolerate outsiders trying to push them around.

Dylan wondered if Peter would be in Anchorage for the rest of the day. He might be hanging out in the big city to avoid talking to the local police. After all, Peter's gun put a .357 slug into Dylan's floor. That would bring up questions in Officer Burl's mind.

Peter usually made an Anchorage run twice a month for his job, and it was about this time.

Burl or one of his officers would talk to Peter in the morning when he returned to work. Maybe Dylan should talk to Peter right afterwards.

It would be a huge risk to face Peter again, but maybe Dylan could reason with him. Maybe he could explain to Peter that, whatever Peter thought he had done, it wasn't true. If Peter has lost his mind, Dylan owed him some help. A man should be able to reason with his best friend. But reason should not be taken for granted.

13

· · · · · · · · · ·

AS DYLAN WALKED a few steps behind the fishermen, he felt the morning's activities in his legs. Looking down at his body, he looked like he had been dragged through the forest. He probably smelled like it too.

Even though many locals at the fish dock and cannery walked around dirty after work, Dylan thought he should try to blend in a little better and get some rest.

Where could he go? It was five o'clock at least. It wouldn't be dark for hours, but sleeping time was quickly approaching. If only he could escape quickly to Lowell Point. He would be cornering himself in the little community. Lowell Point sits past town a few miles at the end of the road. He could rest there in a fishing shed he maintained for Shorty, complete with cot and snacks.

When his security blanket of fishermen suddenly exited the bakery to check out a tacky hole-in-the-wall gift shop, Dylan went along and pretended to be interested in a rack of clothing outside the shop, standing behind it and scanning the boat harbor across the street.

No black SUVs like the one that had rolled up after the accident at Mitch's. He knew military men hung around Seward often: soldiers taking time off from the base in Fairbanks.

There—Dylan saw him. The same outfit the Oxman had worn. He held a gun and stood erect at the ramp leading down to the boat dock.

I guess I can't leave by boat. He figured there would be another guard at the next boat ramp. *How many gunmen does Zwart have?*

The soldier turned his attention from the harbor to the street and shops. Dylan brought a sweatshirt up from the rack in front of him to hide his face, only his sharp, patient eyes showed over the logo, "A Veteran of the Greatland!"

As the soldier turned completely to face the gaudy gift shop, Dylan raised the sweatshirt to hide his face. Right before the cotton and polyester hid his vision, Dylan saw something. No, someone.

Not a soldier, not Zwart, not Peter. Was it Sid? Sid was dead. Could it be a ghost from Dylan's nightmares, standing in front of a whale-watching outfitter?

Dylan fought hard not to lower the sweatshirt from in front of his face for a double take. He wondered if his battered mind was playing a trick on him. Yet a gunman from Zwart was looking, so he kept his curtain up. A few moments later, Dylan casually let the sweatshirt fall, exposing his eyes. The gunman was eyeing the harbor once again, and Dylan scanned the whale watching out-fitter. No ghost there.

Dylan would have to wait until tomorrow to find out about Peter, but he couldn't quell his curiosity about Sydney Green, a spirit from the past.

As Dylan paid a young seasonal employee for the "A Veteran of the Greatland!", he checked the small wad of cash in his wallet. He couldn't keep buying things for much longer.

The predictable evening breeze was picking up, making it appropriate for a trimmed-beard man with muddy pants and a new sweatshirt to put his hood up and his head down.

Now to get to Lowell Point and that fishing shed with the food and cot.

Walking there would be too slow; hitch hiking was too risky. Dylan looked up and down the street for bicycles. Locals often didn't chain up their bikes. Thieves easily get called out in small towns, and tourists don't steal bikes. Dylan saw it. A bike rack across the street displayed three potential getaway tools.

Trying not to draw attention, he crossed the street at a brisk walk. The first bike was an old Schwinn mountain bike. A kryptonite U-lock connected its frame and the rack. The second, a newer lady's hybrid on-road/off-road, was held fast to the rack with a chain. The third bike was a rusty ten-speed. The down tube had the words Iron Horse on it. No lock. Dylan hopped on the Iron Horse as it were his own and pedaled into an alley away from the main street toward Lowell Point.

AFTER TWELVE MINUTES of fierce pedaling, Dylan let out a sigh to find the fishing shed vacant. He stashed the bike under the building, next to two sea kayaks visible behind the shed's short stilts. Inside, he wolfed down Shorty's old granola bars and downed several bottles of water before changing into the clean work clothes stored in the closet.

With food in his uneasy belly, his body nearly collapsed onto the camping cot. Dylan pulled the one wool blanket over his body and covered his head. Would they find him here? Zwart didn't know about this place. And based on Lowell Point's location, he probably would assume Dylan would have taken to the forest. He was so tired. He just needed to rest a little.

His mind rapidly shut down into troubled sleep. The old ghosts joined the image of Mitch bleeding on the floor of his office and the Oxman's neck ripped open with a rusty piton.

Ghosts frequently haunt before sleep. Sometimes they annoy Dylan with their accusations and the way they ignore his excuses. Other times they can terrify Dylan to the point where he screams and wakes with his heart hammering. The worst is when he sees them hiding in the woods and blaming him.

Right now, next to Dylan lay the invisible outline of the ghost that often lingered next to him in bed. The ghost that in these ten years haunted him closely, remained achingly intangible. He unconsciously reached his arms to hold her, but some part of him knew he was dreaming.

Somewhere between wake and sleep, Dylan's mind conjured up a long-ago image of Heather's soft hair floating golden on the pillow and her small breasts rising and falling in a most peaceful trusting sleep rhythm. Dylan kissed her eyes so gently, she didn't notice. He kissed her again and she frowned and rubbed her cheek. He could gaze at her for hours.

Dylan's mind remembered that earlier that day on a picnic bike ride, she peddled through the sunshine looking so pretty he ached. After eating, she had pulled up a golden braid and searched for nonexistent split ends, while she told Dylan that she wanted him to love her as much as she loved him. There was no way she could possibly love him as much as he cherished her.

That night so long ago, as he held her gently, he felt his heart swell. He was so imperfect, and yet she truly loved him. God, she was flawless! A lover and a friend.

Dylan's body jerked upright. A friend! *Peter!* Peter knew about this shed. He could betray him again. Peter could tell Zwart about the shed.

Dylan checked the crooked, battery-powered wall clock and noticed he'd slept through the night. He gathered useful items from the shed.

He had to leave and confront Peter. Peter would tell him why the attempted murder, why the small ruthless army was intent on killing a simple handyman.

Could this whole thing be a revenge attack from Heather's wealthy father? Colonel William Bolton blamed Dylan for her death on Denali. Certainly Bolton had the money and wherewithal to find and hire an army like Zwart's. But why would Peter go along with Bolton? It didn't make sense.

Right before Peter attempted to kill Dylan, he said something about *blood is thicker*. Dylan knew that the phrase *Blood is thicker than water* meant that loyalty tends to follow family ahead of friends. Peter's small family included his mother, affectionately called Baba, living in an assisted care facility in Anchorage and a brother, Illya. This brother lived in Washington D.C. and ran a division of Homeland Security.

Maybe Colonel Bolton had threatened Illya or Baba. In order to protect his family, Peter felt he needed to kill Dylan.

At the harbor yesterday, Dylan had seen a figure that reminded him of Sid Green, his former best friend and mentor. Dylan felt that his own personal ambition had put Sid's wife in danger. Although it didn't really fit his personality, if Sid had somehow survived the Denali disaster, he must want revenge. Pain can change a man. Dylan knew this from experience. But how could Sid arrange for Zwart's army and Peter's attempt to murder Dylan?

Tires crunched on the gravel driveway. Dylan stepped to the window. A solitary black Escalade pulled slowly forward. Dylan was cornered.

14

. . . .

THE SHED HAD two doors: the driveway-facing one, where Dylan had entered, and the back way—a two-foot square hatch designed for loading and unloading kayak gear. This hatchway emptied into the same gravel lot the shed was in. If Dylan exited out the back, he couldn't run without Zwart seeing his back and hearing hiking boots against gravel.

Two men got out of the SUV. Zwart from the driver's seat, his face wearing an expression of hardened confidence and his clothes looking like they were just extracted from a hot ironing board. From the shotgun side of the SUV stepped a skinny man with a ratty face.

Skinnyman bobbled his head around on his bony neck, his eyes greedy.

Dylan thought fast. Leave out the back, and wait until they're inside to walk away.

Two pairs of combat boots crunched gravel. The back hatch closed silently behind Dylan as the front door opened. Dylan could hear boots pounding on the plywood floor.

"He's not here, Sir."

The ratty man's voice reminded Dylan of a cartoon bad guy who sounded as weak and evil as he looked. Dylan imagined him to be the soldier who had gunned down the moose calf earlier.

"I didn't expect him to hide out here, Randall. Peter said he shares this broken down shed with some other fish-brained townies." Zwart's voice rang with brassy poise and power, a contrast to his weedy henchman. "Well let's rig this place in case he comes here. We can leave a little . . . explosive surprise." Randall snickered at his boss's words.

An explosive surprise? Dylan didn't want to leave his post by the back door. He hoped they would mention why they were after him.

"Standard rigging for our big surprise, Captain Zwart?"

"Roger that," barked Zwart. "That dumb mountain man will find out what anti-personnel mines can do. If Mr. Baker opens this door when we're done with it, he'll have a whole belly full of shrapnel to reckon with."

"But Sir, if he shares this shed, might someone other than Mr. Baker trigger the bomb?" Randall seemed excited at the possibility.

"It's a risk we'll take. I've never failed a mission, and I won't start now."

"I'll get the APM, Sir." Dylan thought he heard a ratty chortle as the front door opened and closed.

"We better rig this back hatch door, too," shouted Zwart.

Uh oh. Dylan took a gentle step off the back stoop just in time. The hatch swung abruptly open, resting in the place where Dylan had been standing. He hoped that Zwart had missed the crunch of gravel under his boots. "Yup. Randall, bring two. Mr. Baker might as well blow the whole thing up when he dies." Zwart voice rang from inside the shed.

With a wave of passion, Dylan knew he had to confront Zwart. He had to know why they wanted him dead. What could make this man risk others' lives for his death? Most of all, he was angry.

Randall was returning from the Escalade. Dylan risked a peek around the shed to see him walking head down, absorbed in looking at the box of explosives he was carrying. He seemed to be counting the little bombs in his arms.

"Six, seven. Captain Zwart won't mind a seventh. Heh heh, blow-up Mr. Baker with . . ."

Thud. Randall fell earthward. The keys to the Escalade jingled next to the seven grenades. Then he rose shakily to his knees. Oops, not hard enough.

Thud. Thud. Quickly, Dylan dropped the rock he had used on Randall and replaced it with the handgun from his victim's belt. Just like the Oxman's, it was no halibut gun: a Sig Sauer 1911 tactical .45 with silencer attached. He clicked off the ambidextrous safety.

Two strides had him at the doorway of the shed. As he expected, Zwart was standing by the back hatchway, looking out on the bay. Dylan didn't have time to appreciate the view as he slammed Zwart against the doorframe and laid the cold gun barrel against the back of his head.

"Move and I shoot. I want some answers, Zwart." Dylan's words were resolute, but he wasn't a tough guy who felt comfortable hitting people and pointing guns at them. Only his desperation forced him to play the part of a killer.

Zwart froze with utter calm. He didn't even tremble. "Ah, Mr. Baker. We thought you would have taken to the woods."

He seemed composed, as if a gun to his head was as usual as shaking hands at a business meeting. Had he been in this situation before? Did he know how to extract himself? Dylan used his free hand to yank Zwart's arms behind his back and away from his radio.

"Keep your hands away from your radio." Dylan took a step back. "I'm not kidding, Zwart. One false move. I've already knocked off a few of your men, so what's one more?"

"Yes, Mr. Baker, that nail to my lieutenant's neck was quite disturbing. Have you killed Randall, too?"

"I slit his throat, he's probably bled out by now." Dylan hoped Randall wouldn't regain consciousness while he was questioning Zwart.

"Well, he was rather annoying anyway. You'll have to show me how to do that and not get all bloody. You should be spattered all over." Zwart regarded Dylan's appearance skeptically.

Dylan looked down at his clean hands. *Ask him why he's after you.*

"Why are you after me, Zwart? How am I a threat to national security?" Dylan held the unfamiliar pistol awkwardly.

"I'm simply a mercenary, Mr. Baker. My employers do not disclose their motives." Zwart pulled on his cuffs to straighten the sleeves of his impeccably clean jacket.

"That's a lie, Zwart. You mentioned Denali when we met at the cliff. You know something about me. You said you were hired by the government."

"Ah, yes. That is who we mercenaries do most of our work for, Mr. Baker, the government. And I did read your dossier. I know quite a bit about your boring little life.

"Now, if you think you can threaten information out of me, let me tell you that I have passed worse tests in my tours on duty in the Middle East. I've withstood torture you can't imagine and kept my mouth shut."

"But how . . . "

This was not the first time Zwart faced a gun to his head. He had no trouble turning so quickly that Dylan couldn't think to pull the trigger. It was, however, the first time Dylan had held a gun to a man's head, and his stance was farther away than Zwart expected. Instead of disarming and landing on top, Zwart accidentally pushed Dylan across the room. Dylan never took the gun off his target. Before Dylan could register what was happening, Zwart pulled his own weapon. A standoff.

"Ah, Mr. Baker. If you were going to shoot me, you already would have. You are afraid of killing since you murdered your fiancée and Mr. Alexandrov on Denali. I know people say it was an accident, Mr. Baker, but you and I know you screwed up.

"You are probably wondering why I haven't killed you. Part of my mission is that I am to possibly recover a Bible. Most importantly, I am to silence you before you leak its secrets. "Where's the Bible, Mr. Baker?"

"You want a Bible? But why?"

"Well, if you're not going to cooperate . . ." Zwart's finger started to tighten on his trigger.

Bang. Dylan's pistol bucked in his hand.

Dylan had grazed his target. Zwart clutched his firing arm and spun down to his knee, dropping his pistol. Before he could recover, Dylan kicked him in the face. Hard. This time he didn't hesitate, didn't try to scare the Captain into obeying his orders.

Disoriented due to the gunshot wound, Zwart's reflexes were slow. Dylan tackled the lanky body to the ground and secured his hands behind his back. The abundant fishing line in the cabin served well to bind his hands, then feet. Houdini couldn't break those bonds or escape from something as simple as 30-pound test line.

Zwart struggled to maintain his stony composure. "You son of a bitch, Baker! You shot my arm! Asshole!"

Dylan tried to let him know between vigorous struggles that the wound wasn't deep, had barely grazed the upper arm. There wasn't even much blood, but the impeccable jacket was ruined. Maybe that was the source of Zwart's discomfort.

The gunshot had been fairly quiet because of the silencer, but Zwart's torrent of curses might soon attract the attention of the Lowell Point residents. Dylan gagged Zwart by shoving a filthy fishing rag into his mouth. He examined Zwart's wound once more before leaving, no permanent harm to life or limb.

Regardless, he'd leave him be with his fear of amputation. Dylan felt a tinge of regret that Zwart was so filled with rage. He would have liked to question him further.

Randall was still out cold on the gravel. Dylan dragged him into the shack and laid him across Zwart, who clearly did not like the muddy soldier on top of his clean uniform, especially since they were tied face-to-face. But Dylan's knots would make it a long time before Zwart would be able to get the unconscious soldier off of him.

Dylan smashed their radios with a heavy torque wrench, leaving Zwart without access to backup. He would have to walk, covered with mud and Randall's vomit all the way back to town.

Shutting the door to the fishing shed, he looked around. What now?

The keys to the Escalade twinkled next to APMs in the midday sun. Driving that beast into town would be like wearing Gucci at the Yukon Dave's Pub, but leaving the SUV here would be a giveaway for anyone looking for Zwart.

Dylan ditched the Escalade, literally, in a carved out piece of earth down the lane on Lowell Point. A man from Palmer had once wanted to build a house here and dug the basement out before he ran out of money. The grown-over-bramble-filled hole in the ground swallowed the Escalade with nearly no trace of it showing.

Jogging back to the fishing cabin, Dylan decided his route out of Lowell Point, a place that really had turned out to be the dead end of Seward. He pulled one of the sea kayaks out from under the cabin. In the cockpit was stowed the paddle and PFD.

The boat was a smooth Necky Elaho. It was a little wide for Dylan's liking, making it maneuverable, but less apt to stay on course for long paddles. The second kayak, the Eliza, was designed for the ladies. Dylan always wondered who would buy a hot pink kayak but for this trek, the bright color might actually draw attention away from him.

Dylan pushed the wider kayak back under the cabin and pulled out the Eliza. Inside lay a shorter paddle, a pink PFD, and a flowery floppy hat. Bingo. He shouldered the boat and walked the hundred yards to the beach. Donning his disguise, he climbed into the kayak, and with the grace of a veteran kayaker, launched himself into the blue waters of Resurrection Bay.

Tourists often mistake the bay for a lake. Mountains brace the North, East, and West edges, and a string of sharp-peaked islands block Seward's view of the Gulf of Alaska. Dylan had once heard a woman from Homer say that the height and proximity of the mountains to the town was suffocating. Dylan liked to think they were tenderly hugging Seward.

Atop the water of his protected bay now, Dylan felt the safest he had all day. Sea kayaking always had a way of calming him. Here on the water was where he had begun to find peace with himself.

Dylan paddled further away from shore than usual, although knowing that the presence of a female sea kayaker shouldn't draw too much attention. He wished there was another boat nearby. He'd stand out more alone. Even so, the calm waters of the bay made it popular with kayakers.

Dylan peered out from under his floppy hat. He wanted to take it off and feel the sun on his face. Snow, still stacked high on the tops of the mountains, reflected back bright white: a stark contrast to the deep turquoise of the bay and the light blue of the sky.

Mt. Alice was the tallest peak here. She towered over the bay and across from Seward at nearly six thousand feet from bay to summit. As the range stretches south toward the ocean, the peaks become lower and lower.

Geologists call these drowning mountains. As the northwestern motion of the Pacific tectonic plate compresses the North American plate, this range sinks deeper and deeper. Dylan had once tried to be a mountain— big and invincible. At the time of the accident, he realized that even mountains sink to the depths.

Dylan watched his paddle break the surface of the water, and glide through by the force of his stroke. Two marbled murrelets saw him approach and popped underwater. He wondered if they would dive under his kayak.

Seemingly at peace with the world, Dylan felt pain with each stroke toward his destination. He knew he was facing trouble. He had hidden for ten years from himself and his ghosts, but he wouldn't hide from Peter, from Zwart, and from their accusations.

Denali, Heather, Mr. Alexandrov, a Bible, and Dylan's supposed crimes against his country: Dylan needed to confirm his suspicions, and end this hunt. Each stroke brought him closer to Seward, where he would seek answers from the man who had held a halibut gun to his face yesterday morning. Peter, undoubtedly back from Anchorage by now, knew what this was all about and could explain to Dylan why things had gone so wrong. Or Peter was crazy and needed Dylan's help. Dylan was headed to Peter's office not knowing if he'd face a friend or enemy.

Dylan longed to stay on the water as he sighted a familiar sea otter. The furry marine animal floated comically on its back with face and hind feet out of the water. But every instant on the water was a moment for Zwart to be found and untied, for Dylan to be in danger.

With the help of the current and his long strokes, Dylan quickly found himself with Lowell Point miles behind him, and the southern tip of Seward under his boat.

He grounded the Eliza, stowed his disguise in the cockpit, and cautiously approached the SeaLife Center. Soon he would see Peter. Perhaps the answers to why Peter had tried to shoot Dylan could be found.

Dylan wondered what would happen when he saw Peter. His friend was obviously crazy or under extreme pressure, but Dylan could not imagine a scenario where he could abandon his friend without attempting a rescue.

15

Two Years Earlier

. . . .

THE STORMY OCEAN swells that threaten Seward, Alaska are mere feints compared to the heroic wave wars that rage beyond the neck of Resurrection Bay. Out there the calm bay waters meet the powerful restive Gulf of Alaska forces.

When boats pass by Cape Calisto and become even with the barrier islands protecting the inner waters, they must depend on the whims of the uncaring sea gods who might smite them for their pleasure.

Peter and Dylan started their weekend kayak expedition in full knowledge that a strong south wind could force them to return. Each was hyperaware of the dangers that awaited them. But the trip would be brief, and their ability to turn back reasonably plausible if waters got rough.

The choppy seas should have been regarded as a harbinger of what was to come as they paddled closer to Bear Glacier on the second day of their trip. Decked out in their annoyingly sweaty dry suits, which would limit their exposure to the icy waters in case of a capsize, they cut through the oncoming 18 to 24-inch chop with their graceful Kevlar sea kayaks.

When a kayak overturns, a skilled paddler can perform a rolling maneuver to right the craft. Since only tiny amounts of water can enter a properly sealed sea kayak, a paddler experiences relatively little inconvenience.

If the kayak cannot be rolled, a wet exit must be performed. This operation floods the cockpit with water when the paddler swims from under the overturned boat.

Afterwards, the experienced paddler then must reenter the cockpit of the righted boat, pump out the water, reseal the cockpit and paddle on.

Few kayakers can perform a successful roll on still, flat water. Dylan and Peter both could roll their kayaks—in flat waters.

Bear Glacier is the largest glacier that extends off the Harding Ice Field. Years ago, the glacier stopped pushing a wall of debris, its terminal moraine, and began retreating towards the ice field.

It ends in a pool of its own run off and melt, a lagoon of light turquoise-green water displaying icebergs on its unworldly counterpane. Only small vessels can slip over the moraine at high tide to explore the lagoon.

To paddle among the ice in the cold silty water is to enter a magical world of glowing blue glacial bergs and milky green liquid.

Dylan and Peter spent the afternoon paddling among the icebergs in Bear Glacier's lagoon. To the west Dylan could see a ghost forest.

This stand of eerie white trees was formed during the earthquake of 1964 when the shoreline dropped so deep, the forest could only take in salt water. The salt eventually killed the trees, and left them unable to decompose. They stand like white columns placed haphazardly along a deep green grassy shoreline.

In contrast to the white forest and pale green milky water, the icebergs floated with a blue-white inner glow as if powered by some ancient, inward light. Some bergs looked to be the size of cars or houses, others the size of an Anchorage apartment building.

Peter snapped pictures of the retreating glacier, and Dylan observed some harbor seals with their pups lying like sausages on an iceberg.

Dylan finally convinced Peter to leave their paradise when he tuned into the marine radio weather report to hear that eight-foot swells now faced them beyond the protection of the lagoon: scary paddling, even for the best.

Outside of the lagoon, Dylan breathed rhythmically as his graceful kayak rode each swell. Keeping Peter in his peripheral vision, he strained to see beyond the cloud front.

With each stroke, the water worsened. Swells began to whitecap, breaking like they wanted to punch the sky.

Dylan watched his course, all the while keeping track of the changing waters, constantly adjusting his kayak to hit the waves bow first. Peter's droopy eyes were hard and focused, and his strokes strong and long.

Through the chaos of waves and wind, Dylan's marine radio continued to broadcast the forecast. Ten foot swells at Calisto Head, rain, wind at 25 to 30 knots.

Peter capsized first. He couldn't keep course while hitting the waves head on. Dylan maneuvered quickly to paddle to his friend. Peter rolled his kayak back, but the force of the wave had swept his spare paddle, pump and compass off his deck. His expression read shock. Dylan knew he and Peter had never rolled their boats in such conditions.

In the moment of relief to see Peter resurface, Dylan let down his guard. The wave broke at his side, and despite his low brace with his paddle, and his balance perfected by years of sports, he found himself underwater.

In the summer, the mouth of Resurrection Bay holds waters that vary between thirty-eight and forty-five degrees. It was cold.

A man can't do oval breathing underwater. He can't think when immersed in the icy whirlpool of a Pacific storm. Dylan didn't need to.

His muscles remembered what to do. Bringing the paddle against the side of the boat, and his wrists out of the ocean and into its biting spray, he rotated his shoulders like the hundred times of practice in his past, pushing the water behind him and his back, neck, and finally his head, out of the sea. One breath. One exchange of carbon dioxide for fresh oxygen, and he was under again. Same movements. Were his wrists out the water this time? The swells disorient. A failed roll.

A failed roll forces a critical decision. After a failed roll, the kayaker must decide between two significant choices. To use that last oxygen in his brain and blood attempt another roll, or to pull the spray-skirt that keeps him locked in his boat, and exit his craft: a wet exit.

Dylan didn't remember making the decision. He found himself gasping at the rain, watching Peter struggle to stay in one place, still one with his boat. He had rolled.

Peter shouted against the howling blast, "The wind is also blowing from the East. The cross-wind makes this impossible!"

Back to oval breathing.

Peter shouted above the rain again, "Let's go back to the lagoon before we get into more trouble."

Dylan answered by turning his kayak back. Peter flipped once more before they reached the terminal moraine. Did he feel the same as Dylan had under the water?

The protected lagoon felt eerie and calm. The wind blew above the turquoise pool. If the water had been glass before, it was now cake frosting smoothed over by a rough knife – uniform ripples irritated the surface. Heaven had clouded over, but it was still heaven.

Peter and Dylan assessed their physical conditions. They exchanged an awkward laugh when Dylan admitted he thought he might die before he had righted his kayak.

They drifted toward one of the apartment-sized icebergs. Like moose in a meadow, they felt safer at the edge. Had there been sun, the iceberg would have shaded them with her wide girth.

"God I'm glad we're safe now," Peter sighed leaning back in his seat and exposing his face to the rain.

"We'll wait for this storm to pass, and have daylight enough to get to Calisto Head," Dylan replied.

"Safe at last. I can breathe." Peter had set down his paddle and massaged his hands that were protected by neoprene gloves.

Dylan looked around.

"Safe. Safe. Thank God. By this I know that thou favourest me, because mine enemy doth not triumph over me."

"Peter, is that the scripture that lets you know that God favors you because you are successful?" Dylan asked. "I never went to Sunday school."

"That's how you tell if you are doing things right. God rewards you." Peter pulled out his radio. Scowled at the weak signal, then paddled to the other side of the berg to get a fresh weather report.

With a crack and splash their sheltering iceberg split, sending a 20-foot wave and a new iceberg into the water. Dylan watched it submerge then break the surface, traveling from below, where it had been connected to the monster next to them.

Peter didn't see it pierce their calm. He was on the other side of the iceberg with the radio. Then, with growing speed and intention, the floating ice protecting them from the wind seemed to stagger then start a slow-motion roll. Dylan back-paddled two quick strokes toward safety.

Peter looked straight up at the wall of ice approaching him and purposely overturned, exposing the bottom of his boat to the falling ice. The iceberg slammed into the tough, Kevlar boat and popped Peter out of his kayak like a champagne cork under pressure.

Being a witness to a disturbing traumatic event does not make it easier to observe the next horrible tragedy. Knowing that the pain of watching a loved one die might fade with time did not make watching his best friend's struggles any easier.

All Dylan felt in that moment was the fear, pain and an aching helplessness. The familiarity of situation only reminded him how much he hated it—hated watching someone he loved laugh one moment and be gone the next.

Peter didn't die. The shelf of ice pushed him ten feet down, where he allowed his PFD to bring him to the surface of the disorienting milky waters. Once he broke the surface, Dylan noticed Peter was still clutching his spray skirt and paddle.

Dylan was there to help. Several hours later, the storm abated and a friendly fishing boat responded to their plea with the promise of a rescue. Dylan knew that locals rarely called the Coast Guard: too much paper work.

"Thank God. Thank God," Peter muttered each time he glanced at the ruins of his kayak.

Dylan felt himself filled with a need to protect his friends. If he didn't, it seemed they could be taken from him at any moment.

16

· · · · · · · · · ·

SEWARD RESIDENTS ARE rightfully proud of their SeaLife Center. In all the great state of Alaska, there is only one public aquarium and wildlife rescue center. It shines like a crown showing off graceful steel, glass and masonry on the shores of Resurrection Bay.

In the back of the center are some offices held by Alaska's Fish and Game Department. Peter Ivanov worked as the field agent for this small satellite office. Dylan, knowing Peter should be back from his Anchorage, visit had to find out what Peter knew about all the madness of the past day.

Dylan hoped to find him alone at this time in the early evening. Maybe he could reason with Peter and help him find a way back to normalcy. Thinking that the entrance to Peter's office might be watched, Dylan decided to find an alternate way into the Fish and Game suite of rooms or to somehow disguise himself.

Walking towards the SeaLife Center, Dylan ran across some teens lounging outside a video game resale shop. He asked for directions, appeared confused, then made a deal with the two boys. He would buy them Alaska tourist clothes, ice cream cones and pay their admission, if they would walk him as far as the Bering Sea exhibit in the SeaLife Center.

Wearing identical hats and sweatshirts, the trio walked past a black Escalade illegally parked near the entryway of the Center. Another SUV was just visible in front of Peter's office. Dylan nearly turned back. He felt an odd hollow feeling in his chest. *I should not be here.* He had learned to trust his feelings, but checking out Peter's office and possibly talking to him might be the only way he could discover why these people were trying to kill him.

Zwart's men seemed to be hunting for him everywhere. He hoped his short beard, tourist garb and kids-with-cones would get him where he needed to be.

Dylan and the boys walked right past a large man wearing an earpiece attached to a flesh-colored coil that ran down his thick neck. His mirror dark glasses seemed to look past Dylan and his decoys—probably looking for a single, heavily bearded man.

Once inside the sparkling clean atrium with its slight odor of caged animals, the boys left to look at the birds, and Dylan entered the men's room. He took off his tourist clothes and hid them in the trash. Next to the restrooms, Dylan pretended to drink out of the fountain while he waited for someone to leave via the Employee Only door.

Once through that door, he strode purpose-fully to the staff lounge. Empty. He opened nine lockers before he found a lab coat and ID badge hanging next to some notebooks.

He turned his badge so only the back showed, since he doubted if anyone would believe his name was Trang Ng. Dylan feigned confidence as he entered the empty conference room that formed the back wall to Peter's office. His intuition was screaming at him not to go any farther. *Run! Run!*

Dylan ignored the warnings and proceeded uneasily. He was certain that some answers might be found in Peter's office. From his earlier visits to the SeaLife Center, Dylan knew the conference room closet abutted the closet in Peter's office. Dylan figured he could enter Peter's office by cutting through the closet wall. Dylan found a *reserved* sign, planted it outside the room and started pulling AV equipment out of the corner closet.

After working about 20 minutes pulling out wallboard, Dylan wiggled his upper body through the SeaLife Center's conference room closet and into the Alaska Fish and Game office closet.

From the closet floor, Dylan listened for any sound from the office. Silence. Tearing out the wallboard had covered Dylan with white dust, but also weakened some shelves above Dylan. With a groan, a shelf containing boxes of Alaska F&G publications sagged onto Dylan's back. *Run!* That inner voice screamed again. *You are trapped!*

He had to ignore that voice. Dylan was certain that answers awaited him on the other side. Once he opened the closet door, he would be in Peter's office.

Performing a push-up with the boxes on his back, Dylan reached up to the doorknob and pushed. It seemed stuck. Dylan put his forehead against the door and pushed again. The door opened a crack and hit a chair in Peter's office that made a tremendous squeak. Above him, Dylan could hear more boxes starting to slide down the shelf and stop.

Any movement of his could send dozens of heavy boxes sliding down on him. Dylan felt panic in his stomach when he heard voices getting closer as they approached Peter's office. Dylan knew if he moved now, everything stored above him would come sliding down with a crash.

Dylan was now forced to remain in push-up stance holding up all the boxes with his arms. Dylan couldn't maintain this position for long.

Panic began welling up in his chest. Would this be where he died? If he were in a forest, he would be relaxed and focused. Trapped in this closet, his anxiety level was off the chart. His shoulders were turning numb. Dylan reflexively tran-sitioned into oval breathing.

"Just a simple arrest. Nothing more or less. And you can blog that," a deep voice snapped.

"Simple my foot. You're practically taking over our town," the feisty feminine voice sounded unintim-idated. "Peter, what are these black-suited bullies doing here?"

"Oh Suzie, can't you leave this alone and write about the craft fair?" Peter's slow voice sounded tired. "Captain Zwart here is very busy."

"I'm writing for my readers. They want some answers.

"Captain, why the parade of black vehicles with Alabama plates? You didn't drive these up here from Alabama. I checked with my sources in Anchorage. You didn't use a ferry. What did you do, fly these in just to arrest a shy mountain man?"

Shy? Dylan did not think of himself as shy. He was reclusive, but not a bit shy.

"Ma'am, I told you we are executing a DHS war-rant. It turns out Mr. Baker is a very bad man. We expect to have him in custody by this evening, tomorrow at the latest. That's all I can say. If you want more information, you need to talk to Homeland Security." The voice snapped again in a way to close the conversation.

"I called Homeland Security and they claim they know nothing about Mr. Baker. I checked their website, too. Why won't you show me your badge or your orders?"

"Suzie, please. If it's classified, they can't show that stuff," Peter's voice seemed to plead for her to drop it.

"Peter, don't you 'Suzie please' me. These guys are acting like they own the town. You. You're Alaskan. You know we don't like to be bossed around by strangers," her voice rose. "What do they have to do with Fish and Game? Criminy, Peter. There's been at least one of these ninja Escalades outside your office for two days now."

"Ma'am, you need to leave now. I must talk to Mr. Ivanov," Zwart's voice dismissed her.

"I'm checking on this, Captain Zwart. You think about it and call me. Here's my card. I'm contacting our congressman and finding out from him what's going on, so you had better be telling the truth."

The door slammed as Dylan presumed Suzie left. The pain in Dylan's hands was at a 10. Soon his arms would collapse, the boxes would give away his hiding place and these guys would kill him. Dylan wondered if Peter or Zwart would be the one to pull the trigger.

"Christ, Ivanov, who the hell is she? She's too nosy. If she had bigger breasts, she'd be interesting, but I don't like nosy girls. You need to tell her something so she drops this," the deep voice slammed into Peter. "I have a man who would dearly love to take care of a pretty little thing like that."

"Leave her alone. She's Suzie Alaneo, and she writes for a little thing called the Seward Blogletter. It's basically a gossip rag that goes out every two weeks. No one reads it."

"Alaneo? What's that? A Jap name?"

"It's Hawaiian. This town is full of Russians and Hawaiians." Peter's voice sounded slower than ever.

"Whoever she is, she's asking too many questions. It could get her hurt if she doesn't stop. You got any other women in town? If we are here another six hours, my men are going to need some comfort. Arrange to have a dozen prostitutes sent over to our hotel this evening."

Zwart continued, "Most of my men will take what they want if they can't get it for money. I don't want to clean up after any fights between hotheaded locals and my soldiers. There won't be much left of the locals."

"No way. Seward has a population of about 3,000. I doubt if there is a single prostitute in our whole town. Why do you hire felons? You know you can't trust them."

"My men are specialists. When it's a wet op, you need soldiers who aren't afraid to pull the trigger."

"Zwart, you need to control these thugs. Keep them out in the woods if need be. Out at Caines Head, there's a set of cabins that are only used during hunting season. Take your men out there."

Peter walked across his office to his desk and paused. Fatigue shook Dylan's body so violently, he could see the door vibrate.

"I'll think about that location. Right now nearly all my soldiers are out securing the places you suggested Dylan might hide. You should see how we've rigged his home. It's more dangerous than an Alabama moonshiner on opening day of deer season. If Baker gets even close to his house, he'll be busier than a long tailed cat in a room full of rocking chairs."

"It's guarded and booby-trapped. How do you know one of his dogs won't set off the traps?"

"We have special little traps for those damned dogs."

Peter walked toward the closet door. Dylan's breathing slowly cycled in and out. With sweat dripping off his nose and trembling arms, Dylan could see Peter's dusty shoes near some white wallboard dust on the floor. "I'll be glad when you and your men are gone."

"The best way for you to get rid of us is to get Baker and that Bible of his." Zwart's amazingly shiny shoes appeared next to Peter's.

"If you get Baker, you won't need the Bible." Peter spoke slowly. "Too bad it's not the other way around."

"Don't go soft now. You screwed up your one chance to humanely end this for your friend. Don't make the same mistake twice. You know that he could have arranged for the information in the Bible to get out. Big Brother wants us to get the Bible if possible. It's not something he wants floating around."

"Why is it so hard to get him?" Peter asked as Dylan's arms started a slow collapse.

"You tell me. You had a gun on him and let him get away. We'd all be gone now if you had just had the guts to follow through. You said you wanted to do it yourself. Let's get out of here."

The men moved out of the office, just as Dylan's arms gave way and he tumbled though the closet door, enveloped in a small cloud of white wallboard dust onto the floor.

At that moment, the office door burst open.

17

. . . .

COVERED WITH BOXES of pamphlets and white dust, Dylan lay sprawled on the floor completely helpless. Terrified, he looked up expecting to see a gun poised for a kill shot, but instead saw Suzie Alaneo, a shocked expression on her face. Suzie's long, dark hair, looking like something from a shampoo commercial, framed her Polynesian face and provided a perfect contrast to the green and white colors of her University of Hawaii sweatshirt. Around her neck, a bright, green pendant on a thin gold chain made her eyes seem unnaturally green.

"I'm not stealing anything, I'm just here to get my purse." Suzie squeaked guiltily. She thought Dylan had been waiting to bust her for sneaking back into Peter's office.

"You scared the hell out of me!" Dylan unintentionally barked at Suzie.

"Oh, I scared you! Who pops out of a closet covered in white power?" A somewhat smaller box of pamphlets slid off a shelf and bounced off Dylan's head.

Suzie stifled a giggle.

He stood up his teeth chattering from the adrenaline, brushed the dust off him and flexed his hands and arms to get the circulation back. "Hey. Sorry I spoke like that. I thought you were Zwart and Peter. Don't worry. I'm not security."

"And I'm not here to get my purse, so we're even. You're obviously not security. Why were you hiding in the closet? You certainly don't look like you are one of Zwart's weirdoes."

Suzie looked up at Dylan, her hands pertly on her hips. Dylan assessed her as one of the young athletic-looking Hawaiians who love working in Seward during the summers. Based on the conversation he overheard, Dylan surmised she fancied herself a year-round resident. She also was quite pretty in a girl-next-door way.

"I'm guessing for the same reason you actually returned—to get information. I'm Dylan Baker, the man they are looking for. And I'm not shy. I'm just quiet. I need to find out why they are really after me since I've done nothing wrong."

"I thought they said you were a bearded maniac-killer-rapist. You're not a dangerous terrorist?" Suzie asked, unafraid of the dust-covered approachable man in front of her.

"I'm not, nor have I ever been a terrorist. I'm just a hunting guide and handyman. I've lived up in a small cabin on Shorty's land for the last ten years hunting, fishing, guiding and fixing things for people. I don't have a phone or a computer, just a couple of dogs." Dylan looked at Suzie earnestly, his brown eyes wide.

"You are that quiet, hairy guy who fixed my neighbor's furnace a couple years ago," Suzie looked hard at Dylan.

"Who's your neighbor? The Knitting Barn? Yeah, I fixed her furnace two summers ago." Dylan was starting to get feeling back in his hands.

"Nancy Pierce's knitting business. That's it. I don't know how much you heard, but I'm Suzie Alaneo." Suzie studied Dylan for a moment. "They told me you shot a National Park ranger, Mitch Graham. His body has already been flown to Washington for DHS forensics." It was becoming obvious Suzie was uneasy about being near Dylan as she back away a step, unconsciously fiddling with her necklace.

"That's another lie. Mitch was injured in a fall, but someone shot him after I left to get help. They conveniently blamed it on me." Dylan brushed the white dust out of his hair.

"He was shot twice at close range with armor-piercing bullets. I talked to one of the local investigators." Suzie took another step back.

"Suzie, he wasn't shot when I left him. Zwart's men use that kind of ammo. No one in Seward would have any use for expensive bullets like that. I bet they shot him to bring heat onto me." Dylan paced in the small office flicking dust from his short beard.

"Well it worked. Everyone is after you. Why do Peter and Zwart want you dead?" Suzie's green eyes followed Dylan.

"I don't know. I always thought Peter was my best friend. Yesterday, he came to my house out of the blue, pointed his halibut revolver at me and tried for a kill shot. Captain Zwart and his men have been chasing me all over the woods. They have high-tech weapons and electronics, and they shoot to kill."

"You say you didn't kill Mitch. Zwart said you were a killer. Are you?" She pushed her dark bangs to the side.

"I kill what I eat, and I eat what I kill. Anyone who eats meat or wears leather is responsible for killing animals directly or indirectly. With me the animals have a sporting chance."

"No Dylan. What I mean are you a killer of people?" Suzie tensed for his answer.

Dylan looked down. "Ten years ago, some people died in a climbing incident I was leading. I didn't kill them on purpose. Yesterday Zwart and a man started shooting at me. One of them attacked me, and I killed him. But it was him or me."

Dylan wiped non-existent blood from his hands. His face showed anguish "I didn't want to, but it was him or me. I may have hurt some of Zwart's men with booby traps I set when they were chasing me through the woods.

"I could have turned the tables and hunted them. It would have been easy, but I don't want any more blood on my hands. I just want to be left alone." Dylan looked down. His grief bubbled to the surface unbidden. His hands were still shaking but he seemed unable to cry. *I wonder why I opened up to this girl. I've never told anyone about the accident.*

Though suspicious, Suzie seemed to relax a bit. "Let's do what we came here to do. Let's see if we can figure out why Peter is involved and why these men are after you."

Suzie started lifting papers and looking in folders. Dylan followed her lead and looked through the papers in the trashcan.

After five minutes, Suzie found Dylan's application to work for Alaska Fish and Game. Scrawled on a yellow note attached to the application was: VERIFY SS#!

"Did Peter have you verify your social security number?" Suzie showed Dylan the note. "Maybe this is how you came to the attention of Zwart. You gave Peter the wrong social security number and they confused you with someone else."

"Yes, he made a special trip out to my cabin the day before he tried to kill me. I had given him the correct number the first time." Dylan looked closely at his application. He remembered how odd it felt to be filling out the form after so many years in the woods.

"That's so strange," Suzie pondered. "If Homeland Security honestly thinks you are a terrorist, they could have easily found you through a bank account, a tax filing or a credit card application."

"Suzie, I've lived in the woods for the last ten years. I can't remember when I entered any personal information onto a form or a computer." Just then the old fax machine started to rumble. They looked at the paper feeding out. It was all in Russian.

"Can you read Russian?" Suzie showed the fax to Dylan.

"No, but Peter's family is Russian. It's not strange that they communicate by fax. Peter complains that many computers don't have Russian character sets installed." Dylan gestured to the fax. "This looks like a stanza from a poem." Dylan and Suzie squinted at the Russian words.

Suzie pointed to a Cyrillic letter that looked like a w attached to an upside down w. "Hey, this looks like the symbol on my grandmother's necklace!" Her hand went unconsciously to her neck.

"Let's get online." Suzie sat down at Peter's computer and moved the mouse. "Good. It hasn't timed out. I won't need a password." A few minutes later the translation appeared on the screen, *Psalm 41:11, By this I know that thou favourest me, because mine enemy doth not triumph over me.*

"I've heard another Russian quoting that Psalm," said Dylan. Just then they heard footsteps in the hall that faded as the passerby entered another office.

"I think we've been here long enough. Let's get out of here." Suzie put the paper into her pocket.

After a few minutes, a man wearing the official Alaska tourist costume of sweatshirt and hat exited the SeaLife center walking with Suzie Alaneo. The Escalade parked near Peter's office was gone, but the one out front was still taking up more space than needed in front of the tourist entrance.

Suzie put her hand on his arm as if they were a couple.

As they walked away from the SeaLife Center, Dylan's quirky smile was barely visible, "Suzie Alaneo. I do know that name. Where did I see it? Ah, yes. The rummage sale and potluck blog: *The Seward Recycle*?"

"Funny. It's the *Seward Blogletter*. And, for your information, more people in Seward read my blog than USA Today." Suzie paused and added, "On the first and third Thursday of each month."

Dylan looked down at her hand on his arm. He'd forgotten how sweet human touch could be.

"They keep asking me for a Bible," Dylan blurted, making sure his arm remained easy for her to hold.

"A Bible?" Suzie asked.

"Zwart is looking for a Bible as part of his job. I think I know what Bible he's looking for. And I think I know where that Bible is." Dylan turned toward her, his face white. *Why am I confiding to a reporter?*

"Where? Let's take a look at it."

"It's in a grave." Dylan's chest seemed to swell with emotion. Was it the touch or the grave that caused his heart to throb?

"Tell me about this Bible," Suzie pulled her hand away. She had changed from a friend to a reporter.

"Why do you want to know?" Dylan's voice choked slightly with emotion.

"It's my business to know, I'm a reporter, and I'm going to write this story."

"Suzie, these guys aren't playing for fun. You do not want to get involved."

"It's not up to you to decide if a reporter should become involved in a story. The story decides, and I'm going to go with you to get that Bible."

Dylan observed Suzie's determination.

"Nope, you don't want to go with me; it's in a place that's hard to get to."

"Dylan Baker, who trusted you when you were breaking into Peter's office? You need to let me come with you."

She put her hand on his arm sending an emotional spark through Dylan. "Besides, it's part of your disguise to have a woman with you. They're probably looking for a loner."

Dylan realized he would not be able to dissuade her from following him. "OK. I need to collect some things from my cabin, and I'm worried about my dogs. Let's meet at Shorty's in 45 minutes. Bring everything you need for an overnight hike. I'll fill you in then."

To get the Bible, Dylan would have to go back to a place he had worked so hard to escape. A place more alone than silence and colder than death: the tomb on Mt. Alice.

And he knew he'd need to take this stubborn Hawaiian with him.

18

· · · · · · · · · ·

DYLAN HAD TO CONSIDER Heather's father again. The Colonel had ruled Allied Energy like he did his marines: callously and uncompromisingly. He gave his employees no option but stunning success. Pretty much everyone who worked for the huge energy company hated Bolton, unless they owned stock in the firm.

It's not often that a military leader can find such naked success in the corporate world, but Colonel Bolton had the attitude that he could force the world to accommodate his style. His unshakeable belief that God was on his side gave him an aura of divine malevolence.

The Colonel arrogantly basked in the glories of his military and business exploits. To enter his huge office, a visitor was forced to walk down a painfully bright trophy wall. Each golf trophy, presidential handshake photo, and community award reflected light from dozens of spotlights.

Among these honors were glossy photos of his gorgeous wife and young children. The photographer had arranged the family members around Bolton like sycophants around Pharaoh. Looking at the two flawless, beautiful children and smiling super-model wife, one might think Billy Bolton had it all.

On the outside, Bolton's family looked like a warm sanctuary of Christian love, but inside it was a cold hell of fear and anxiety. As dictatorial as the colonel was in business, he was more so in his own castle. He demanded perfection at all times from Billy Jr. and Heather. What he accomplished was a cheerless and anxious family whose members could never please their ruler.

Each family member dealt with the situation differently. Mrs. Bolton dulled the pain of the emotional abuse by fading into a bottle. When he turned 15, Junior "accidentally" hung himself to escape the prison of unrealistic expectations.

Instead of offering reassurance to his wife and daughter, Bolton spent the days following Junior's death making certain that all reports referred to the event as a "tragic accident". If it was possible, Bolton retreated even farther from his family into a sort of religious hysteria.

Heather, the strongest of all, changed her last name, left home at sixteen and eventually ended up on the staff of a climbing magazine.

Shortly after Dylan and Heather met, Bolton unexpectedly showed up to have a "man to man" talk with Dylan. It was clear that Bolton hated Dylan. What caused this powerful dislike mystified Dylan. He wondered if it was because Bolton was a religious zealot and viewed Dylan as a heathen.

Their first conversation was an interrogation about Dylan's religious beliefs. At the time, Dylan thought Bolton only wanted to discuss religion so that Dylan would get the message that Bolton believed Heather to be a virgin and better stay that way and woe be it to he who violated her.

Once, Dylan found some bugging devices in his room and showed them to Heather. Heather reacted guiltily, as if she believed Bolton had those put there. But she weakly told Dylan it was probably a competing magazine trying to learn trade secrets. They found similar hidden bugs in Heather's room and car. After that, the lovers sought intimacy in places they knew to be free of surveillance.

After the bugs were pulled out, a pair of military-looking thugs who warned him not to dishonor Miss Bolton attacked and beat Dylan. When Heather heard of the beating, she took out a restraining order on The Colonel, and in a love-conquers-all pact, decided to surreptitiously continue their relationship. Both Dylan and Heather were astonished at the power and depth of their feelings for each other.

When some thugs reappeared at another photo location, Heather sent a letter to her father saying she would write a tell-all book about him if he didn't back off. Knowing that his cherished public image was more important to him than his billions, the thugs stopped coming. Heather and Dylan believed themselves to be free from Bolton's spies.

Bolton's intrusions probably pushed Dylan and Heather closer together, united by being common prey to her obsessed father. Heather helped Dylan with his freelance work as a guide. She had insisted on a contract with the Russian so that Dylan and Sid would be paid an absurd amount of money even if the trip were called off.

There was a 90% chance the climb would be cancelled since winter conditions on Denali usually involved extreme cold, short arctic days and 150 mph winds. A typical summer trip lasts three weeks. The chances of getting a long stretch of decent climbing weather was slim to none.

Dylan pushed the memory of his last night with Heather out of his mind. Certainly Bolton had the money and wherewithal to find and employ an army like Zwart's. Bolton was such a religious fanatic; he might think Dylan had Heather's old Bible. But why would Peter go along with Bolton? It didn't make sense.

Right after Peter pointed a gun at Dylan, he said something about *blood is thicker*. Dylan knew that the phrase *Blood is thicker than water* meant that loyalty tends to follow family ahead of friends.

Peter's small family included his mother, affectionately called Baba, living in an assisted care facility in Anchorage and a brother, Illya. This brother lived in Washington D.C. and ran a division of Homeland Security.

Maybe Colonel Bolton had threatened Illya or Baba. It could be that Peter felt he needed to kill Dylan to protect his family. Dylan wondered if he should have focused these last hours on Bolton and not Peter.

19

. . . .

AS DYLAN TOOK a roundabout route to his cabin, he had been tempted to whistle for Doolie and Bergen. Their master often spoiled the dogs, and he worried that a morning without their usual routine would have the pups anxious.

Betrayed by Peter and Mitch, Dylan didn't think he had ever loved his dogs more. *I'll never wake up to find Bergen holding a gun to my head, and Doolie is way too smart to be fooled by Zwart's lies.*

Approaching his cabin he felt a growing sense of anxiety instead of joyful anticipation for seeing his dogs. Fear focused his attention for the possible trap ahead. Hadn't he heard Zwart tell Randall that a similar grenade trap would be set at his cabin?

Dylan picked up his pace. Zwart may have commanded a few of his henchmen to stay and guard his home. Now he was jogging.

Would those assholes Zwart hired hurt Doolie and Bergen?

Doolie was wise. He would stay out of their way. But Bergen had a way of trying to be friends with everyone, despite obvious dangers. Dylan slowed to a creep as he approached the clearing of his cabin keeping his breathing nearly silent.

At first the area seemed deserted. Afternoon light reflected off the soggy spruce needles gathered on his wooden roof and highlighted the drifting motes of pollen in the calm air. The familiar peace cheered Dylan. However, the clearing had looked the same yesterday at this time, before Peter with his gun, before Zwart and his bombs, before Mitch and his blood . . .

Voices. Dylan focused on the sound. He remained invisible in the perimeter of the clearing, and inched forward until he could see the speakers from behind. Two men in black fatigues, the same uniform as both Oxman and Randall, sat on the edge of the cliff that Dylan had used for his escape. He strained to hear what they were saying.

"And see that? That's Charles's dried blood right down there on that ledge. Stabbed him with a nail or something! In the throat!"

Charles. Oxman has a name. I killed Charles. Dylan wiped his hands unconsciously on his pants.

"Zwart made it sound like it was going to be an easy mission. I thought this guy was a shy hermit?"

"He must have done something nasty. Zwart really has it in for him."

Shy? These guys don't know shit, Dylan leaned in to hear better and sized up the two men. They were bigger than Randall, though without the height of Zwart or the girth of Oxman, *Charles.*

Dylan thought the one on the right could have been Mitch from the back. They shared broad shoulders. He wondered if these guys were at all like his friend, just doing their jobs.

The Mitch-like-man spoke again. "Damn. I'm bored. I was hoping to kill something this time. Did you know Foxtrot shot a moose baby? Where's that dog that keeps running around here, maybe I'll shoot it."

Not like Mitch!

Dylan scanned the clearing and surrounding forest for his dogs: a spruce, some devil's club, roots, and another spruce. *Doolie!* Almost directly across from him, between twin trees stood Doolie, his head above the undergrowth. In relief Dylan let out a sigh. The henchmen missed it, but the dog perked up. *Stay Doolie. Don't give me away.* Dylan held up his right hand in a halt signal, Doolie saw his master and understood.

Now to get rid of these guys. Dylan crept near the edge of the clearing toward the cliff until he was in a line with the fatigues. Slowly, he drew the gun he had taken off Randall. *Silencer. Perfect.* He leaned over the cliff in order to take aim, still hidden by the vegetation. *If they would only look away.*

As if on cue, Doolie barked. Dylan lost his focus for a second to look back at the dog. Doolie wasn't even looking at him. Instead, he was up on all fours looking into the forest, as if barking to hidden friend. Dylan fired twice.

The rocks at the base of cliff made a sound like a baseball on an aluminum bat, the short rock fall produced by the shots had the desired effect. The fatigues turned their glances away from Doolie and down the cliff.

"He's there! At the bottom of the cliff! I bet he was trying to climb back up, I told you, man, told you he would come back to the cliff!"

"Do you think it's really him?" His question was more of a remark than an inquiry.

"They always return to the scene of the crime, idiot. Let's use these ropes to climb down and get him."

"Those ropes look skinny. And besides, I can't rock climb!"

"You don't need to. God, you're dense. We just use these ropes—these ropes that were used to recover Charles' body—they have to be strong."

"Shouldn't we radio Zwart?"

"No way. Zwart will steal all our fun. Let's get him ourselves."

Dylan watched like a proud hunter as they fell into his trap. He waited patiently until they were off the ropes at the base of the cliff, and then he untied the ropes from their anchors and watched them drift down the cliff.

If they were able to find their way out of the forest onto the road, it would be a two-hour walk back to the cabin. If they called Zwart to admit they were lost, they'd get chewed out and maybe get docked some pay. Dylan had bought himself some time.

At Dylan's whistle, Doolie came. The old dog didn't seem to have the bounce in his step he had yesterday morning.

"Are you hurt?" Dylan inspected his dog. Nothing seemed wrong, but Doolie wouldn't stop whining and looking at the cabin. "Where's Bergen?" At his own question, Dylan followed Doolie's nervous glance to his log house. Another whine started there, a younger dog's cries that turned into howls.

Dylan felt his face get hot. *In the house? They rigged his home with explosives and left his dog inside? What kind of sick bastards would leave a dog to bait an explosive trap?*

He suddenly wished he hadn't waited until the fatigues were safely down on the ground before releasing the ropes. Bergen was a clumsy pup, constantly tripping over his own paws. Dylan couldn't imagine how he hadn't accidentally blown up the cabin.

Assuming Zwart's boast about grenades in the cabin was true, he had to check it out.

"Stay here, boy," he said, patting Doolie on the head. Dylan started cautiously toward Bergen's whines and the cabin he had so lovingly built. He searched the ground surrounding the cabin. Zwart's guards had been perched on the cliff edge, maybe to look over the view, but perhaps because if they guarded any closer, they would be setting off a perimeter trap.

A few steps closer. Scan the area. A few more steps. Dylan glanced back to make sure Doolie wasn't following him. What he saw behind him made his jaw drop.

Sunlight reflected off a hair-thin wire, which seemed to disappear into the ground on both sides. Looking closer, Dylan realized that the wire was exposed because he had disturbed it while inspecting Doolie moments earlier. Had he already set off a delay timer?

He was confused. Zwart had made it sound like he used crude traps, ones that, if activated, would blow up like land mines. Dylan had clearly fallen for a perimeter trap of some kind, yet he was still standing. Had he set off a silent alarm? Were Zwart's men on their way again? Dylan had to assume that Zwart's men were on their way, either from the guards who had climbed the ropes or some kind of silent alarm.

Anxious, but sharply focused, Dylan backtracked and slowly followed the wire to where it was no longer visible. The wire disappeared into a hole, the size to fit a grenade, but empty. The end of the wire was a loop, perfect to fit over the pin of a grenade.

Dylan understood how the trap worked. The unknowing would pull the trip wire, thereby pulling out the pin of the grenade in the hole, and thus blowing up the earth close to him. But where was the grenade? Had the men left the trap unfinished?

Bergen whined again from inside the cabin. Dylan hoped the inside trap was equally unfinished. Yet the incompetence of the perimeter wiring felt eerie and inconsistent with Zwart's precise personality. Dylan would have preferred to face a consistent opponent.

He made it to the house without spotting more wires. The front and back door would be rigged for sure, so he approached the window first. His eyes barely reached the bottom of the window. Zwart's orders must have been more serious about this trap than that for the fishing shed. No less than ten grenades were set about three feet from the front and back doors.

Like the perimeter trap, the bombs were set to go off when the wires wrapped around the pins were pulled. Each wire ran from a pin to the doorknob. The doors each opened out, so pulling open the door would pull the pin, sparking the chemical fuse inside. The windows seemed untouched, but Dylan couldn't discount a strand of the nearly invisible wire lurking nearby.

Bergen sat between the two traps cruelly tied with a short rope, wagging his entire body joyfully at seeing his master. His captors must have realized his hyper nature and the liability that he might set off the trap early. As Bergen's antics increased, it was clear to Dylan that he might free himself from the nearly chewed-through rope.

Dylan had to be quick. Getting into the house wasn't a problem. Dylan, with his slight climber's frame, easily slid through the ice block hatch and came up the stairs. The thumping from Bergen's struggles made Dylan rush faster than he wanted to.

The frantic reunion with Bergen was far too short. Bergen clearly wanted to crawl into Dylan's lap and exchange canine kisses for Dylan's rough petting. But Bergen had to settle for Dylan's urging to stay. His eager whining melted Dylan's heart as he untied his sweet dog.

Getting Bergen out without setting off any of the traps would be another problem. Before now, Dylan had always enjoyed Berg's large size for a lab. But even if he could somehow lift his pup through the ice block hatch and turn him sideways, Berg's shoulders wouldn't easily fit through the crack. He could chop out the hatch, but then he'd still need to lift the wiggling joyful pup six feet up, and soldiers must be getting close. There had to be another way. Outside Doolie barked a quick warning: strangers were approaching!

The door. Having built the house himself, Dylan knew that by simply removing the pins from the hinges of the doors, he could swing the door the opposite way, keeping the handle unmoving, while the other end of the door opened enough for Bergen and him to escape. It would have to do.

Looking out the window, Dylan could just see black clad soldiers far down the path, but approaching quickly.

"Looks like we better hurry. And I need to teach you about stranger danger, Boy."

Calming Bergen with slow pets and soft words, he looked again at the bombs dangling malevolently near the door. It was more real now, being inside with them. Yet facing death wasn't new to him. Before opening the door, he glanced at the wall of tools for what he would need for the journey ahead: rope, harness, his climbing bag complete with carabineers, chalk, and headlamp. He'd also need some backpacking gear, camping items and warm clothes. He tossed some cooking utensils onto his pile. He would be able to camp in a remote site not on any map. Dylan looked forward to being some place where he could not be found.

He'd worry about food when he got to Mt. Alice. There was plenty of food available on the mountain. He threw the necessary gear into an open pack and placed it by the front door. Shushing Bergen, he set to work on the hinges. The pins had been there for nearly ten years, they were difficult to remove, but Dylan was a handyman. Except for the bomb dangling at his elbow, this was a job like any other.

With the pins undone but the door still balanced in place, he led Bergen carefully by his collar. His tail was a huge hazard, as it could easily hit a wire. Dylan didn't have a plan in case this happened. The time delay, two to six seconds, might be enough for him to jump out, but he didn't know if he'd have the strength to leave his dog. Inch by inch, he scooted the door open, checking with each movement that the doorknob stayed in place, without moving the wires and pulling the pins.

He stopped when the crack seemed big enough to fit Bergen. Bergen pushed his nose through the narrow opening, ready to launch. *No need to push my luck.* He guided his dog through the crack and let out a sigh.

Outside he heard an approaching soldier yell ahead for the guard to turn on their radios.

"Go sit with Doolie." He smiled, seeing Bergen streak off toward his friend waiting patiently beyond the clearing.

Dylan tossed his pack out the door, and was nearly out when he realized his ropes were still on the floor.

Then it happened. The door, no longer on its hinges, and losing the supportive contact with Dylan's back, fell outward, pulling ten grenade pins with it.

The phenomenon was strange. Dylan felt as if invisible hands had grabbed hold of his jacket, wrenched him off the porch and down behind a nearby boulder. The only other thing he could remember before his body flew off the porch and his head hit the dirt, was the bright purple flash of the explosion.

Dylan came to with warm waves caressing his nose and eyes. Bergen nudged his belly with his wet nose while Doolie licked his face.

He knew he had only been out seconds. As he raised his body, a wave of nausea passed over him and he lay back down. How did he get so far from his house? Did the explosion push him away?

Rolling gently to one side, he felt a tug on his jacket. *Did I feel hands pulling me?* It was then he realized the blast had deafened him. Then came the vomit. *Glad I didn't eat much today.*

Dylan's headache prevented him from dwelling on the ruin of his cabin. The months he had spent constructing the walls, the floors. He tried not to think of all the tools now destroyed in the blast. He knew the basement must be caved in, along with his food stocks, meat and grain he had hunted or bargained for. Everything Dylan had, he had worked for. Never had he thought it would be destroyed this way. An unnatural disaster.

When he felt he could sit up, he looked at the ruins of his cabin. The new wave of nausea had nothing to do with his head injury. It was seeing the loss. The little fires and glowing mess made him think of the red blood on his hands earlier that day. Destruction was following him.

Nearby the soldiers writhed on the fern-covered ground. They had been injured in this blast. Dylan's survival instincts told him he had to leave before more soldiers showed up.

So much destruction! If he lived out the days ahead, he could dwell on his losses. Right now there was no time to grieve.

Knowing his voice was making noise, but unable to hear much he spoke to his dogs. "Come on, boys. I have some things to do.

"Let's see if Shorty is still my friend."

20

. . . .

SHAKING NEAR-DEATH experiences were not new to Dylan, yet as he and the dogs walked a new path toward town, he couldn't stop thinking about the explosion. He could still sense the feeling of hands on the back of his jacket. Was he crazy? *It was the explosion. No one could have pulled me from the house.*

Still, he felt uneasy, and a creeping sensation that started deep in his stomach told him he was being watched. Dylan stopped. Doolie heeled and perked up his ears, one front paw motionless in the air.

"Hear anything?" Apparently Doolie didn't, he began to trot on. *Perhaps it was just the wind through the spruce.* Dylan's hearing was starting to return. The boulder must have shielded him from the most harmful parts of the explosion.

This land belonged to Shorty. The cabin, the cliff, the path, the trees were all on Shorty's land. Looking back, Dylan surmised that Shorty hadn't been up here much since he showed Dylan the clearing for the cabin ten years ago. Shorty's bad leg prevented him from hiking—puttering around his store and fishing left the old man tired enough these days.

Dylan remembered hiking up to the clearing that day. Shorty's steps had been slow, but Dylan had enjoyed the walk. An old man even then, Dylan admired the fire within that seemed to fuel him with a younger man's energy.

Shorty and his wife had moved to Alaska from Savage, Minnesota after he served in the Korean War. His bad leg was a testament to his service, and Dylan always wondered if he bore internal scars. His leg worsened each year.

A familiar winter sight was Shorty massaging the cold knee joint as he surveyed his shop from the counter stool. Dylan once suggested that Shorty move to Arizona since the cold was bad for his leg. Shorty's look hit harder than bullets. Dylan never mentioned Arizona again.

Dylan's young legs carried him to town quickly. By the end of the walk his hearing had largely returned, and the sight of Doolie and Bergen by his side offered him a feeling of comfort and normalcy. As Dylan watched Bergen chasing a bee, he wondered about what to do with the pups if Shorty, like Mitch, believed Zwart's lies. Where could he leave them while he confronted his past on Mt. Alice?

The dogs stayed close as he tiptoed through Seward. With a deep breath and a hope that Shorty was on his side, he slipped through the back door of the old man's store.

The shop smelled like rubber and oak. Two customers stood at the register fumbling with fishing tackle. Shorty sat on a stool behind the counter with his back to Dylan, but he could hear him explaining something to the customers.

"You'll want to annoy those reds into biting your lure. You won't catch anything, otherwise." Dylan loved to hear Shorty talk. He spoke in a rhythm, as though someone set a metronome a little slower than normal speech, and Shorty followed its beat a little more ardently than the normal. Every tenth beat or so, his voice would give a crack.

He continued to talk to the customers. "Well that's why the lure is so shiny!"

The counter was a clutter of little boxes full of trinkets for sale. Fishing lures, candy, magazines, sunglasses, and key chains made a fortress around the cash register. The customers had set their tackle on the one empty space. Behind the counter sat a framed black and white photo of a woman with a bob and a lacey dress, Shorty's late wife, Ann Marie.

She died shortly after Dylan moved to Seward. Once, when Dylan had offhandedly asked about her, he saw a mirror of his own pain in the old man's eyes. Although they never spoke of Dylan's past, he felt that Shorty sensed his heartache. Now he wondered if never speaking up about his past had left his friends open to Zwart's lies. The antidote to Zwart's poison was the truth. Had Dylan hidden the medicine?

Shorty bagged the tackle. "Alright, you take care now. Come back and let me know how ya fare. I'll take a cut of your catch for my advice, ha ha!" His voice cracked on the word *catch*. It was as if he had used all his steady tones in his youth.

The dogs ran to greet Shorty first. They often stayed at the shop when Dylan ran errands in town, or fished in the bay. Shorty always said they liked him because he kept treats behind the counter, but Dylan said they adored him because dogs can sense an honest man.

Dylan took a tentative step forward. Did Zwart have a spy in his friend's shop? Would Shorty pull a gun? He watched the old man's back as Doolie nudged Shorty's knee with his nose. Bergen's tail beat against the counter, eyes cast up at Shorty. The old man didn't tense at the sight of the dogs. He reached behind the key chains to get the usual treat. When he turned around, Dylan stepped back.

"No need to look scared, Dylan, no government scouts here."

"Shorty, what happened?" Behind his glasses, Shorty's left eye was swollen shut—both eyes were black, looking like the remains of a punch to the nose. The pools under his eyes were as dark as the bay in winter, and they seemed to have robbed all the ruddy flush from his cheeks.

His face, usually alight with enthusiasm, seemed void of that spark, and Dylan knew that if he stepped closer he would notice the old man's wrinkled skin that always hid behind his youthful vibe.

"No worries, Dylan, just some bad men decided to rough me up. Came in this morning. Man, they had some whoppers to tell about you! I told 'em not a word was true. They didn't like that." Shorty's voice cracked more than usual. He was still sitting down.

"Oh God, I can't believe . . . Shorty why? I mean . . . I'm so . . ."

"You're not responsible! I dare say I let my tongue run away from me. 'Representing my country', they said! A load of phooey. They didn't like what I said about you, Dylan." He tapped the counter in thought, and then smiled genuinely. "Come over here, boy, don't just stand there with your mouth open!"

Dylan looked at his feet and unrooted them from the dark wooden plank floor. It was unlike Shorty to not get off his stool. He wondered what injury prevented him from walking over to Dylan.

"Shorty, you look awful." It was true. A closer look made the bruising look sickly. No wonder those customers were fumbling with the tackle, they probably were avoiding his face.

"It's not so bad. You know I take aspirin for the strokes, makes my blood thin, you see. Don't clot so fast like it should, that's why the bruises look so bad. They didn't hit me real hard."

"Shorty, you should see a doctor about that eye, and why aren't you standing?"

"I got a little kicked, Dylan. Don't look at me like that! I've seen worse! Anyway, that was nothing about you. I started talking about honorable service and my days in the army." A brief flush overwhelmed Shorty's cheeks for the moment he spoke of his service

"I wouldn't take back a word! Now tell me what these bastards want and what you're going to do about it. I want you to get 'em, good." Shorty rubbed his leg as he spoke.

Bergen whined.

"Dylan, your knuckles are all white. Unclench your fists, boy!"

Dylan didn't tell Shorty where he was going or what he would do, but he filled him in on the lies Zwart had told Mitch, and on the mystery of Peter's involvement.

Shorty told him to take anything he needed from the shop, and to leave the dogs with him. Both men looked up as the bell over the door tinkled, and Suzie walked into the store.

"Hey Shorty! Oh!" Suzie stopped in her tracks. "What happened?"

Dylan, dirty and battered from the explosion, turned towards Suzie. "Dylan! My God! What's with you guys?"

Dylan looked at Suzie. "I'll tell you on the trail. Let's get going. We'll go to a place no knows about. We can relax a bit."

With fresh packs of supplies and a handshake, Dylan, his knuckles still white, led Suzie out the back into the Seward sunshine.

21

. . . .

DYLAN AND SUZIE started down the alley behind the store as Shorty closed the back door.

Within a few moments Suzie understood Shorty's encounter with Zwart and the consequences of Shorty's decision to decline discussing any information concerning Dylan.

"Where are we going now? The store? Dylan, you didn't buy any food. I get it. You want to travel light. Not eat."

"We don't need much food. Mt. Alice is a natural grocery store, and they might recognize me at the store. Besides, we'll be in a place where no one could find us. We can pause to catch our breath."

Suzie paused for a moment. "I'm willing to eat weeds, but can we buy some coffee?"

"Sure. First we need to get a bow at my friend's house." They resumed a rapid pace down the alleyway.

"A bow! You mean archery? I'm pretty good at shooting bows. I used to teach archery while I was a camp counselor."

"Great! You're in charge of dinner."

After weaving around the cars parked perpendicular to the wooden porches adorning the storefronts on Third Avenue, they rounded the corner onto Jefferson Street.

Adjacent to a modest church, Dylan crossed the street, opened the blue picket fence gate and walked up to the porch of a small, grey house, which looked too elegant for the neighborhood.

Hidden under a potted plant was a house key. Suzie followed him around the house, and they entered through a back door. The beautiful house, carefully built in the craftsman style had the look of a home not lived in.

"Who lives here?"

"Dave Clark. You may know him. *Do You Love Me*, Dylan hummed. "Or *Glad All Over*" Dylan attempted to lighten the mood as he beat air drums and sang the oldie.

No reaction from Suzie. *The line between funny and dumb can be razor thin,* Dylan thought.

She wondered if he were trying to distract her after seeing Shorty's injuries.

"You're going to have to listen to more oldies. Anyway, the owner is the "other" Dave Clark. He runs several hardware stores in Georgia and is one of my best hunting clients.

"I put the roof on this place, and he thinks I undercharged him. He told me I could use his gear any time."

Suzie shrugged and followed Dylan downstairs to a large metal door. Dylan punched in a key code, waited for a substantial *thunk* from inside the door and held it open for Suzie.

An amazing array of bows, shotguns and hunting rifles decorated one huge wall. "Pick out a bow you feel comfortable with, while I pick out the arrows."

After trying several bows, a beaming Suzie showed Dylan a large, wicked-looking compound bow. "How's this?"

The complex and amazing bow could have been a prop for a science fiction movie. "That's a Bowtech Insanity CPX fully decked out. The draw would be too much for a woman. It's designed for a person with much longer arms who hunts big game." Dylan looked back to the wall for a better choice.

Thunk. A practice arrow bounced off of the floor three inches from Dylan's foot.

"OK, maybe the draw isn't too much for you." Seeing Suzie's grin, Dylan selected a different tact, "How about this one?"

Dylan handed Suzie a simple pink women's compound bow. "Sorry for the color. Let me see you draw it. For a person your height, you probably want a 26-inch draw."

After satisfying himself that she had the right bow, he showed her the arrows. "These are flu-flus. Have you ever used them?"

"These look weird. They don't have a point and the feathers are too big and look like clown decorations."

"Wait until you see them fly, Suzie. You'll love them."

Dylan thought back to when he first let loose a flu-flu.

GROWING UP ON a berry farm near Hood River, Oregon, Dylan had plenty of bird hunting expeditions with friends. Hunting did not call to Dylan at that time. He went mostly for the companionship with his friends. Then his buddy Cahoon introduced him to hunting birds with a bow. Although only 14, bow-hunting birds suddenly gave Dylan a focus he had never before experienced.

Cahoon and Dylan constructed arrows called flu-flus. They had huge bright feathers that caused the arrows to rapidly lose speed. This made them easy to find and reuse. It also gave the arrow the most satisfying ripping sound as it lived its short, powerful life.

The boys would take their backpacks, bows, homemade arrows and spend days hunting grouse while camped out on the Columbia River Plateau. Rarely were they able to actually bag an animal, but a lucky shot of Dylan's knocked one down their first bow hunt and hooked Dylan forever on this type of hunting. That night Dylan stared into the flames cooking the boys' grouse stew. All he could think about was hunting the next morning.

Years later when Dylan looked over the bow hunting treasure he had earned from roofing Dave Clarks' cabin, he was delighted to find several sets of custom-made flu-flus. Each of the arrows had probably cost Clark well over a hundred dollars. Some were fit with whistling arrowheads. These would add an eerie scream to the ripping sound of the flu-flu.

There was no arrow more fun to shoot than these screaming flu-flus. On the hills near close to timber stands, Dylan would have a whistling arrow notched, so if he flushed and shot at a grouse, the rip/scream might flush a second bird in time to shoot the next arrow.

Dylan hunted because he had to eat, but when he hunted birds with these arrows, he completely enjoyed time wandering the hills with his dogs and remembering innocent moments in Oregon so long ago.

"WHAT ABOUT THESE ARROWS?" Suzie pressed on the tip of a hunting arrow and three razor-sharp blades snapped open. "Whoa!"

"Those are for big game. We don't want to kill something we have to pack out. Careful, they are very sharp."

Suzie walked over to an impressive selection of hunting and military gear. She pointed up at an amazing shotgun. "That's a Benelli M4 Super 90. Looks like it has the 7+1 internal tube magazine. Can we take it?"

"Where did you learn that, girl? No, we can't take it. How do you know so much?"

"My dad collected guns." Suzie gestured to the room. "Not like this guy."

"Your dad? What's to hunt in Hawaii except feral pigs?"

"Hey, don't knock feral pig hunting. You howlies know nothing. Look up axis deer sometime. We have terrific big game hunting in Hawaii. My dad loved hunting and his guns. He was so proud of his assortment I got the grand tour and quizzes every time he added something."

"Check out the shells Dave has for that gun: monolithic-solids with full metal jacket and tungsten steel inserts. It's overkill for an elephant. We don't need to take this heavy, expensive and pretty-much worthless-in-Alaska gun. This is not the right ammo for big game around here. It would ruin all the meat."

Dylan pulled a gorgeous hunting rifle with scope off the wall. "This is a 30 caliber Remington 700 XCR II with a Nikon Monarch scope. With the 300 ultra magnum ammo, a good shooter could take down a moose with one shot every time."

"Can we take that?"

"No. Do you want to pack out a moose?"

"No. But you need some better self-defense than this small bow and tipless arrows. Did you forget some bad guys are after us?"

"Of course I didn't forget, but we're going some-where that no one knows about."

"Fine, take a small gun." Suzie looked over at the wall of pistols. "How about that little one?" Suzie gestured to a subcompact pistol.

Dylan hefted the small weapon then picked up a magazine and looked at it. "It's a Glock 42, and it only holds 6 shots. Looks like .38 caliber. I don't think this will stop a big soldier unless I get a lucky shot."

"OK. I got my light bow and headless arrows. You got a pistol that can't stop anyone. I guess we're ready for a fight. "

"Seriously, Suzie. We don't need a gun, but I'll throw this into my pack. "

"How do we get to the trail head for this Mt. Alice climb?" Suzie picked up her pink bow and quiver of arrows.

"That's your job. We go to Yukon Dave's Pub." Dylan pulled the iron door closed as they left the house.

"OK. I need to make a quick call to my sister. She was expecting me for dinner tomorrow. I'm going to be dining and vacationing on Mt Alice instead. Yeah!"

SUZIE APPROACHED the rather rough looking fisherman walking out of Yukon Dave's Pub. "Hey, can you give me and my friend a ride to Bear Lake?"

"Sure little lady. Where's your friend?"

Within a few moments, a battered Dodge pickup pulled out onto the street headed north. Watching Seward retreat as they skirted Resurrection Bay, Dylan and Suzie relaxed for a moment and enjoyed the afternoon.

Quickly, the road turned to gravel and they knew they would soon start their climb to Mt. Alice's snowy shoulders. Dylan's mind was a mix of relief at getting out of town, and anxiety about digging up the Denali artifacts. Maybe prowling the bird hunting grounds that he and Peter had so often visited would distract him from his concerns.

13

A Year Earlier

. . . .

THE RIPPING SOUND of the flu-flu arrow was not followed by the thunk of a blunt projectile hitting its target. The "thunk" was what you listened for when hunting ptarmigan, the small chicken-like birds that populate the arctic regions. Peter might be having better luck on the other side of the willow thicket. Dylan listened carefully through the wind for the distance-softened rip of Peter's arrow.

Dylan had seen some falcons circling up high and followed them to a large covey of ptarmigan. About 50 birds were feeding in groups of two or three in some willows. If they got lucky, Doolie, Peter and Dylan would have a terrific dinner tonight.

The late fall wind blew out of the south at 20 knots. Hitting a one-pound bird with an arrow is hard enough. Hitting a skittish wild ptarmigan in a crosswind was even harder. The moment a ptarmigan landed on the ground, it became invisible—its feather color blending into the rocks or snow depending on the season. The only chance of getting one was to catch one roosting on a branch or taking flight. On second thought, Peter and Dylan might be having granola bars for dinner.

Outsiders say that ptarmigans are dumb because they tend not to burst into flight when approached. When they are flushed, they'll only fly about 100 yards before landing again to disappear on the ground. Dumb or not, if Peter and Dylan didn't get a clutch of birds, they'd only have enough food for the two-day walk out of the hills, instead of a seven-day bird hunting trip. It would be merely a hungry four-day snowshoe trek around the early winter valleys near Crescent Lake.

Dylan felt the sharp wind pause. He heard a male ptarmigan drumming near its territory, then the *sizzle-thunk* of a flu-flu hitting its target. Peter got lucky. They might still have a great dinner tonight.

Over the next few hours, Dylan and Peter got about six birds in all. The victorious huntsman would get the Alaskan hunter's candy: the hearts and livers of freshly killed birds. Doolie would get what the two friends didn't want.

That night the frying pan, bubbling with a half-inch of bacon fat, smoked over the fire while the saw-toothed mountains behind burned purpley-pink in the sunset. Peter, by far the better cook, bragged about his secret seasoning crumbs as he laid the ptarmigan breasts into the sizzling fat.

Dylan finished setting up the tent and banked snow around it to shelter it from a biting wind that had sprung up. Usually they would linger by the campfire swapping stories or just watching the flames, but Dylan knew the weather would chase them into the tent earlier than usual this evening.

As they hunched near the fire to eat with Doolie between them, Peter talked about his family. His oldest sister had married a University of Alaska economics professor and had two little girls. His younger sister ran a bed-and-breakfast in Anchorage. His brother had served in the military and afterwards taken a civilian job in Langley, Virginia using his Russian skills in a cushy government career.

"Dylan, I wouldn't trade places with any of them for anything," said Peter as he nibbled on a ptarmigan bone, his prominent Adam's apple bobbing. "My brother's stuck in an office all day long coordinating information sources. Me? I get to live here, hunt, fish, hike and boat with my friends. I'm truly free."

"I know how you feel." Dylan wiped the special seasoning from his chin. "It would be impossible to explain to anyone how the mountains looked today, how it feels to have a successful hunt or how good this food is. It's not only the fresh air but some intangible connection with nature and the earth that keeps bringing me back."

"How come you never talk about your family, Dylan? You know about my sisters, brother and my parents. I don't know anything about your family."

Dylan played with Doolie's ears. "There's not much to tell about my family. My parents had a security dog business, but died in an accident. My Aunt Zoe raised me until I was 18 then took off with a boyfriend. I'm pretty much my own family. Let's throw hatchets to see who cleans up."

Peter knew that their old after dinner game of throwing hatchets into a stump would probably mean that Dylan would do the clean up. Peter had an uncanny way of always hitting his target. "Hey Dylan, you packed most of the weight for trip. I'll do the clean-up."

"We'll do the clean-up together." Dylan picked up a folding shovel and prepared to bury the organic waste.

Soapy dishes began to rattle in the pot. "OK. How about those Nanooks? I heard they beat Michigan State. Want to go up to one of their games sometime?" It was clear that Peter would avoid saying anything to make Dylan uncomfortable. He was just that kind of friend.

"I love hockey, but Fairbanks is pretty far for a hockey game."

Doolie stared hard at the men's plates, and knew he'd get to lick them before they'd go into the wash water. He got to go on these hunts as a guest. Dogs weren't much help on a bird bow hunt. However Doolie carried most of his own food and was allowed to sleep in the tent if he didn't have gas.

Dylan looked up at Peter's serious, droopy face reflecting the campfire light. He wished he had told Peter that he had abandoned the few and distant family members he knew about, and everything else in his first life when he fled the horror of the Denali disaster. Despite the light talk, Dylan did not feel free. He'd lived in Seward for years and felt trapped in this terrible crystal paradise. A man with no past or future who stared at a life that didn't change. Maybe some day he'd get the courage to rejoin society.

His share of the clean-up done, Dylan looked at Peter. "I'm turning in." Dylan left the yellow-warm campfire to Peter and Doolie to crawl into his icy sleeping bag and lonely dreams.

23

. . . .

SUZIE AND DYLAN walked the shoreline path toward the trailhead for their Mt. Alice ascent. With Resurrection Bay on their right, Suzie noticed a sea otter bob up just off shore. The curious creature regarded the pair unafraid. Another head broke the surface. It was a pup and the two communicated silently.

As the older otter began grooming, Dylan thought back to the first time he had seen a Resurrection Bay sea otter. He was returning from Mt. Alice in a rented kayak. Still full of self-loathing, the creature had offered him a sense of serenity that Dylan longed to possess.

As he watched the otters go about their business, it occurred to Dylan that he should do the same. He should look for redemption in the daily routine of caring for his physical and social needs. In a way, the otter showed Dylan that peace could be his if he could let it come to him. He could enjoy the rhythm of labor and relaxation that was the life of the otter.

Dylan watched Suzie's light, carefree walk despite the weight of her backpack. How he longed to have that grace! Dylan walked the shoreline trail carrying weight far exceeding his backpack.

Years ago he had escaped from deepest depression by retreating into the Alaska woods. By putting all his energy into survival, he had allowed his mind to slowly heal from the trauma of the Denali disaster.

Now his best friend was trying to kill him, he was a suspect in the murder of another friend, and a small army of ruthless soldiers was out to destroy him and what he held dear. To discover why all this was happening, Dylan would need to undo the very act that started his healing.

He would exhume the Denali arti-facts buried so long ago: an entombment that allowed him to begin a steep, vertical climb out of hellish guilt.

From this side of the bay, he could see the harbor, Mt. Marathon and Lowell Point. Seeing these sites offered a feeling of calm he didn't expect. He had become a part of this place.

Dylan took over the lead to show Suzie a nearly invisible side trail that would lead them to a camping spot Dylan loved. As Suzie walked on, Dylan used a Sitka spruce branch to brush away any footprints that might reveal the trail to his secret camping Shangri-La.

The trail wound away from the bay and into a dense spruce forest. The relatively mild winters near the bay and the frequent summer rains made for a temperate rainforest that always put a spell on Dylan. This kind of forest made him feel like he belonged to something important, and he wondered if Suzie felt the same way.

The trail swung past a creek full of spawning salmon and ringed with noisy gulls and sharp-eyed eagles all waiting for the feast of salmon eggs and spawned out fish carcasses.

Dylan stopped to watch. The magnificent fish, each the size of his leg, were busy building and defending their nests before exhaustion would kill them. Their bodies would decay on the bank giving nutrients to the forest and filling the stream with bugs for the hatchlings to eat. After a big splash brought him out of his reverie, Dylan resumed his journey noticing that Suzie was far ahead of him.

The path wound past a stand of silvery-barked alders. As they climbed in companionable silence, Dylan realized the depression that had threatened him minutes ago, had been forced into the back corners of his mind by Alaska, a force superior to anything humans could fathom.

Dylan still worried that the closer he got to the burial site, the heavier his footsteps would become. He had to shake off these destructive feelings. This Mt. Alice climb should be no different from other ascents.

As if by a signal, the woods abruptly stopped and a sunny flower-filled meadow lay humming before them. He could hear Suzie's sharp intake of breath as she viewed the Alaska garden before her.

The beauty of this patch of heaven pushed Peter and Zwart into the background of Dylan's mind. Dread and fatigue were replaced by a sense that the mountain had been granting him more power and energy. This perfect meadow. All of nature was working at a feverish pitch to prepare for the coming winter.

Dylan led Suzie to the north side of the meadow near some large boulders and a spring that flowed so crystalline pure, that it appeared to be carved from some kind of living glass. By the fire pit and firm, stone-free plots, it was clear to Suzie that this was someone's secret camping spot.

"We are completely safe here. No one knows about this place. We can just pay attention to this meadow and relax." Dylan's face seemed peaceful and confident.

"If no one knows about this place, how come there's a parking lot and trail head down the mountain?" Suzie wanted to know.

"To get to that south trail from here, you'd have to cross this huge meadow. Most hikers just stay on the path and walk right past this area." Dylan shook out his tent.

They set up camp quickly as the sun hung low over the Harding Ice Field to the west.

"OK master of the woods, what's for dinner?" Suzie asked as she munched a trail bar.

"We're having wild salad unless you can get us some fresh ptarmigan. You carried that pink bow all the way up here, time to put it to use.

"Great, show me the bird, and I'll shoot it. "

"It took me a long summer to learn how to shoot birds with a bow. Let's have a lesson first." Dylan rolled up a ball of weeds and put it on a log about 10 yards away.

"OK. Go for it." What followed was the wonderful ripping sound of the flu-flu as Suzie released the arrow. On her second shot, she hit the ball of weeds and sent it over the log.

"See? I told you I knew how to shoot a bow."

"There's more to it when the target is alive. If it's moving, you need to shoot ahead of it. Try hitting it when I throw it. I want you to hit it as it's ascending."

Dylan demonstrated by taking her bow, throwing up the weed ball and hitting it with that wonderful ripping sound.

Suzie stood back and tried it as Dylan threw up ball after ball for her. This proved to be so challenging that Suzie could rarely get a hit even if she was 10 feet from it.

As the sun started its slow set, Dylan handed the weedball to Suzie, "I'm going to gather a salad before it gets too dark. If you want, you can keep practicing. The birds are going to roost over on that side of meadow in about 30 minutes. If you're going to get a bird, it will be there. Come back by dark and enjoy a salad by the fire with me.

"Get ready to cook a brace of ptarmigan. I will learn this."

As Dylan browsed the meadow for dinner, the steady ripping of Suzie's arrows formed a counterpoint to the natural meadow sounds. The evening light turned the Mt. Alice summit rosy colors and the meadow prepared for sleep.

Standing on a ledge his arms full of plants, Dylan looked west toward Seward. The Kenai Fjords shone greenly in the slanting sunlight. Mists clung to sparkling glaciers, rivers of ancient ice that seemed to glow from within by a powerful bluish atomic light.

Tiny Seward perched on a fan-shaped terminal moraine. Everywhere else, grand mountains pushed their massive chests right to the edge of the water. The bay burst with life: whales, salmon, clouds of rich plankton. Food for birds, otters, bears and handymen. Without understanding it, emo-tions swelled up in his chest. Gratitude showed clearly in his face. This was his, and he was this. *God, I love this place!*

The peace of Dylan's life had been shattered by a secret that might be revealed in the Bible buried near the summit of Mt. Alice. Dylan realized that Suzie's support would allow him to face painful memories.

Dylan suddenly became aware that he hadn't heard the ripping sound of the flu-flu arrows for a long time. What was up with Suzie?

24

· · · · · · · · · ·

THE EVENING SUN flickered through the trees as Zwart's team approached the entrance to the north Mt. Alice trail. A distant beach campfire contributed haze to the hillside. Only a few forest sounds challenged the breaking of twigs and the shuffling of army boots. "Circle up." The six deadly looking, night-vision-equipped, black-clad soldiers ambled to the meeting point indicated.

Zwart assessed their readiness with a few quick glances. "Kilo, your night-vision cords are too long. You'll catch one on a branch. Echo, you are placing too much of your weight on your heels. As a result you are making twice as much noise as you should when you walk". Both soldiers acknowledged the recommendations.

Zwart's attention shifted to the situation at hand. This mission had to succeed. The commander was pissed. Mission results to date have been unacceptable. As of this moment, things were going to change.

"Here's what we know. A fisherman at Yukon Dave's Pub reported giving a ride to a man fitting Dylan's description. The man, accompanied by a woman, was taken to Bear Lake. We believe this man is our target. They have a several hour head start. Our first objective is to neutralize both Dylan and the woman—two very dangerous targets. Shoot to kill. Afterwards, we can determine if they have the Bible."

Zwart paused while he confirmed eye contact with each soldier. "I'm going level with you. To date, our mission metrics have been pathetic. Historically, this squad's performance was based on honor.

"We are willing to sacrifice to complete the mission. For those of you who have let this fresh mountain air fog your minds, *honor* means perseverance, muscle, and blood. It is time to up our game! Fall in. Echo, you're sniper." He pointed a manicured finger at an amazingly fit female soldier, "Tango, you're lead."

Tango snapped to ready. "Yes, Sir."

The soldiers checked their weapons and prepared for an assault. Their world became green-on-grey as they powered up their night vision goggles. Tango smiled toward Foxtrot, "I'll give you the "moose sign" if I see any suspicious movement." Several men snickered. The night vision equipment hid Foxtrot's moose-cub-shooting embarrassment.

Insensitive to early evening darkness enhanced by the dense forest, cat-like Tango started up the same north trail that Dylan and Suzie used earlier that day. With only slightly more noise, the rest of the soldiers and Zwart followed. Tango skillfully scouted the trail and moved the group quickly along.

A commotion in the dense ferns snapped up her complete attention. A small, green, roly-poly bear cub tumbled out of the bushes and peered surprised at the soldiers. Tango let loose an automatic blast of silenced fire that nearly cut the cub in half and then spoke into her sleeve advising the team of her actions.

The soft shuffle behind and to the left of Tango heralded Zwart's approach. "Tango, focus on increasing your efficiency. You could have accomplished the same result with 50% less ordinance. Also, check your sites— the first three shots were low."

"Yes, Sir. Thank you, Sir." Tango smiled sensing a compliment embedded in the suggestions for improvement.

25

. . . .

"YOU'VE BEEN BUSY." Suzie appeared in the campsite carrying two fat birds. Suzie looked over the meadow greens Dylan had laid out. He'd made a salad and a pan of tea from devil's club shoots and other herbs. Shorty had told him the tea would help a man think clearer and cure diabetes, but Dylan liked the taste and soothing warmth of it.

Suzie threw the birds down on the cutting board triumphantly. "You dress these and cook them, I'll clean up and put everything away."

As Suzie went to wash up, Dylan's "Nice birds!" comment elicited a smile. Watching Suzie's feminine walk to the spring, Dylan felt an unfamiliar emotional stirring welling up.

Since he lost Heather on Denali, his interest in women had also been buried. Quickly he busied himself with getting the birds ready to cook. *This is not the time to resurrect long-repressed desires.*

Suzie won the hatchet throw to see who did the clean up. *She's distracting me in this peaceful place,* Dylan thought.

Later, as the two small tents glowed in the dark under the amazing power of their candle lanterns, Suzie spoke through the Alaska night silence between the walls of the two tents, "Dylan, where do you see yourself in five years?"

The wait for a reply was so long, that Suzie thought he must be asleep. "Five years? I don't know. I guess if I survive this madness, I'll do what I'm doing now. Since moving to these woods, I haven't really made any plans."

Suzie blew out her candle. "If you asked me this a while back, I would have said I wanted a houseful of kids. I wanted nosy neighbors coming over with their urchins for play dates. And I wanted to write something besides a blog, maybe a Pulitzer-winning news story."

"Are you going to do that by yourself?"

"I'll get the Pulitzer by myself, but the other parts may require assistance. I guess I want someone to share my dreams with; someone who lets me gaze at him as he shaves in the morning and rub his sore shoulders at night."

Suzie paused introspectively. "I guess I see myself at a juncture. I know the endpoint: a significant contribution as a writer. I'd like to find a life partner, too. But which do I pursue first? Being a writer first and a partner second leaves me with a different life than being a partner first and a writer second."

Suzie tried to peer through the tents walls to see Dylan. "Don't you want a life partner?"

Again, silence. Suzie wondered if she heard a choking sound from his tent. "Yes. But I don't think anyone would want me."

"What are you talking about? You are handsome and smart, even if you are a bit strange. After you recover emotionally, you'll be a fine man for someone who wants to live in the woods and eat weeds."

"You think so?" Dylan sounded so hopeful: it made Suzie smile. Dylan paused introspectively. "I'm not a writer. The only thing I ever create was a technique to remove carbon dioxide from a test tube. "

Suzie's smile grew into a grin. "So did you make millions on it?"

"No, it was too inefficient."

She decided to change the subject. "I saw a yearling black bear over on the south side of the meadow. Just as you suggested, I stood still, then backed away slowly while maintaining eye contact. I wonder if I'm the only girl in Alaska who doesn't have bear protocol memorized."

"Good job. If that bear had attacked you, you'd need to fight back. Hitting its nose or eye with a rock or stick would be best."

While Dylan lay in the quiet of the woods, his candle lantern blown out, his mind called up one of his early encounters with bears.

YEARS AGO WHEN he was new to bow hunting but thought he knew what to do, he found a sturdy tree close to where several game trails crossed. In it, he'd built a roost a month before hunting season and returned on opening day to sit on his perch and wait for the deer. If Dylan could get a decent-sized buck, he could eat for a month and trade some jerky for rice and vegetables. He needed this food.

Just before dawn, Dylan scaled the tree to discover that the seat he had made had been chewed up by squirrels and was now the size of a playing card. He hoped the wait would not be long. Many painful hours later, Dylan decided his butt could not be more uncomfortable when a doe stepped daintily out of a thicket. It had picked its way within 50 yards of Dylan's tree, when a magnificent 10-point buck emerged, following the doe. It's heavily muscled neck held the huge rack with ease.

Dylan needed the buck about 25 yards or closer to get a perfect shot. The doe walked past his tree and the buck seemed to follow as if on autopilot. At 30 yards, the buck stopped and stared intensely up at Dylan's perch. Had he noticed Dylan's scent? Dylan knew he held the most effective, high tech hunting bow ever made. His breathing, the bow stabilizers, and his laser sharp focus held the bow rock-solid on target. This might be the only shot he would get today. Behind him the doe suddenly leaped down the trail.

The buck whirled just as Dylan released his arrow. The arrowhead appeared tiny at first look. Upon impact, three surgical steel blades would snap open to make a huge uncloseable wound. In just moments, the deer would bleed out, lose consciousness and fall.

But that didn't happen. Dylan had taken the shot too soon: a typical rookie's mistake. It would have been ok if he had missed his buck entirely, but instead, the arrow had hit the forest king in the belly. With amazing strength and agility, the buck spun around in mid-air and vanished down a game path.

Dylan would need to track this animal, perhaps for many hours, to get a kill shot. He would then need to somehow get the meat back to his cabin for processing. What had started as a simple day hunt was now going cause the buck unspeakable misery, and Dylan would put in uncounted hours of backcountry labor. What an idiot he had been! Always wait for the shot. *Always wait for the shot.*

Eager to end the suffering of the buck and get tracking, Dylan lowered his bow to the ground using a string. Just as he did this, three black balls of fur tumbled into view. What's this? Holy shit! Black bear cubs. The sow crunched out of a thicket behind the cubs.

Dylan froze, hoping they would amble on. As the mother sniffed the greeny-blood mark where Dylan had gut-shot the deer, the curious cubs started climbing his tree. Each of these cubs weighed about 70 pounds and would bite. How to get these nosy cubs away? Soon the closest one was nearly to Dylan's boot.

Dylan had his hunting knife handy, but he didn't want to hurt these cubs. He yelled at them. It was as if he had thrown acid in their faces. They bawled, backed down the tree and ran into a thicket.

The moment Dylan yelled, the sow became furious. She charged the tree, leaped onto it and started climbing. Roaring with anger, she approached Dylan's hunting platform. Dylan pulled his bow up past the enraged bear to his platform and notched an arrow. He could send a deadly arrow down the throat of this enraged animal, but if he killed this sow, it would be killing four bears. The cubs could not fend for them-selves yet.

He screamed at the bear and made himself as large as he could. This didn't intimidate the angry mother bear in the least, but a cry from one of the cubs diverted her. She descended and followed her cub's cry into the thicket.

Dylan waited for the forest to become quiet again. Uneasy about an angry sow nearby, Dylan wanted to go back to his cabin. Dylan knew that wasn't a choice open to him—ethics and hunger forced him to proceed deeper into the forest.

Dylan hoped the buck would seek water then rest. It was not to be so. For the next 20 hours Dylan tracked the buck, which eerily bellowed its misery to the forest. Dylan had never heard anything like it. With each echoing buck cry, Dylan vowed never to take a shot until the situation was perfect. For years the pitiful buck bellows would linger with Dylan, joining the sound-track to his night terrors.

IN THE DARKNESS, SUZIE SPOKE, breaking into Dylan's memories. "But, I had my bow. I could've shot that bear if it charged."

"That bow would not stop a bear. Not unless you got a lucky shot and put an arrow up its nose."

"OK. If a mean black bear attacks me, I'll hit it with a stick or rock. Or shoot an arrow up its nose. Who hasn't seen the bear attack warnings on bulletin boards peppering the campgrounds?"

"Really, I don't think you need to worry. I've lived in the woods for 10 years and although I've seen black bear cubs I've have never been attacked by a monster black bear. A brown bear once charged me, but with brown bears you just play dead and they leave." When Dylan noticed no response from Suzie, he figured she was asleep.

"Suzie, you are safe now," Dylan whispered.

26

· · · · · · · · · · ·

TANGO LOOKED DOWN at her hands: two more modafinil pills. These should keep her going and ready for combat after climbing this ridiculous mountain all night. The false trail laid by Dylan had cost her team hours of wasted wandering among the absurdly dark forests on the sides of Mt. Alice and had really pissed her off. No one makes Tango look stupid. She decided to make Dylan suffer for this indignation.

She stared at the tents 500 meters across the meadow from her vantage point: no movement. Likely the subjects were sleeping in. Tango slowly and quietly retreated into the brush to give a report to Zwart. Her report would be concise and perfectly aligned with Zwart's SOPs.

Tango focused on silent movement through the forest without leaving a trace of her passage. She frequently glanced over her shoulder to confirm the faint trail she followed remained undisturbed.

Rather proud of her skills, she acknowledged Kilo's nod as she entered Zwart's camp. Kilo received a status report from Tango and prepared to stake out the meadow while Tango spoke with Zwart.

Now that Tango had located the targets, the squad could prepare for the assault. The mercenary's camp exemplified mobile combat efficiency.

Each self-sufficient team member had arranged his or her combat and survival tools for an instantaneous departure. Zwart had directed the sniper to soften up the targets before anyone got close. The others spread out in the woods as a flanking maneuver to prevent escape.

A few minutes later the meadow, now glistening from a light rain, stretched out before the team. The sound of a .50 caliber rifle shot was to be the signal to move in. Subjects were only to be taken alive if they immediately surrendered.

Movement on the far side of the meadow snapped her consciousness into full battle mode. Tango radioed an update to the squad. The subjects were packing up their camp and preparing to move out. Across the large meadow, a public hiking trail would lead down to a parking lot/trail head or upwards to the summit of Mt. Alice. They could be making a break for it.

As the rain increased to pelting waves flowing across the meadow, Zwart and Echo appeared at the meadow's edge about 100 feet west of Tango's position. At Zwart's signal, Echo immediately began preparing his sniper rifle. "Do you have a clear shot?" Zwart's radio voice was both sharp and soft in Echo's ear.

Echo approached a fallen tree to use as a shooting platform. He attached the tripod, balanced the Barrett M107 .50 caliber sniper rifle with its Schmitt and Bender scope, and stared into the lens. For a moment no one moved. "Not sure, Sir. They are pretty far and that wind is not consistent." As if to emphasize the point, a sharp blast of wind blew the cap off one of the soldiers.

Dylan and Suzie could be seen walking away from the assault team, apparently unaware of their peril.

"Give it a try", Zwart commanded.

Echo tracked their movements trying to anticipate a pattern as Dylan and the reporter moved through the waves of pelting rain.

Slowly his finger tightened on the trigger of his Barrett about to send 18 kilojoules of naked power towards Dylan's body.

27

· · · · · · · · · · ·

UNAWARE THAT A DEADLY six-person attack team was nearly at their campsite, Dylan pushed his sleeping bag into his pack. He wasn't sure why he was experiencing a deep feeling of dread.

His conscious mind told him it was the weather, which was giving all the signs of a violent summer storm blowing off the 1,000-square-mile Harding Ice Field. A mountaintop is a bad place to hunker down to withstand one of these amazing storms.

"I don't see why we have to have just a granola bar and water for breakfast. I know you have some coffee in your pack." Suzie munched dourly on her breakfast. Unlike most inexperienced backpackers, she had packed her gear quickly and was nearly ready to move out.

"I don't like this storm. Up here it can get really dicey. We'll need to go down and come up another day." Dylan hoisted his pack and swung it around expertly to his back.

"Oh no you don't. We came up here and we're going to get that Bible." Suzie started resolutely across the meadow as treetops tossed, grasses flattened to the earth and small branches rolled and bounced. Forest debris flew across her path in a horizontal plane.

"You don't even know where it is," Dylan found himself yelling to be heard as he followed her. The deep dread he felt earlier became even more profound.

Unbidden, images of Boris insisting on ignoring the Denali storm, and Dylan's subsequent capitulation flooded his mind.

Suzie hiked purposefully across the meadow even as gusts made her appear to stumble sometimes. She was going to get the Bible with or without Dylan's help. Dylan's dread increased. This situation was so much like hiking with Boris.

As Dylan caught up to her, he wondered if his dark feelings had anything to do with facing the burial chamber for the Denali artifacts he'd collected. In his mind he could see Heather's necklace, Boris's Bible and other objects. Maybe he was just afraid of letting something out: something that would drive him back into the woods for another ten years.

Just then, during a lull in the wind, his pack lurched as if someone had thrown a punch into the bottom right corner. He saw a piece of his orange tent and part of his mess kit fly out in front of him.

"What the heck?" Why did the tent piece burst out in front of him when the wind was blowing from the right? A deep rolling boom thundered across the meadow.

"Thunder," said Suzie confidently.

"Get down!" yelled Dylan as he pushed her forward. A crater the size of a dinner plate opened in front of them just as a sheet of rain slammed the meadow.

"Someone's shooting." Dylan yelled through the wind and rain. Suzie looked scared as she rubbed her palm where her hands stopped her fall.

"What can we do?" Suzie yelled back. "We're in the open."

Dylan looked back to the direction from which the shot had come. With the sudden appearance of the rain, visibility had sudden dropped from 500 to 20 yards. "We run. Now!"

Nearly picking Suzie up by her pack, Dylan led Suzie onto the left fork toward the south trailhead.

Quickly, Dylan pulled the remains of his orange tent out of the opening in the pack made by a .50 Caliber M1022 sniper bullet fired from 1000 yards.

As they ran, Suzie felt as if she were under water, so heavy was the rainfall. "Slow down! I can't breathe!" Suzie turned to Dylan. "Let's drop our packs. We can run faster."

Dylan struggled with indecision. Suzie was exhausted. Downhill would be much easier for her. *Sid! What should I do?* Dylan looked downhill where the rain seemed to intensify. He glanced uphill where the trail seemed brighter. "No, we'll need them." Dylan yelled. "Whoever is after us will think we are going down the mountain like any sane person. We'll let them think that, but go up instead. I know of a cave that can give us shelter."

Suzie nodded. "OK. You lead."

Despite the poor visibility and slippery trail, Dylan went unerringly to the trail marker that showed the distance to the parking lot trailhead. He signaled Suzie to wait while he threw off his pack and ran down the trail just out of sight. He wrapped his orange tent around a tree and quickly returned to Suzie.

Throwing on his pack he signaled for her to follow. This part of the trail was mostly on loose flat rocks that would make it impossible for anyone to track a quarry. As they ascended, Dylan gained confidence that their pursuers would be unable to find them. The weather was just too bad and their direction would be impossible to find.

He suddenly remembered another time his trail was impossible to find. That time Zwart tracked him with a tiny GPS. Could he be tracked this time?

28
Many Years Earlier
. . . .

DYLAN FELT NAKED. He clung to the cliff with none of the gear that allowed him to be a world-famous climber.

Indeed, he was nearly naked: wearing nothing but silk shorts and a chalk bag. Climbing up a crack on a warm, absurdly smooth Mexican ocean cliff face, Dylan felt the thrill that stone gives to climbers.

The route radiated magic. A parking-lot-sized flake of stone, thin as a boot-sole, had Dylan climbing using his chalk-covered fists as cams. Thirty feet up the cracks seemed quarried by some god-like mason—the joints appeared so perfect. Rapture filled Dylan with a rush of joy as he ascended a crevice. *God, I love this!*

Months earlier, when Dylan asked Sid how he learned to climb so well, the quiet man just arranged a trip to Mexico and said, "I'll show you."

Sid started Dylan's training by showing him how to dive. They began at nine feet and gradually moved up until Dylan was comfortable diving at 90 feet, just like the Olympic high divers. Dylan loved the diving. It allowed him to use his climbing ability to ascend steep cliffs in the Mexican heat, and then dive into the dark cooling waters below.

After the diving, they moved to a camping spot away from Acapulco to a place divers avoided. Despite the perfect waters, divers never came to the famous wall of smooth stone, de Precipicio Cristal, because it was impossible to climb. The stone walls hovered over the deep Pacific Ocean waters as if daring a climber. Sid climbed them.

Dylan started following Sid's lead. In no time, Dylan was independent. If he slipped, he could rotate in the air and dive safely into the amazing blue waters below.

At fifty feet up, the morning sun on his bare back felt warm, and the crack he had been using for holds narrowed from leg holds, to fist holds then to the most subtle of fingertip holds. This rock face was where Sid said he learned the secrets of his skill.

Dylan finally reached the end of his climb. The route up the face ended. At this point, what did Sid expect him to learn? There was virtually no way to gain any more altitude. The next hold was physically impossible to reach. Wishing he could rest hanging on a rope, Dylan realized he needed to make a decision. His hands and toes would quickly fatigue. Climbers must keep moving or rest. Pausing in this precarious spot was a bad plan. He bought some seconds by chalking up his hands.

He searched for any minute protrusion that might offer him a hold. He saw a tiny finger-sized crack far to his left and rearranged his current holds to get a few inches closer, but it made no difference. The hold was too far for any sane climber to attempt.

"Go for it," Sid called from below.

Dylan would actually need to leap. What if he didn't make it?

"Dylan, just find out if you can get it. If you miss, you'll know what you can do."

Dylan knew that to delay would be to attempt the leap with tired muscles. He leapt, but while airborne, cast a quick look downward. His hand missed the crevice. As he fell the 50 feet down to enter the blue ocean waters, he planned what he would do on his next try.

When he surfaced and swam to the base, Sid was already above the spot where Dylan had fallen and holding himself horizontal with his hands on one wall and feet on another.

"You look like a hammock," Dylan called up.

"Yeah, this really makes my abs burn, but if you put yourself in this same spot, I'll take an awesome photo from above." Sid gestured to his ever present camera hanging on his belt.

The two friends spent a few more weeks on the Mexican ocean cliffs exploring their own limits and becoming comfortable trusting their weight to nearly imperceptible bumps in the rock face.

More than climbing skills, Dylan learned to control his emotions. At a time when he should be terrified, Dylan learned to put that emotion aside and coldly evaluate the potential success of a move.

Under Sid's guidance, Dylan probed the boundaries of his body and mind. He learned that the mind is far more important to climbing success. He used breathing to focus his attention. He could push terror aside and see exactly what he needed in order to complete his goal.

Dylan possessed superior physical strength compared with his mentor. Yet Sid was a better climber due to his intimate knowledge of what he could and could not do. Sid never let emotions interfere with his climbing. Sid took no unnecessary risks and rarely experienced failure.

Dylan felt all too familiar with failure.

29

· · · · · · · · · · ·

NO LONGER CONCERNED that they could be
tracked, GPS or not, Dylan urged Suzie onward.

As they gained altitude, the rain changed to
rain/snow mix. Dylan knew they would be unable to
warm up if they didn't get shelter soon. Suzie was
slowing down: the altitude, the stress of fear and the
cold were all taking their toll.

At a rest stop, Dylan pulled several heavier items
from her pack and shoved them into his. He struggled
with his pack where the sniper's bullet had damaged it.
"Suzie, do you have some string or even dental floss
handy? I've got to tie this up." He showed her the
gaping hole in his pack.

Suzie drew off her wool sock hat and pulled a yellow ribbon from her hair. "Here. I don't need it now."

Her hand plopped into his with the ribbon and remained there a moment longer than necessary.

There. Human touch. Dylan was again amazed at how powerful it was. He felt flooded with emotion, but knew this wasn't the time to think about it. "We got to keep going. The cave isn't far."

But it was.

About an hour later, Dylan carried Suzie's pack as she stumbled dumbly behind him. Her jacket had let in moisture, plus her sweat had left her body wet. She would be hypothermic soon, if he didn't get her to a safe place. Rain/snow was changing to blowing snow, and it seemed to accumulate on Suzie. At some point, she lost her hat and didn't notice. She wore Dylan's hat too far back on her head and he had to keep adjusting it.

Brushing off her head and shoulders, Dylan assessed her condition. Her speech was slowing. Not good. She was shivering, which was a good sign. As soon as she stopped shivering, it would mean she might not be able to warm up without interventions that Dylan didn't have.

"Come, on. We're almost there." Dylan tried to put on a confident voice. He was taking her to a place he didn't want to go, a haunted place, but a place he must enter in order to save her. Sometimes Dylan hated himself for being so timid.

Dylan encouraged Suzie to drink some water and eat. Her body needed to stay hydrated, and she had to have some calories to maintain the spark of warmth that still lingered in her core. Dylan knew that they just had to work through a field of car-sized boulders to get to the cave. A deep clap of thunder erupted from just behind them. Suzie flinched.

"It's just some Mt. Alice thunder, Suzie. No one is shooting up here. We'll be in our dry cave as soon as we cross this boulder field." Dylan hoped the cave would still be there. Most of the stones atop Mt. Alice were unstable which made it bad for climbers looking for some vertical routes, but fine for hikers.

To Suzie, it seemed Dylan stopped abruptly before a heap of bowling ball sized stones near a pile of huge boulders. He threw down the packs and started throwing stones this way and that. In a few minutes, she could see a black opening leading to a space created by the two giant stones leaning against each other.

Later, she wouldn't remember scrambling down into the dark space, but woke up in the dim light of her candle lantern illuminating a space about 20 feet long by 6 feet wide and a sharply sloping narrow ceiling about 10 feet high. The floor was pebbly, but Suzie was lying in her sleeping bag with Dylan's wrapped around her. A warm towel lay on her head and another lay around her throat.

"Good, you're awake. Drink this," Dylan offered her a cup of hot sugary lemonade from a mix they had brought. Their camp stove hissed under a bubbling pot of water, and she could see her clothes hanging on lines near one end of the cave. Her hand strayed to find her green necklace still in place.

"Sorry. I had to take off your wet clothes. Don't worry. I didn't peek." Dylan offered her more hot lemonade as he hid a smile. "I'm making a soup from our leftovers from yesterday and snowmelt. Also, for future hikes, you need to get some better waterproof breathable gear. And don't wear cotton."

He reached over and felt her panties on the line. "Hey these are dry." He tossed them to her, but she just closed her green eyes and let sleep overtake her. She knew she was safe and soon to be warm.

Dylan woke her several times over the next hours to give her more warm lemonade mix and a delicious hot wild soup. She drank it obediently then slept. Once she appeared warm enough, he unwrapped his sleeping bag from around her, climbed into it and scooted next to her so their bags were offering warmth to each other.

Exhaustion beckoned Dylan towards sleep, but knowing that the entombed objects he buried ten years ago were just on the other side of the cave under a make-shift alter made him uneasy. Eventually the comforting warmth from Suzie's nearby body gave him the confidence to sleep, blissfully unaware of the disappointment he would face in the morning.

SUZIE AWOKE STILL FEELING cold. On the opposite side of the cave, Dylan hunched over their ever hissing stove.

"Got any more hot lemonade mix?" Suzie was surprised how groggy her voice sounded.

"Coming right up, but first I need to drink my coffee. We only have one mug, one mess kit and no pistol due to the rip in my pack from that gun shot." Dylan slurped the coffee.

"Wait, you have coffee? That smell woke me up. I like mine with cream and two sugars." Suzie sat up. She felt dizzy and fell back onto her air mattress.

"Sorry. No cream or sugar. I can put lemonade mix in it for you." Dylan looked doubtful. "You should probably avoid caffeine for a few days. You were pretty hypothermic." Dylan pointed a spoon at her. "I'll have some hot lemonade and oatmeal ready in a few minutes.

"I am so hungry!" Suzie announced then fell back asleep. Dylan prepared her breakfast and wrapped it up in a dry towel to keep it warm. He would let her sleep. This would delay the point when he would disinter the Bible and other Denali artifacts.

The moment when the buried items actually came out of the ground proved anticlimactic. He had left the cave to get some water and when he returned, Suzie was sitting cross-legged on her sleeping bag eating oatmeal and looking through the Bible. She had located, dug up the Bible and returned the other items to the cave alter.

"Dylan, this is a Jerusalem cross. See? It's carved to resemble the cross worn by the Crusaders." Suzie opened the Bible and thumbed through it.

"This Bible looks really old. It's an antique and all in Russian. I wonder what Zwart wants with it?" A bit of oatmeal clung to her cheek as she examined the tome.

Dylan looked hard at the book. He hadn't remembered that the wooden covers had a large Jerusalem cross carved on it or the gilded page edges. As Suzie exam-ined the book, a piece of paper fell out.

"Hey. Here is an old bank note from 1882! It's a five-dollar bill drawing on the First National Bank of Juneau. I bet it's worth something."

Replacing the money, Suzie turned back to the cover and ran her hand over the Jerusalem cross. "It's like a big fancy plus sign with little plus signs in each quarter. Each mark for one of the five wounds of Jesus."

Dylan peered closer, "Do you see any reason why Zwart would want this?"

"Nothing obvious. There are some very old-looking pencil marks on some of the pages, but they look over 100 years old. It could be the key to a book cipher or something like that. Or it could have a microdot somewhere in it. Do spies still use micro-dots?" Suzie examined a random page.

Suzie handed Dylan her empty bowl. "I'm taking a nap, then we're going to town and hide out in my apart-ment where we can examine this more carefully."

Dylan reached over and picked the piece of oat-meal from Suzie's cheek and flicked it into a dark corner of the cave. She smiled at him, crawled into her sleeping bag and fell instantly asleep.

Dylan didn't know why Zwart wanted this Bible. The heavy disappointment he felt surprised him. It was as if he got a punch to the stomach before he could tighten his muscles. Dylan had wanted answers from the Bible and now had more questions.

He hoped that finding the answers would not mean more killing.

30

· · · · · · · · · · ·

THE KNITTING BARN tried to attract tourists with a garish paint job covering a smallish 1940's-style home. The downstairs was crammed with knit items ranging from true works of stunning fabric art to gaudy kitsch.

Upstairs were the living quarters and a wide, open room for classes or large projects. The back of the house held a small kitchen and private living room. Nancy Pierce had purchased the business six years ago when her husband died in a fishing accident.

Across the gravel alley was a boxy nondescript duplex containing a dark, downstairs apartment that Suzie Alaneo had rented and from which she cobbled together *The Seward Blogletter* twice a month.

It was Nancy who explained that a good number of Seward residents did not use their computers for local news, so Suzie printed a number of copies of her blog. Suzie used Nancy's upstairs project room and Nancy's help to assemble each printed issue and pass them out to the Sea Star Café, the bakery and Shorty's Tackle Shop.

Now in its fourth year, Suzie had readers from nearly 30 states and five countries. Visitors would vacation in Seward, fall in love with true Alaska quaintness, find the free blogletter and follow it online to retain the flavor of Seward.

Dylan and Suzie strolled with a carefree gait after picking up the dogs at Shorty's. Bergen surged ahead and Doolie followed as they walked through the gravel alleys toward Suzie's apartment. The uneventful, relaxing return journey from Mt. Alice gave them a feeling of confidence and a growing sense of intimacy.

Suzie looked obviously tired and yearned for her dark but cozy apartment but agreed with Dylan that they should approach her home carefully since it might be watched. In the long Seward twilight, as they walked behind the Knitting Barn, Nancy Pierce was taking laundry and knitting-ware off her clothes line and talking to the bold feral bunnies that populate Seward.

"Hi Suzie. Look how soaking wet everything on my clothes line is." Nancy held up a fuzzy, but dripping potholder. "Whoa. Nice looking bow and arrows!" Nancy's gaze shifted from the arrows to Suzie. "You look like you got caught out in the rain, too."

"Hi Nancy. We got soaked, but we're OK." Suzie held onto Dylan's arm as they approached Nancy's backyard. Bergen shoved his nose curiously into the laundry basket. The bunnies had all vanished.

"Bergen, stop that. Those are clean." Dylan patted his knee to distract the pup from the interesting smells in Nancy's laundry.

"Oh. You're Dylan Baker, my heater-repair-man. I didn't recognize you. You look nice without your huge beard." Nancy picked up her white plastic basket. "What's this I hear that the police are looking for you?"

"It was a case of mistaken identity," Dylan smiled through his exhaustion.

"I thought so. Suzie, are you having Dylan work on your furnace? Those other repairmen said they were fixing it. What's up?"

"Repairmen?" Suzie's voice sounded strained.

"Why do you say they were working on her furnace?" Dylan grabbed Bergen's collar to quell the young dog's fascination with Nancy's laundry.

"It was the weirdest thing. Two big black SUVs park behind your apartment, about five men, not from around here, I know all the locals. Well, they take tools inside, and leave about an hour later.

"Since when does it take that many people to fix a furnace? It looked strange to me. So I went over to your garden to pick some beans and asked them what they were doing at your place, they said fixing the furnace and to mind my own business."

"Nancy, nothing was wrong with my furnace. Those men were not fixing it." Dylan could tell Suzie was getting angry. "Nancy, I need your help. I think those fake repairmen want to hurt me because they think I'm helping Dylan."

"You are helping Dylan," Nancy put herself between the curious nose of Bergen and her New Zealand possum-wool tea cozies. "I'll call Officer Burl. He'll deal with any fake repairmen."

"Let's not bother Burl unless we have more information." Suzie reasoned.

"It's no bother. It's his job." Nancy picked up her laundry basket and walked toward her house.

"Nancy, Burl doesn't know Dylan's not the person he's looking for. Until he figures that out, we need to keep Burl away from Dylan." Suzie looked over at Dylan playing with his dogs. "Dylan has some things to do that can prove his innocence, but he can't do that if Burl finds out he's here."

"Of course Dylan's not a criminal," Nancy smiled at Dylan romping with his dogs on her damp lawn.

"Until we can straighten this out, can we rest at your house?" Suzie's eyes looked tired.

"You can stay here all you want. You look beat. Want some dinner? I made two meat loaves this evening. I can fix you guys supper in a jiffy."

"You don't know how good that sounds, Nancy." Clearly it made Suzie tired to consider fixing dinner.

"OK. Don't lift a finger. Just find a seat in the living room, and I'll bring you both a tray." Nancy led them past a collection of bird feeders and up some damp, seed-strewn concrete stairs to the back of her shop.

Twenty minutes later she brought two fragrant steaming trays out to her back living room to find everyone asleep.

Bergen woke up when she entered the room and followed her back into the kitchen as she put the meals in the oven to stay warm. She managed to extract a ball of yarn from his mouth. "I'm going to have to keep an eye on you, Bergen. I don't want you to chew up anything." Nancy wrote a note to Dylan and Suzie explaining she'd be back and where to find their meals.

"I'm teaching an evening class over at the Senior Center. Bergen, how about you come with me so you don't get into any mischief while I'm away?"

Nancy held the door open as Bergen stood rooted to the floor, his tail thumped against the oven door with a deep rhythm.

Doolie walked stiffly in and regarded Nancy and Bergen with his gray muzzle and solemn eyes. Bergen made no effort to accompany Nancy out the door.

"Not coming? Well, you two behave yourselves. And Bergen, don't chew up anything."

Nancy let herself out into the Alaska twilight.

HOURS LATER SUZIE awoke in the dark living room amongst the other sleepers. "Nancy?" Suzie called softly as she padded into Nancy's cluttered, warm kitchen. As she was reading the note, Dylan and Doolie joined her.

"How about dinner and a Russian Bible? We can figure out why that Bible is so valuable." Suzie served the meal and Dylan poured glasses of milk. They put the Russian Bible on the kitchen table between them and started looking for anything that might be interesting to Zwart.

They finished their meal in near silence as each page was turned and the pretty, carved covers examined.

"The grain on these covers is beautiful, and I love the Jerusalem cross carved into it." Suzie held the book under one of the powerful magnifying glasses Nancy used for needlework projects. "Aside from the wooden covers, I just don't see anything special about this Bible. It's in Russian and it's a New Testament with Psalms, but nothing has been written in since it was printed back in 1989. It's pretty, but I don't think it's rare. There are probably thousands of Bibles like this."

"Maybe you were right. Perhaps there's a micro-dot or something glued onto one of the pages," offered Dylan weakly as he finished washing the dishes.

"I think we would have noticed it. We've both been through this book several times now." Suzie pulled a slobbery saltshaker from Bergen's mouth. "I wonder if Nancy has something for him to chew on?"

"His favorite are my socks, but I'm wearing them until I can get some fresh ones." Suzie pulled a pair of pink wool socks from a display rack, laid some money on the cash box and handed them to Dylan. "I know they are a bad color for you, but they are clean and high-quality wool. You can give your old socks to Bergen so he stays out of mischief."

Dylan eyed the pink socks doubtfully, but followed Suzie's suggestion. "Thanks for the present." Wearing pink socks and feeling silly, Dylan took the Bible, flipped through it again and set it down on the table, "They are probably looking for a different Bible. Getting this one was a waste of time."

Suzie noticed how discouraged Dylan looked. "It hasn't been a waste. I learned to shoot a flu-flu, didn't I?" She dished up absurdly large bowls of ice cream for each of them. Suzie had read somewhere that Alaskans ate more ice cream per capita than any other state, and felt she had to keep up the tradition.

They took their bowls into the living room and settled again into the comfortable chairs they had slept in earlier. "Suzie, I'm so sorry I brought you into this. You should stay far away from me until this whole thing ends."

"Dylan, you didn't bring me into this. I jumped in with both feet trying to get a story for my blog."

"We should tell Nancy some of the details of what's happening so she can avoid being of interest to Zwart. And Suzie, you should go somewhere and hold up until these thugs leave. I'm concerned that they left a trap at your place."

"They probably just searched for you and left. By the way, some people here say Nancy is a busybody, but she's one of my best friends. I don't think we could discourage her from helping us." Suzie picked nuts out of her ice cream daintily and ate them.

Dylan heard a crunching sound from the kitchen and got up to see what Bergen was chewing.

From the kitchen, Suzie heard Dylan say, "No Bergen. Bad dog!"

Returning to Suzie in the living room, Dylan brought in a well-chewed Jerusalem Bible.

"So much for this. If they wanted it in good condition, it's toast now." He tossed the pulpy mess into a trashcan and sat down to finish his ice cream.

Bergen kept staring at the trashcan like a squirrel was about to leap out.

"Dylan, I don't think you should leave that chewed up Bible in there, Bergen is going to yield to temptation and pull it out for more chewing. Plus it has that old bank note in it." Suzie took her empty ice cream bowl to the warm kitchen, on her way back stopping to pull the soggy and broken Bible out of the trash. From behind him, Dylan heard her gasp.

"Dylan! Look at this!" Suzie held out the Bible.

"What is it?" Dylan was next to her in an instant looking at the broken and splintered covers.

"A cavity has been carved out of the inside of the cover and this was hidden there," Suzie held up a square, flat piece of black plastic about the size of a small wheat cracker.

"What is it?"

"It's a compact flash memory card: a CF card. I used these with my old camera. You've never seen one? Boy have you been in the woods a long time. I bet this is what Zwart has been looking for since he got here."

"So it has pictures on it—like film? What pictures would be worth killing for?"

"It may not have photos. It's usually used for images, but it could have anything on it: documents, pictures, video. It can have anything on it that can be saved on a computer. This is an old one, only 128k of space."

"It's probably no good. For ten years it's been in a frozen dry-bag up on Mt. Alice."

"Dylan, this isn't a hard drive. No moving parts. They last forever." Suzie turned over the CF card in her hand.

Dylan examined the card. "Can we see what's on it?"

"Maybe Nancy has a card reader. If she does, we can see if it has anything that might interest Zwart."

A sharp bark from Bergen and deep growl from Doolie interrupted them. The dogs charged the door. It opened and Nancy came in turning the growls to tail wagging.

She smiled at them. "You're awake and both here. I thought I saw a light in your apartment as I walked up." Nancy put a basket of knitting supplies on the table. "Did you like the meatloaf? It's my mother's family recipe."

Suzie put a hand on her arm. "Nancy, we have something to tell you." Nancy looked startled. "You may be in danger."

"Oh thank goodness! I thought you were going to say you didn't like the meatloaf."

"Nancy, some bad men are after Dylan. They might try to hurt you or us. We're trying to figure out why."

Nancy regarded Suzie with a doubtful expression. "OK. Some bad guys are after Dylan and might hurt me. Tell me how I can help." Nancy put her hands on her amble hips.

"Do you have a compact flash card reader? We have a card we need to examine." Suzie held up the CF card.

"I sure do. It's the fastest way to get the video out of my trusty old camcorder. But it can wait until morning. It's almost midnight! You are staying here tonight. There's a queen sized air mattress and pump in the project room. On the top shelf are some sleeping bags. You two need to rest."

Nancy extracted a soggy TV remote from Bergen. I think I'll walk Bergen over to Shorty's in the morning. I love dogs, but Doolie is more suited to guarding a knitting shop. You two get up there and go to sleep. The card can wait. It will still be here in the morning."

Suzie could barely keep her eyes open as she got ready for bed. Dylan got the mattress and sleeping bags laid out. "I think Nancy thinks we know each other better than we do," Suzie said as she washed her face.

Dylan felt awkward. Did Suzie think he would want to use the queen-sized bed for more than sleep? When he came back from the bathroom, Suzie was asleep in her sleeping bag. Dylan took minutes to carefully climb into his bag so he wouldn't wake her.

As soon as he settled on his side of the mattress, Suzie rolled over and leaned her head against his shoulder. She slept with her mouth open—just like Heather. Tonight he would not sleep with Heather's ghost. He would sleep with a real person.

Dylan's arm started to throb where Suzie's head lay. It didn't matter. He held as still as a stone enjoying the trusting human affection. Suzie lay like that half the night. Dylan's arm was asleep and profoundly uncomfortable. Calmed and soothed by Suzie's presence, Dylan slept better than he had for months despite his arm losing all circulation.

Next door, in Suzie's house, a light flickered and went out.

31

· · · · · · · · · · ·

DYLAN OPENED HIS EYES the next morning to find Suzie's sleeping bag unzipped and unoccupied. The sunlight through the window told him it was about nine. He never slept in.

Pulling himself into a sitting position in his sleeping bag, he looked around Nancy's project room. He didn't know if a head rush or remembering yesterday's events made him dizzy.

He lay back down as Suzie walked out the bathroom with a towel wrapped around her head. She wore some of Nancy's clothes, looking very pert in her baggy attire. "I don't think I've ever slept that sound. Amazing what exhaustion will do for you."

Rubbing his arm, Dylan agreed. "We should look at that card now. I slept well too, but I can't wait to find out why Zwart and Peter want to kill me."

"You're going to need to wait until after breakfast. I'm starving." Suzie threw her damp towel at Dylan.

Downstairs they found a note on the kitchen table explaining that Nancy was out walking Bergen over to Shorty's place, and they should make themselves at home.

A half-hour later, sitting at the table with Suzie, a cup of coffee, toast, bacon, eggs and a red-checkered cloth napkin made Dylan yearn for a simple domestic life. He wanted to cling to the peace and contentment of this moment. He wanted nothing strange or new to happen. He just wanted to gaze at Suzie when she wasn't looking.

Her face glowed in the golden morning sunshine slanting into the cheerful yellow kitchen, a bluegrass melody blared from the local radio station. Yet the CF card seemed to throb with menace from its place near the sink.

Suzie seemed reluctant to face their problem, too. She stalled while she finished her breakfast. "You like this song, Dylan?" she ran her toast around the pool of egg yolk on her plate.

Dylan moved his thoughts from her graceful fingers to the radio. "I don't know it," he admitted.

"Really? I thought you outdoorsmen all loved this stuff." She hummed along with it for a few moments.

Dylan knew climbers who brought guitars to their climbing sites and sang to reflect on life at the end of the day. Dylan always spent those nights planning the next ascent in his tent. He could be caught nursing his dreams, not making melodies.

"Maybe you'd smile more if you let some music in your life," Suzie teased. She played an air mandolin to the tune. Dylan would have given anything at that moment to impress her with music.

Too soon, they had finished the kitchen clean up and sat before Nancy's new Mac nestled in her cluttered front-room office. It seemed all screen to Dylan, but he feigned familiarity with it. As Suzie plugged in Nancy's card reader and inserted the CF card, Dylan felt his pulse quickening. What would they learn? Would Suzie see the contents and despise him? What could be on that card that was so powerful?

The first thing Suzie did when the image of the card appeared on the screen was to copy it to the hard drive. Then she attempted to view several of the files from the hard drive copies. None would open. An error message kept appearing explaining that the files were unreadable.

"What's wrong?" Dylan jumped at the sound of his own voice.

"This computer might be too new to read these ten-year-old files. Plus, this Mac may not be able to read old PC files."

Dylan looked crushed. All that effort for some files which can't be read?

"Look, Dylan. We need to find a computer with 10 year-old software." Suzie ejected the card reader.

"How do we do that? This is little Seward, Alaska, not a big city with lots of computer museums."

"If the files on these are only 10 years old, we don't need a museum. Probably one of the donated computers at the Senior Center has what we need."

Dylan didn't respond. He was out of his element.

Dylan decided to shelve his internal questions about hardware verses software. He was visualizing a quick alleyway route to the senior center, when Suzie pushed her chair back.

Dylan looked at the remains of the chewed up Bible. "I wonder how the Bible verse we found in Peter's office fits in with this Bible. Or are they unrelated?"

"I've wondered about that, too. There's the actual Bible. We know its significance now—it held the CF card, the bank note and old pencil notes. Then there's the Bible verse. You said Peter's family is religious?

Maybe they knew the Russian on your Denali climb and were part of a religious organization that quoted that win-at-all-costs message. And maybe they have some sketchy government secrets as part of their biblical fraternity. Maybe this CF card has some information on it that Peter's brother needs, and he sent Zwart to get it!"

Dylan played with Doolie's ears and watched Suzie shutting down the Mac. Dylan couldn't help smiling at Suzie. There was so much energy in that little body. He expected that soon they would learn the secrets from the Jerusalem Bible.

32

· · · · · · · · · · ·

KNOWING SHORTY WAS moving more slowly than
normal, Dylan decided to collect Bergen before he could
chew up everything in the shop.

There was also a chance that Zwart might continue to
harass Shorty since he must be getting more desperate to
get the Bible, and Dylan wanted to warn his old friend.
He could collect Bergen, and tell Shorty to take a
vacation.

Dylan walked the back alleys to the woods then cut
west toward the docks. He would have to cross an inter-
section, busy by Seward standards, a large open parking
lot and the railroad tracks to get to Shorty's tackle shop.
An insistent feeling of dread made Dylan's steps move
faster than he wanted. His goal was to appear casual, but
his gait conveyed urgency.

If Zwart had a man watching Suzie's apartment, what would they do to Shorty? Anyone in town would say that Shorty was probably Dylan's best friend besides Peter. But then, Shorty was pretty much friendly to everyone.

Once he alerted Shorty to Zwart's need to get the Bible, he could collect Bergen and get Suzie to a safe place while they unraveled the secrets of the CF card.

Shorty had family a few miles away in Moose Pass. He could stay with them for the duration. How would he get the overly stubborn Shorty to leave? His obstinate old friend was so fearless and yet so fragile.

An eerie feeling came over Dylan as he broke cover and strode towards Shorty's lonely little tackle shop. It was the same feeling that crept over Dylan when he knew he was being stalked by a backwoods predator.

From experience, Dylan knew the best course of action in the woods would be to back away, put cover between him and his hunter and flee. Shorty was too good a friend for Dylan to run.

As he came closer to the tackle shop, the sub-conscious warnings in Dylan's mind were loud and insistent: *Get away! Now!* Dylan wondered if these warnings were just an overreaction to his recent hyper-vigilance.

By walking the tracks, Dylan was able to approach Shorty's shop from behind. There was the battered old white van, a large white paper under the wiper. His scalp prickling with danger, Dylan put himself between the van and the shop so a distant sharpshooter would have trouble getting a clean shot. He scooted under the van and pulled the paper down where he could see it. Spreading it out he saw a crudely written note.

Any visitor to Shorty's tackle shop would find dozens of precise, handmade signs indicating what's on special, what the fish are hitting and directions for rigging fishing poles. These signs all have the distinct slant of left-handed Shorty, but the legibility of a mechanical engineer. The note Dylan held had Shorty's mechanical-engineer-letters, but these were slanted right-handed and poorly made: as if Shorty had written them right-handed.

The message stunned Dylan. It was clearly a suicide note: "I can't take it anymore. I'm ending it."

Dylan knew that Shorty would never kill himself. He was having too much fun and held onto too many long-term goals.

What would he find in the shop? Would Shorty be dead? Was there a trap laid for him? Uncharacteristically, the curtains were all pulled shut and the front door had the big CLOSED sign on it. *Why would Shorty close shop at a peak shopping time?*

Dylan snaked around to the back door to listen. Silence. He attempted to open the door—locked. Just then, he heard the whine of a dog. Bergen? Maybe Bergen and Shorty were just fine.

Dylan debated what to do. If it were a trap, Zwart would have both entrances rigged with explosives or covered by a sharpshooter. Dylan worked his way around the shop to the dockside of the building. Shorty's living quarters were in the back of the shop. Dylan shoved a rusting snow shovel blade into a back window crack and pushed with all his might.

The lock splintered and the window swung open. The reassuring rubber and oak smells instantly wafted out to him. Dylan launched himself over the sill and onto a shelf loaded with spinning reels. Instantly, large rough hands pinned Dylan down, his legs still partly out the window. He felt nylon zip cords cuff his hands behind his back and bind his legs together as he was pulled through the window.

He looked over to see Shorty zip-tied to a chair, his left hand a pulpy mess of ground meat and bone, and Bergen hogtied in front of him. Shorty appeared to be barely conscious, and Bergen looked relieved to see his beloved master, the bloody zip ties obviously causing the pup great pain. His jaws were taped shut, so only his pleading eyes and whines communicated his desperate joy to Dylan. All his attention on Shorty and Bergen, Dylan barely took in the explosive devices partially rigged to the front door.

"Welcome Mr. Baker. You took far longer to get here than we expected." Zwart and a black-clad soldier with spiky blond hair and an ID patch naming him *Victor*, put Dylan into a high-backed old chair and efficiently attached Dylan's legs and arms to the chair. Escape would be impossible. Zwart closed the window and drew the curtains.

"We won't need them any more." Zwart jerked his head toward Bergen and Shorty. Victor pulled on surgical gloves. He picked up an old .32 Ruger revolver that Shorty kept behind the counter and coldly put a bullet into Shorty's head. Without wasting any motion, the soldier quickly fired into Bergen's head. Shorty's body spasmed a few times then became still. Bergen instantly became motionless: one of his dead eyes still on Dylan. Victor carefully pressed the gun into Dylan's right hand, and then placed it on a nearby table.

Zwart looked at Dylan. "So sorry to do that, Mr. Baker, but you made it necessary by your lack of cooperation. Just imagine, if you had just surrendered when I first gave you the chance, no one would be dead. We'd have the Bible and be gone. You would be out fishing. You've caused a great deal of destruction."

Dylan stared dumbly through the gun smoke. An amazing amount of blood ran down Shorty's cheek and dripped off his grey beard. *What? What just happened? Am I dreaming this?*

"We're going to take you for questioning, then release you. None of this was necessary." Zwart brushed some non-existent lint of his pristine white-bandaged arm.

Dylan's eyes drifted down to Bergen. He lay still as if at rest. A huge black emptiness inside made Dylan realize his friend and dog were gone. What else could he lose?

"Soon my men will take care of that skinny Hawaiian bitch. It's too bad. All you needed to do was to answer some questions and hand over the Bible."

Dylan gasped for air. He suddenly couldn't breathe. He would die and all his friends, too. And his dogs! Panic forced his heart rate up.

"You never wanted information. You just wanted me dead." Dylan gasped.

"Mr. Baker. You seem agitated. I didn't expect that." Zwart pulled a battered chair around, placed it in front of Dylan and sat facing him.

"Zwart, you never cared what I had to say." Sweat mingled with fear on Dylan's face.

"You are certainly right about that. My boss recently decided he dearly wants to know what you know. We have carte blanche in regard to you." Zwart nodded at Victor, who'd put on fresh gloves.

Dylan gulped air like he couldn't get enough. He turned away from the grizzly scene in front of him.

"You've been so cool up until now." Zwart looked amused and gently patted Dylan's cheek. "This means your interrogation will be much easier." Zwart turned toward his assistant. "Sergeant, find some scissors. We'll begin by removing Mr. Baker's eyelids. We want him to see what he's done to his friends."

Realization washed over Dylan. Zwart was an expert. He had taken extreme measures to unbalance his prey, and it had worked. Zwart had control over Dylan's body, but Dylan knew how to control his emotions.

Sid's lessons on oval breathing came back to him. Peace began washing over him. The only way out of this situation would be to first get control over himself.

The sergeant carefully laid out scissors, a small knife, a corkscrew and various fishing and boating tools in front of Dylan. These were meant to further disquiet Dylan. Never for a moment did he doubt that Zwart would use the instruments to get the information he wanted or just have some sick fun.

"You seem to have calmed yourself, Mr. Baker. Perhaps you are reconciled to your situation. Before I let the good sergeant here have his way with you, maybe you'll tell me what you know about Peter's brother and Boris Alexandrov's Bible? Perhaps we can let you go unharmed." Zwart picked up an 11 inch locking C clamp covered with bits of Shorty's hand.

Zwart plopped into the chair facing Dylan. The sergeant stood behind while Zwart played with the clamp. "Why don't you first tell me about Peter's brother?"

Dylan managed to convey poise. "Zwart, I can't believe what a screw-up you are. Whoever hired you got burned. You've lost valuable resources, killed several innocent people and now the situation will be too complex for you to get away. You don't have the Bible, and even though you have me, I know nothing about why you are doing all this. You've been a complete failure, undone by a few dumb Alaskan hicks like me. You can't release me. I'll come after you, so kill me and get it over with."

The slap was expected. Dylan rolled his head as best he could to lessen the power of the blow's impact. The rickety old chair offered some slack as it wobbled. His mouth filled with blood, and he saw Zwart nod at Victor. "Your turn, Sergeant," Zwart hissed. "Mr. Baker, you have no idea who you are dealing with. The authorities will not want to mess with me."

Outside the shop, the crunch of gravel announced the arrival of a car. Dylan could hear car doors slam. Moments later the front door to the tackle shop rattled.

"It's local cops," Sergeant reported as he peered through some curtains in the front room.

One thought hung in Dylan's mind. *I'm going to die.*

33

Many Years Earlier

. . . .

HIS CLIMBING GLOVE, in tatters, had yielded to six hours of abrasive, granite mountain face. His youthful ambition to pull off another stunning solo first assent was also in shreds.

Dylan Baker, the rock star of the climbing world, had met his match: Northern Italy's The Devil's Finger. His glove was gone, his fingernails were gone, and his confidence had fallen over 1,000 feet to where he had started his solo climb on the uncon-querable Dolomite.

"I'm going to die. I'm going to die. I'm going to die," started from some secret part of his mind and built up to explode out of his parched lips. No matter how skilled a climber, that person needs water, rest and focus. Dylan had been out of all three for at least an hour. He couldn't go up any more, nor could he descend. Why had he tried this alone?

The sun vanished as a chill cloud wrapped its icy breath around the last flicker of warmth in Dylan's body. Without that last bit of warmth, Dylan knew he would start to become hypothermic and his body would choose his method of death without consulting his brain.

"I'm going to die. I'm going to die." It became a chant that Dylan whispered to himself. His chant was interrupted by a sharp click. Dylan knew that sound, it was the gate of a six-inch offset-D carabineer snapping home. He felt the lightest touch at his waist, twisted his head around to see a red climbing rope attached to his harness.

He looked up to see a climber, trailing a red line, appearing to liquidly flow upwards toward a crack that Dylan had been trying to reach for the last hour. Dylan could see the climber had reached the crack, installed a camming device and had pulled up another line with a duffel. Dylan looked away and his body just shook with relief and fatigue. He wasn't going to die. This guy was setting up a portaledge—a sleeping platform that Dylan stupidly had not brought.

It seemed just an instant later that a familiar voice said, "Hey Dylan, you ready to take a rest?"

Dylan craned his neck up, there was Sidney Green smiling down at him. Sid Green! He was the wizard freelance photographer. Dylan knew Sid had to be able to climb, but to climb at this level of skill was above world class.

Sid was more than master climber. Dylan had found a man who used his ambition as a tool, instead of being a tool to ambition.

That night, sharing the portaledge and letting his body rest for the morning climb out, Dylan made a decision. He needed a mentor. Quiet Sidney Green became Dylan's teacher: the man Dylan could always rely on. Dylan's rock.

34

· · · · · · · · · · ·

"KEEP QUIET. They'll go away." Zwart put a huge strip of duct tape over Dylan's stubby beard then picked up his machine pistol.

Boots on gravel circled the tackle shop. Zwart and Sergeant followed the footsteps with their guns. The steps stopped at the broken window.

"Shorty, are you there? It's me, Burl." The window rattled. "Shorty? We need to talk." Dylan heard Burl radio for backup.

Zwart swore, opened the back door and stepped out. "Officer, I'm Captain Zwart, Homeland Security. This is a federal stakeout. You need to leave now."

"Oh I need to leave, eh? Well cool your jets, Corporal. We've had more ruckus in Seward since you've arrived than the time that Australian guy won the salmon derby. I need to talk to Shorty. His friend, Dylan Baker, is wanted for questioning in the death of Mitch Handel, a federal employee and my good friend."

"Shorty's not here and you must leave immediately. You are interfering with Homeland Security."

It was the wrong thing to say. Alaskans are generally polite to everyone, but they hate having arrogant outsiders telling them what to do. Burl pumped a round into his shotgun. "I'm interfering? Let me tell you something Mr. Pretty-Boy major or whatever. My job is to protect the citizens of this town, and no outsider with fancy nails is going to stop me. You can shove Homeland Security up your butt. You're in Alaska now."

Zwart reddened, but didn't move. "My men are holding Dylan Baker inside. We need to take him to Washington for questioning." Zwart looked over his shoulder at the big sergeant.

"Zwart, you want Baker? You can just get him the way prisoners are always transferred to federal custody: bring federal charges and get federal papers. Right now I have local charges, so we need to talk to him. Hand him over." Burl started to push his way inside. Zwart's hand tightened on his machine pistol.

Zwart watched another police car approaching up the highway, its lights flashing. "OK, I'll bring him out. You wait here." It was clear that Zwart did not want Burl and his officers in the shop.

"Sergeant, bring out Baker." Zwart's voice called into the shop. Dylan twisted in his chair to try to stress the rickety old piece of furniture.

"Stop moving," the big sergeant ordered. He bent down to cut Dylan's legs free. As he was cutting Dylan's left arm free, Dylan's right arm pulled the armrest out of the old chair and clubbed Sergeant a sharp blow to the side of his head.

As soon as Sergeant was down, like lightning Dylan hit him twice more with the armrest—hard enough to kill a trophy halibut. Sergeant rolled senseless onto his side, moaning. Dylan strode to the bathroom, cut the zip ties, opened the window near the white van, and slithered out into Alaska.

Dylan had no trouble avoiding the federal versus local battle at the front of the shop. He had no trouble getting himself blocks away to a dirt road alleyway and out of sight. He did have problems comprehending what was happening around him. Shorty dead? His sweet Bergen dead?

This must be his fault, but how did this all come about? Hadn't he paid his debt? All the suffering, the loneliness, the guilt. Must he endure more for his mistakes on Denali? So many people gone because of him.

His ankle gave out and his knees hit the wet dirt. He spat saliva and blood in front of him—the remains of Zwart's slap. The injury was a joke compared to what others had suffered. He wanted to cry but all he could manage was to spit another mouthful of blood into the mud.

He looked up. The sun hit the mountains. They lit up with pure sparkling snow and deep forest greens. A shaft of sunlight hit a mountain peak just above gossamer floating mists.

This happened often in Seward, whether he was happily fishing with Peter or dwelling in his dark despair. He stood up and kept walking. His ghosts weighed him down. Sid, Shorty, Bergen, Mitch, Oxman, Heather, Boris . . . Knowing that Bergen's death weighed on him heavier that Boris's death cause guilt to surge through Dylan.

A bird chirped.

Dylan fell to his knees again. His shoulders shook and his face convulsed.

He vomited. His mouth no longer tasted of blood, but of acid and shame. *I lost my sweet Bergen and dear Shorty.*

The gulls would clean up his half-digested breakfast. How was it that only an hour ago he was enjoying his morning with Suzie, and now Shorty and Bergen were lifeless in the tackle shop?

Dylan didn't know where to go. Without standing, he scooted and crawled a few feet to lean against a garden shed that backed into this alley. He struggled to attain stillness. It wasn't self-pity, but emotional shock that was moving his world. Slowly his shoulders stopped shaking, but he couldn't cry. He ached to cry.

It wasn't the sun playing with the clouds, bunnies hiding shyly under the shed, or the dogs barking in the adjacent lot that helped him think clearly. But his surroundings came into normal view again while he sat, limp against the garden shed, in the alley only a quick jog away from his dead friends.

He knew if they went after Shorty, Suzie might be next. He felt himself drop into oval breathing when thinking of Suzie. If he didn't know how to manage his heartache but, he did know what to do when confronted with ominous threats.

His body once more under his control, Dylan felt a surge of calm but explosive power running through his muscles. He stood up and jogged toward the Knitting Barn.

35

. . . .

SUZIE KNEW IMMEDIATELY that Dylan's typical silky composure had been savagely rent. His eye looked puffy from where Zwart had struck him, and the skin around his wrists was brutally chafed. Blood oozed from zip-tie burns. Sparing her the gruesome details, Dylan told her that Shorty and Bergen had been killed.

"Dylan." Suzie's voice sounded so soft to him. She drew him to her and gave him a soothing hug. "I'm so sorry!"

Time seemed to stop as Dylan allowed her comforting hug to start his long healing process. Later he would be unable to say just how long Suzie held him.

Somehow, she seemed to be able to manage her grief by turning the situation into a problem that needed to be solved.

"Dylan, this is escalating. We need to halt Zwart and all this craziness. If the local police didn't think you were Mitch's killer, we could talk to them. We can't go to the feds because Zwart is the fed." Suzie led Dylan into the bathroom and pulled a first aid kit from a shelf.

"I feel such a heavy burden on me. My friends Mitch and Shorty—dead. Peter. I've spent so many happy times with him. Now he's my enemy. It seems like somebody dies every time Zwart comes near me. So much death. And I feel terrible about how much I miss Bergen."

Suzie dabbed disinfectant on Dylan's wrists. "This has got to cease. We need to find out what's on that memory card and use the information to halt Zwart. Let's go over to my little basement apartment next door. The upstairs people are out of town, so it should be quiet there. Besides, my laptop, at least, is not a Mac. Maybe the software on it can open the files."

"I don't think so, Suzie. Remember what Nancy said, the repairmen you didn't call? They were in there "fixing" things? Zwart's men may have your home under close watch or it may be rigged with explosives." His wrists wrapped in gauze, Dylan put Nancy's first aid kit back up on a bathroom shelf.

"So we check to make sure it's safe before getting the laptop. Besides, anybody who came there yesterday is gone by now." Suzie grabbed a sweatshirt, took Dylan's hand and led him outside the back door in into the afternoon sun to begin a stake out of her apartment.

To Suzie, it seemed she and Dylan spent an absurd amount of time looking for a surveillance team. Dylan appeared to be completely comfortable just waiting and watching in silence. Always accused of being a bit hyperactive, Suzie began to regret letting Dylan do this let's-wait-here-forever thing.

Finally they approached Suzie's front door. Suzie could sense the tension in Dylan as they became closer. She could hear his breathing and observe his intense concentration.

Before entering, they again sneaked around the entire perimeter looking for evidence of tampering. Dylan could tell Suzie was getting impatient with his cautious approach to her home. Their plan was that Suzie would enter her apartment, grab the card reader, her old laptop, and a change of clothes, and then leave.

"Dylan, once I'm inside, I'm safe. The doors are made from solid old-growth planks. I doubt a bulldozer could get through them." Suzie seemed eager to get into the comfort of her home.

"What I'm worried about is that someone is in there waiting for you. Stay here, I'm going over to that old greenhouse and find something we can use as a weapon. I'll enter your place by that back window you said doesn't lock, then I'll let you in the front door."

Dylan silently loped over to a dilapidated greenhouse and disappeared into the tangle of weeds embracing it.

Suzie looked at her home. It called to her. Maybe she just longed for something normal, like her kitchen. Maybe she wanted to stop all the craziness and have her life back. It could just be a strange impulsive act, but Suzie couldn't wait. As soon as Dylan was gone, she moved.

From across the yard Dylan turned to show her a screwdriver he'd found. He saw Suzie put her key in the front door. With a sharp click audible across the yard, the heavy dead bolt slid open. She swung the door open staying outside to be greeted by the moist and comforting earthy smell of her basement apartment.

She paused outside, noticing nothing amiss except her rug was not where it usually was. Dylan hissed, "Suzie, wait!"

She walked in and flipped the light switch. The lights did not come on. A pang of fear surged though her chest. With shaking fingers, she flipped them again—up and down. No luck. She hoped those repairmen had accidently left a breaker switch off.

"Suzie, get out!" Dylan's voice conveyed an urgency that almost made her leave.

Suzie turned to call out to Dylan that she was coming, when a strong hand brought a powerful smelling cloth over her face and an iron grip around her chest. Her legs kicked the air ineffectually as she was lifted off the floor.

Unable to scream or hit, Suzie felt herself drift off to a dark and terrible calmness as the strong arms carried her across space. Dylan saw a figure close the massive door with a solid clunk followed by the authoritative click of a deadbolt sealing her in.

Knowing it was useless to attempt to open the front door, Dylan ran around back to pry open Suzie's back window as quietly as possible.

Sliding like liquid into the dark room, Dylan pushed open the curtains on the windows to let in some light. Shelves of books and a dusty stationary bike were all he could make out. This must be Suzie's storage room.

Careful not to make any noise, Dylan crossed the room and put his ear to the door. He could hear one side of a soft emotionless conversation.

"Suzie. Suzie. I didn't give you much. Time to wake up. We have work to do."

Dylan's breathing became deep and oval. *They have Suzie. How many are they?*

The pleasant male voice sounded quiet and distant, like a medical professional performing routine benign tasks.

"Suzie, the sooner you wake, the sooner we can get started." Dylan heard a rustle like plastic as the voice spoke. His movements fluid and silent, Dylan took a full minute to turn the doorknob in order to maintain silence.

"Suzie, you need to be awake to feel everything." A snipping sound and a feminine groggy groan. "The first cuts are the best. Come. Come and awake."

Dylan pushed opened the door slowly, so slowly, someone watching would have been unable to be certain that it was truly moving.

"Suzie, the others all showed me their terror before they started to beg." Snip. "Show me your eyes. Maybe I should just cut off your nipples. That would wake you up."

Dylan could view just enough of the kitchen to see the floor covered with plastic sheeting.

Snip. "Too bad you have such small tits." Snip.

From the black back storeroom, Dylan caught a glimpse of a bespectacled, well-groomed man holding some scissors and a scalpel. If Dylan had met him on the street, he would have thought he was an insurance salesman or a middle school science teacher who happened to dress in black military fatigues.

He looked outlandishly ordinary and spoke with a practiced emotionless voice. Dylan could not see Suzie, but he could tell this soldier had probably secured her to a kitchen chair.

"This might do it." Snip.

"Ouch!" Suzie's voice suddenly sounded groggy but awake. "You cut me. Who the hell are you?"

"Oh. A feisty one. This will be a very long, wonderful afternoon. A truly wonderful afternoon! I hope you last longer than the others." The male voice spoke softly and reasonably: like a benign remark about the weather.

Dylan risked pushing his body around the door for a look. He could see Suzie taped to a chair, her clothes cut into ribbons and blood running down from her ear and making a dark line along her chin and dripping onto her shredded shirt.

Dylan pulled quickly back into the room. *I think he is the only soldier in there.*

He could hear Sid's voice in his head: *Climb as quickly as possible. Never pause. Never overprotect. Never think. Always move. Move!*

Dylan could see the backroom wall and an enormous bookshelf framed the door. He kicked off his shoes and put the screwdriver between his teeth. Putting his rope-burned hands on the bookshelf and his feet against the wall, he lightly climbed up so he was like a hammock strung above the backroom doorway. He clung horizontally above the door, his back against the ceiling.

He called into the kitchen using a calm conversational tone. "Hello? Suzie? I have the Bible. I found it hidden here in the back room." Dylan reached down and turned on the light.

A soft rustle from the kitchen told him the soldier was coming after him. He saw the silencer on the machine pistol enter the room first. It swung professionally around the room, fired a three round burst into a laundry basket filled with sheets and towels. After a beat, the soft-voiced man entered the room in a military hyper-vigilant manner.

Dylan expected the screwdriver to experience more resistance when he stabbed it downward into the top of the man's skull. It was like pushing the screwdriver into a watermelon. What surprised Dylan even more was that the screwdriver, buried six inches into the man's head, seemed to have no affect on him.

The gun swung up toward Dylan. One hundred percent of Dylan's concentration was on the barrel. He dropped from his ceiling perch, both hands catching the gun barrel as it coughed and a chunk of cheap linoleum burst out of the floor. Dylan's body crashed against his soft-voiced foe, oddly wearing a screwdriver handle on his head like some crazy Halloween prop.

Dylan was an expert hunter. He'd harvested thousands of game animals in the most humane manner possible. Why wouldn't this guy go down with a metal rod in his brain?

They rolled on the floor, the man obviously a trained fighter. Three rapid punches to Dylan's face made a huge white flash that filled Dylan's vision.

Dylan was definitely not a trained fighter. Once he'd been in a bar fight with a drunk cowboy who said all climbers were fairies. Dylan had gotten a lucky punch early in the fight and the cowboy had decided he didn't mind sharing the bar with fairies.

Hoping for another lucky punch, Dylan awkwardly aimed a fist at his attacker's face. The soldier skillfully ducked so Dylan missed the face but landed a smart blow on the screwdriver handle.

What happened next was like a switch suddenly thrown inside the man's head. He became instantly limp and collapsed. The screwdriver's blade must have finally done some serious damage inside the man's skull.

"Suzie!" Dylan stumbled into the kitchen.

Blood running down her neck, shredded clothes, slumped and taped to her own kitchen chair – Suzie looked like she had been through hell. Still drugged, she had a dull and unconcerned glaze in her eyes which looked more gray than green. Dylan couldn't see the tough spirit from which came that alert cry when the man had cut her. Whatever he had used to drug her had her as unconcerned as a mother watching her baby sleep.

"Suzie." Dylan tried to keep his voice calm. He didn't want her to realize that a killer had abused her.

She groaned.

Dylan had no trouble cutting her free with a kitchen knife. But he didn't feel safe yet. *What if that soldier alerted backup when Suzie walked in?*

He touched her shredded shirt. Underneath, her simple black bra and green necklace remained intact. Dylan wondered what bespectacled guy's problem could be. To him, her breasts looked perfect.

He wanted to leave this place. Fast. Not only was he wary of reinforcements coming, he half expected a bomb to go off or soldiers to pop out of the woodwork. Plus, basements made Dylan uncomfortable. He liked to go up, not down.

He couldn't take Suzie outside looking like this. He would draw attention with a beat-up, bloody woman on his arm. Fresh clothes and less ear-blood on the neck were in order.

Looking around the cozy apartment, he had no trouble finding Suzie's room. A contrast to his cabin, Suzie's walls displayed blown up photos of Alaska and Hawaii instead of saws, axes, and ropes. On the dresser he found a picture of her and an attractive man in front of Exit Glacier in Seward. *A boyfriend?* Dylan had just assumed she was single. A closer look made it obvious it was a brother.

He felt awkward opening a dresser drawer in search of a replacement shirt. He hoped she wouldn't think he had pried when she realized he'd gone into her room.

"There's my computer," Suzie, standing in the doorway, drunkenly gestured to a battered laptop charging on a card table. "Grab that card reader in the bowl, too."

Dylan had a hard time deciding if he should put the sweatshirt he found over her shredded shirt or take it off. Blood dried on the collar. Fortunately Suzie started nodding and blinking as he dabbed her neck with a wet kitchen rag.

"Dylan?" she asked groggily.

He pulled his hand away from her neck as though he'd been caught doing something wrong.

"What happened?"

"One of Zwart's men got a hold of you for a few minutes. I'm just trying to get you cleaned up so we can leave fast."

"My shirt is cut up." She sounded drunk. He felt relieved she hadn't snapped at him like she had at her captor.

"I got you this blouse and sweatshirt from your bedroom." Dylan extended the garments to her.

"That's my painting shirt. And I sleep in that sweatshirt. You suck at picking out clothes." She seemed unconcerned that Zwart's men were here. He hoped she had forgotten the whole thing.

"Suzie put this on. Please," She took the top from Dylan and set it in her lap. Just when he thought she had forgotten the task he'd given, she pulled the shredded shirt off over her head. He helped her button the fresh top and pull the clean top and sweatshirt.

Without the blood and in the clean clothes, she would turn fewer heads.

"We need a safe house, Suzie. And we need to find out what Zwart is after. We'll clean up at Nancy's house, but we'll need to find some place Zwart won't think of looking for us."

Suzie looked up at him and smiled drunkenly, "The Senior Center."

BACK AT NANCY'S house, Doolie looked on as Dylan used disinfectant to clean and superglue to close the wound on Suzie's ear. He gave her a Tylenol he found in the now-depleted first aid kit to ease her headache and sore ear. Oddly, he felt no guilt about killing the sadistic soldier with the screwdriver and worried about his lack of feelings.

Suzie fell asleep sitting on the toilet. Dylan had to suppress his embarrassment and lead her to a bed for a nap. While she snored softly, Dylan held Doolie and shook. Would Suzie be next? Would Nancy? Would Doolie?

Looking down at the laptop and card reader, he wondered if it had been worth the trouble to get it.

36

. . . .

DYLAN WALKED SUZIE to the Senior Center
carrying their packs and gear from their Mt. Alice trek.
They entered a large attic storage room. On a sagging
couch, Suzie took another substantial nap. Upon
wakening, she seemed groggy, but determined. Little
memory of the events in her home came back to her.

She turned her attention to the man sitting next to her
and fixed him with a look from her green eyes. "Dylan,
we need to find out what's on this CF card right now."
She stood. Wobbled. Then carefully walked over to the
dusty computer at the desk.

"Whenever someone in Seward buys a new
computer, they donate their old one to the school or this
Senior Center for the tax deduction. This building has an
attic full of Osborns, Commodores, IBMs and just about
any old computer you can imagine. I'm betting this old
workhorse right here will be able to read that CF card.

It's not too old, but it should be about right to read 10-year-old files."

Suzie, seeming to pull together her old energy, dug around in a drawer for an adapter to get her card reader into the computer. Finally she found an old dry printer, which had the right adapter and used that. She hoped the old computer would be able to recognize and read the contents of the CF card.

While they waited for the huge monitor to lumber to life, Dylan allowed a sense of anticipation to build in him. This might answer all his questions. He would find out why his friends Peter and Mitch tried to kill him. Why Zwart and his band of felons were so determined to kill him. Maybe Dylan's world would suddenly make sense. He appeared so anxious, that Suzie sent him downstairs to borrow the laser printer in the office. No one would need it until the following day.

As the dim monitor began to brighten, Dylan watched Suzie try to open the files. Each attempt was met with an error message. His hopes began to fade.

"Let's try booting this computer with these Windows 98 disks." Suzie blew the dust off a stack of disks, put one in the drive and restarted the computer. She looked so self-assured, Dylan tried to grasp and hold on to her confidence. He felt it slipping through his fingers when the computer froze. A hollow cold doom waited below him, and he was slipping. These files were probably unreadable or encrypted.

As Suzie briskly worked through the process of installing the new operating system, Dylan fought the gloom, but let his mind wander to their next step. Where he possessed patience in the woods, Suzie could stare down a progress bar with a stone-like equanimity.

Moments later Suzie whooped. "Look, I got one open. It's a low-res photograph within an old Works document. The newer operating systems can't open these old Works files."

Slowly the old computer displayed the photograph line by line from the top down. They could see some men seated at an outdoor café with the background signs in Russian.

"That's Boris!" The words erupted from Dylan like something he'd been holding down for ages.

"Who?"

"It's a young Boris Alexandrov. He was a client of mine years ago on the Denali climb." Dylan stared intently at the photo as it finished loadıng. Under the photo was some writing in Russian. Suzie hit the print button and followed the steps to save the file as a standard pdf. Suzie worked as if her actions required no conscious thought.

"That looks like Russian writing. Can you read Russian?"

Dylan shook his head.

"What else do you notice?" Suzie zoomed in on the photo.

"It's Boris and someone at a Russian café. I can't tell who the other man is, but he looks familiar." Suzie hit the PRINT button. When nothing happened, she went on line, located the printer driver for the laser, loaded it up, restarted the computer then watched the printer do its thing. Dylan wondered how she knew so much about computers as he watched her continue to open and print documents from the CF drive.

As the modern laser printer shuttered and served up sheet after sheet of paper, Dylan picked them up. Mesmerized, Dylan examined the printouts. Suzie brought up the next file. "It's another photo. These have the look of surveillance photos. I don't think the men knew they were being photographed."

As they studied the printouts, it was clear the photographer had caught the second man with a better shot.

"It's Peter!" Suzie shouted as the grainy photo resolved.

"No, Peter has lighter hair, and he's skinny. This guy looks like a weight lifter. It really resembles him, though." Dylan bit his lip.

"Why can't it be Peter a long time ago?" Suzie begged.

"I know it's not him. Look, more Russian at the bottom."

"Peter has a brother. Could it be him?" Suzie stared up at Dylan.

"Oh my God! You might be right. Print it and we'll try to find out." Dylan impatiently waited for the old computer to chug through the tasks Suzie was asking it to do.

When Suzie tried to open the next file, she got an *insufficient memory* error.

"I'm going to pull some memory out of another computer and put it in this one. I bet we can open all of these files."

Dylan groaned at the delay. "What can I do to make it go faster?"

"Dylan, you are driving me crazy with your impatience. Why don't you clean my pink compound bow, or you can help by walking over to the Sea Star Café and get us some coffee and muffins."

"I can't go out there; someone might recognize me." Dylan stroked his small beard.

"No one in Seward has ever seen you with a short beard. Wear your tourist outfit and my huge dark glasses. You'll be just another tourist."

"Those are girls' dark glasses. I'll look funny." Dylan held out Suzie's outlandishly large dark glasses.

"With the girl-glasses and your pink socks, no one who knows you will suspect anything." With a small screwdriver in her mouth, Suzie began shutting down the computer and pulling out plugs.

Wearing the glasses, Dylan checked his wallet and walked the back alleys to the café.

The café, looking like it was lovingly built into an old church, had a new girl on duty—one of the many seasonal workers who kept Seward working. While she prepared his order, she complained that her replacement should have been there an hour ago. She interrupted her work several times to call her boss and complain.

Dylan, anxious about being recognized, tried to keep his face down. He found himself fretting about Suzie's safety. What would Zwart do next? Could they stop him? Dylan found himself anxious about what they would learn from the CF files, while trying to feign patience as the pretty barista finally completed his order.

He had to force himself to carry the paper bag in a casual manner as he returned to the senior center and entered through the back door.

Relief flooded over him when he saw Suzie safe and looking triumphant as the computer was once again coming to life. Nearby, an-other computer appeared to have exploded, as parts lay scattered over a table.

"I did it. I installed the memory from another ma-chine. We'll try to open the other files." She accepted a hot paper cup from Dylan and pinched off a chunk of muffin as another file opened.

It was a sound file. Clearly two men spoke in Russian. The sound of rustling papers filled in gaps be-tween the conversations.

"What are they saying?" Suzie asked.

"How should I know? I can only say *cheers* and *thank you*."

Suddenly they both recognized some English words: *Langley Virginia* and *top secret.* "We got to get this translated," Dylan put down his cup. "Peter's brother works in Langley, Virginia."

"I'm going to open all these files and save them so any computer can open them. You just eat your muffin."

As Dylan reached for the remaining muffin, Suzie studied the screen. "Look! This next file is all Russian words. I wonder if it's a transcript of the recorded conversation?"

"We can take this stuff to the library and have Karina translate it."

"No need. We can use an internet translator to get an idea of what it says. Too bad the internet is so slow here." Suzie continued to alternate between rapid commands to the computer and waiting while the old machine followed her instructions.

Hours later, Suzie looked over the stack of papers between them on the table littered with coffee cups, muffin wrappers and computer parts, "Is this what I think it is?"

Dylan held one of the translated pages, "It looks to me that this shows someone is selling the names of CIA field agents to Russian mafia."

"This is going to cause huge national attention. Once Russia knows who these people are, their lives are in danger. We have to get this information out to the authorities." Suzie looked stricken.

"Yes, but who can we trust? The government thinks I am a criminal. It seems like they are trying to kill me and anyone they think I've talked to."

"Maybe the guys trying to kill you are Russians. I bet they think you knew all this long ago and they want to cover it up. They are guessing that's why you've been living off the grid."

"Off the grid?

"Yes, keeping your name off any government or private document so they couldn't find you."

"I wasn't avoiding the government. I was trying to find a way to recover from the pain of losing my fiancée and friends. As soon as this is all over, I'll need to mourn the loss of my Seward friends and Bergen. I wonder if I'll be off another ten years."

"Nonsense, Dylan. You're a different man now. Plus, you felt responsible for those Denali deaths. No way, are you responsible for Zwart's actions."

"My brain agrees with you, but I still feel that, once this all stops, I'm going to crash like last time."

"Let's work on stopping this nightmare. If we go to the government, they'll just tell their agent Zwart where you are."

"What can we do?"

"Let's do what I do best, get this information out to the public where they can't suppress it. I'm going to write my blog right now."

"How does that work?"

"Here's what happens. You get a new ink cartridge at the stationary store. This one is dry, and I really need to finish printing up hard copies of all these documents. Then I will write up the blog post, publish the information on my web site, e-mail the print version to my Anchorage printer. She'll print and mail the paper edition to my print subscribers and send me 50 copies for local business to pass out." Suzie looked up at Dylan, who looked ridiculous in her glasses, tourist hat and pink socks.

"What if Zwart is able to stop your newsletter? He's pretty smart."

"He can't." Suzie sounded confident as she tried not to laugh at Dylan's appearance.

"Let's say he can stop it. Shouldn't we get a backup plan to release this information?"

Suzie brought up the Homeland Security site. She found a tab labeled *Citizen Tips*. "Here's what else we can do. I can upload the contents of this CF card to this site. We have a 1200-baud landline modem and Windows 98. What could go wrong?"

After numerous freezes, Suzie got the old computer to begin uploading the information. A long green progress bar appeared on the screen and gave the impression of not progressing.

"Shouldn't that bar be moving?" Dylan taped the computer screen with his finger.

"It's a really slow modem. It might take 18 to 24 hours to complete the upload—if the computer doesn't freeze.

"How would you even know if it froze?"

Dylan realized it would be another long wait. As a hunter, Dylan possessed infinite patience, but he sucked at waiting for computers.

He yearned to collect Doolie from Nancy and enter his Alaskan woods to think. To think about what will happen when the world finds out that Peter's brother, then a CIA agent, now a top Homeland Security official, had sold the identities of field agents to Russian criminals. These agents likely died horrible deaths as they were mined for information.

Illya would stop at nothing to prevent the proof of his duplicity from coming to life. Illya believed that God favored his actions. *By this I know that thou favourest me, because mine enemy doth not triumph over me.*

No wonder Peter had turned against Dylan. *Blood is thicker than water.* Illya must have convinced him that Dylan wanted to destroy Peter's Russian family.

All this death to protect Illya from prosecution! Dylan wondered if Zwart knew he was working for a traitor.

He felt Suzie's arms tenderly encircle his waist from behind. The sweetness of her touch, and the knowledge that she trusted him so completely fired long repressed feelings in him. He wanted her. He wanted her body and her love.

She laid her head against his back, and he felt her arms tighten around his waist. Dylan froze, not wanting the moment to end and embarrassed by his obvious physical response to her touch.

"Dylan." Suzie turned him around and pressed herself against him her green eyes looking deep into his. "I want you to kiss me."

With the gentlest touch, he lifted her chin and delicately brought his lips to hers. He softly gave her a sweet, slow kiss, but it was obvious she wanted more. Unnoticed, the big glasses fell to the floor while passion seemed to explode and their kisses became deeper and more urgent.

Footsteps on the stairs broke the spell.

"Anyone up here?" an elderly man's voice called from the stairwell.

"Ted? It's me, Suzie Alano. We're nearly done." Suzie had to gasp to catch her breath, and somehow Dylan's shirt was on the floor.

"You are not using up all the printer ink are you? The cartridges are pricy." It was clear the voice was concerned.

"Dylan is leaving right now to get some more ink, so don't worry." Suzie handed Dylan his shirt, Alaska hat and her glasses.

He drew on the shirt, glasses, pulled his Alaska hat low over his face and headed for the stationery store wondering how Suzie could just turn off her passion.

Suzie likes me. She likes me for a boyfriend. Dylan suddenly felt like he was 17 and in love.

37

. . . .

DYLAN STOOD in the line at the Seward Stationery and Ice Cream Store eager to get printer ink. As he waited his turn, a feeling of dread started to creep into his mind.

Suddenly, what he wanted to do was to run back to the Senior Center to check on Suzie. It didn't make any sense to do that. He'd told the clerk what he wanted, paid for his order, and a girl was prowling the shelves in the back trying to find the cartridge he needed.

Dylan could not name anything that would point to additional danger surrounding Suzie. Outwardly he appeared composed as two elderly women, one wearing a flamboyant purple dress and floppy hat and the other wearing worn, threadbare men's working clothes, called out a question about a laptop battery to the girl looking for his ink.

The feeling of dread seemed to escalate as the women then asked about some flyers they'd ordered. Dylan looked out the front window at some bunnies foraging on the lawn and tried to suppress his urge to run.

As a hunter and wilderness survivor, he had learned to trust his feelings. He knew that there was no reason to believe that something was wrong with Suzie, but his internal alarm bells were clanging incessantly. Something had set them off.

The chubby-faced Asian girl behind the counter triumphantly held up his order.

"Did you have a coupon?" she smiled.

"Coupon?" Dylan wanted to leave the store. It was taking all his self-control to remain calm.

"Yes you get half off your second cartridge with the coupon" she explained.

"I don't have a coupon." Suddenly, tossing several bills on the counter, Dylan turned and rushed out of the shop leaving the new cartridge on the counter. In the background he could hear the girl say, "But Sir, you paid for this one."

Dylan slowed and appeared to calmly walk as he approached the back entrance of the Senior Center. Inside, he galloped up the stairs to the attic storage room where he and Suzie had been working.

"Suzie?" A quick glance showed that she wasn't there. He checked across the hall to the bathroom. "Suzie, are you in here?"

Dylan flew from room to room in a rapid search for Suzie. Downstairs Dylan dashed into the kitchen to see if she was getting a snack. He nearly ran into an older bald man dressed sharply in a sport jacket and slacks. The man wore a nametag that declared he was *Ted*.

"Whoa. Are you OK?" Ted looked concerned.

"Yeah. Just looking for Suzie. I am supposed to bring her a printer cartridge."

"Suzie Alaneo? She left with those rude soldiers. They told me she had an interview, but they took all that camping gear you brought in. I was hoping you weren't planning on leaving it here. I have enough stuff to organize."

Dylan froze. He thought about Shorty and Bergen. He thought about how small Suzie seemed. Zwart would not hesitate to hurt or kill her.

"Which way did they go?" Dylan tried not to act upset.

The corded phone on the wall interrupted the man's answer. Ted gestured vaguely up the street, turned from Dylan and answered the phone. After a brief conversation, he handed the phone to Dylan.

"It's for you." Ted looked confused as he handed the phone to Dylan.

"Mr. Baker. My team missed you somehow." Zwart's smooth voice started an adrenaline avalanche through Dylan's body.

"Where's Suzie?" *Breathe. Don't become distracted.*

"Why, she's safe with me. You have my word as a soldier, she will not be harmed, that is, if you bring the Bible to us this evening."

"Where is she right now? I can bring it right now," Dylan felt himself returning to calm. Maybe he won't harm her.

"Mr. Baker. Tonight she'll be at the Marathon Hunting Camp. Just bring the Bible, agree to chat with us a bit, and we'll release Miss Alaneo.

"It's too bad you just didn't offer to give us the Bible a few days ago. Then we could have left you and Ms. Alaneo alone. As it is, we need to have a serious talk with you."

"I can bring it to you right now if you release her unharmed."

"Sorry Mr. Baker. That's not an option. We need her help stopping some emails she sent to Anchorage regarding a confidential Homeland Security operation. Besides, I can't talk to you about this. We don't negotiate with terrorists."

Outside Dylan heard the squeal of brakes as two Escalades bounded up the curb in front of the Senior Center.

An assault team burst into the room astonishing Ted as he held the phone awkwardly.

"Where is he?" barked the skinny, overly tattooed squad leader flashing an official looking DHS paper.

"Where is . . ." Ted looked down at the silenced weapons and the red laser dots drawing tight circles on his chest. "Wait. Don't shoot. There's nothing here of value," Ted's eyes wandered over to the donation jar.

"Where is Baker?" barked the leader again.

Ted turned toward the back door, which stood ajar. The leader gestured at two of his men who rushed through the doors. They came back shortly.

"There's an open window and below it a dumpster. He could have gotten away."

"How the hell could he get away? I was just listening to him talk with Captain Zwart over the radio. We'll need to wait until tonight if he's dumb enough to attempt to rescue that skinny bitch."

38

· · · · · · · · · · ·

DYLAN KNEW HOW to prepare for a hunting trip. He could predict which gear would be needed to make the trip successful. This was different. This time, Dylan was thinking that he would need to kill not one prey, but perhaps dozens.

Unlike hunting animals, his quarry this time could be rendered inefficient by manipulating their emotions.

As he surveyed Dave Clark's impressive armory, Dylan didn't stop to ponder his choices. Dylan worked like an expert chef choosing which knives, pans and pots would be needed to make a familiar menu.

He pulled the Benelli shotgun off the shelf and laid it on the table. From a drawer he pulled out several boxes of shells: each shell overkill for any Alaskan big game animal. If fired at a whale, it would strike with such force that an 18-inch diameter by 30-inches deep area of flesh and bone would be instantly changed to a pink sludge.

Next he brought down the 30-caliber Remington 700 XCR II with the Nikon Monarch scope and several boxes of 300 ultra magnum ammo. This rifle, even in the hands of a beginner, could accurately put a metal slug into a moose's eye from 500 yards.

The bow, an Insanity CPX, would fire a high-tech hunting arrow with an aircraft aluminum inner body, surgical stainless steel blades and titanium tip at over 320 feet per second. The razor-sharp blades would snap open on impact creating a wound with maximum bleed-out capability.

Dylan put his deadly tools into bags and headed toward the ruins of his cabin. He needed a distraction for the soldiers he'd be facing, and it was buried in a can near his outhouse.

DYLAN QUIETLY APPROACHED the privy behind the ruins of his cabin and pulled a board off the back of the blackened outhouse. He then slid a rock to the side and pulled out a small, heavy dry bag. He opened the bag to reveal a stash of Pandas: Chinese gold coins about the size of nickels. He stuffed the bag into his daypack.

Through the night, Dylan worked grimly to build the hunting roosts and lures that would allow him to quickly kill his deadly prey. All the while, he had to tell himself that this was justified. If he didn't kill Zwart and his army of murders, they would kill more innocents. These were the evil men who killed Shorty and held Suzie prisoner. He hoped Suzie was still a prisoner and not dead.

As Dylan approached the Marathon Camp, a series of rustic cabins usually only occupied during hunting season, his footsteps became heavy. Dylan had never hunted humans before. It took all his self-control to imagine this hunt, and he hoped he could carry it through if needed. Perhaps Zwart would let Suzie go.

Maybe all he wanted was the Bible, but a part of Dylan's brain knew Zwart was setting a trap.

39

. . . .

THE BLACK ESCALADE bounced up the rutted road to the front of the outlying cabin. "Hey, Rookie. Zwart said the cabin is unlocked. Go in and light the lanterns. I'll get the little lady." Rookie nodded and entered the dusty cabin.

Bravo walked back to the rear gate as it opened. Suzie's wrists were bound to the car seat with zip ties, and a bag covered her head. Suzie's yells had already been somewhat discouraged with a backhand slap across her face. "Well little lady, we've arrived. May I help you out?" Bravo brought out a too-large hunting knife and cut her ties.

"Let me go. Dylan will hurt you when he finds out how you are treated me." Suzie's voice sounded muffled but amazingly brave through the hood. "He'll hurt you if don't let me go right now."

Bravo moved away from the SUV and stopped in front of the cabin. "Your friend isn't here, but I am. I'm sorry. I will need to do another search. Zwart is a stickler for details."

Bravo's hands began at Suzie's ankles and lightly touched every surface up to the base of her neck. As he moved, Suzie felt her fear and anger rise.

"You're a monster. Dylan told me what to do with monsters." For a bear, she should go for the eye or the nose.

"A monster? Really? You know, if we are lucky, I won't get any additional orders from Zwart until tomorrow. He just wanted you alive in case you are needed as a trade." The cabin light reflected off of his yellowed teeth and amazingly large tongue stud.

Hoisting Suzie over his shoulder, using a hand on her butt for stabilization, Bravo carried her into the tiny kitchen and roughly placed her in a chair. "Hey, Rookie, I need some more zip ties."

"I didn't bring any. Zwart told you to keep her secure. Use the ties you brought."

Bravo tore up a soiled dishtowel and used the strips to bind Suzie to the only chair in the room.

His smile grew bigger as he mentally thanked Zwart for selecting him for this tactical mission. Zwart would not be disappointed.

"Rookie, secure the SUV. Take it over to Zwart's cabin. It's not that far."

Bravo roughly pulled the hood off Suzie's head. She gasped and took stock of her surroundings. She found herself in one of the basic, dusty-woods smelling, early-1900s cabins that dotted the forests surrounding Seward. A small kitchen window, framed by faded yellow curtains, provided a glimpse into the darkened late summer forest. The kitchen table was cluttered with Suzie's things Bravo must have brought from the Senior

Center: camping equipment, the pink compound bow and flu-flu arrows.

Piled high with ashes, the cold fireplace over-looked a couch and a doorway into a bedroom. The soldier towered above her as he methodically removed military gear from a backpack. The dishtowel that bound her insured that she and the chair would move as one or not all. Had Suzie's restricted wrists not distracted her, she might have chuckled at the cross-stitch design on the wall declaring that you should *Untie Your Dreams.*

"Bravo, I don't think I should leave you alone. Remember what Zwart said."

"Don't worry. Nothing's going to happen to her." Bravo looked at Suzie's small neck.

"What about Kinshasa? You were supposed to guard those girls in that school. None of them were supposed to be raped and strangled."

Bravo fixed Rookie with a hard stare. "I'm in charge here. Go move the vehicle. This cabin should appear deserted to any casual inspection." Rookie could see Bravo was in a dangerous mood. Better to risk being chewed out by Zwart than a beating by Bravo.

Suzie found herself working her hands against the coarse cloth bindings while her captors argued.

"Anyway, that forest wild man will never find his way here. Get moving."

Resigned to his busy-work tasks, Rookie shrugged and departed. Bravo turned his attention to Suzie, slouching in the chair. Cold hands secured her ankles to the front legs of the wooden chair before spending several moments resting on her knee. Bravo seemed to be dropping into some kind of ritual trance as he stared at Suzie's body.

Suddenly a pounding on the door broke his reverie.

Suzie instantly thought: *Dylan?*

In one graceful motion, Bravo pulled his Desert Eagle, a huge Israeli-made .50 caliber pistol from his holster and approached the door.

"Dylan! He's got a gun!" Suzie yelled. Bravo turned to look at her and his big gun followed his gaze.

The rickety door slammed open, and Rookie hit Bravo with a sharp, sideways body block knocking the gun into the woodpile.

"What the fuck?" Bravo threw Rookie across the room. "Do you know how close you came to being shot?"

"Hey! I thought that Dylan guy was in here. Why didn't you gag the prisoner? That's SOP for a hostage." Rookie rubbed his shoulder where it hit the wall.

"I decide what's SOP out here in the field you shit head. Look, my gun's all dirty." Bravo blew bark dust off his shiny mini-canon. "I've decided that SOP is also a perimeter check. Get started."

"I'm not going to get blamed if you go apeshit on that prisoner." Rookie watched the massive chrome Desert Eagle come up. "What are you going to do with that cannon? Shoot holes in engine blocks?" Rookie turned to leave.

"Shut up. Now complete a perimeter check." Rookie looked at Bravo, then at his hand on the Suzie's knee. Rookie's face expressionless, he turned, picked up his rifle and walked outside.

Marshalling her strength, "You should let me go. Dylan will kill you if you hurt me."

Bravo exhaled in an abbreviated chuckle. "Whatever. My assignment is to wait for my orders. But, it would be a shame if we couldn't have any fun while Zwart makes up his mind." Bravo picked up a blunt-tipped flu-flu arrow from the table and touched Suzie's chin. Then he used the arrow to open Suzie's shirt sending a button skidding across the floor.

"So what's with the pink bow and these blunt arrows?' Bravo inspected the whistle on the tip of one of the arrows.

"They are for shooting birds. Untie me and I'll show you how they work." Suzie continued to work her hands on the shredded dishtowel bindings.

"I think these are good for undressing a bird." Bravo approached the next button on Suzie's shirt.

Irritation jumped to the forefront before Suzie had time to think. "What's with you guys? Did your interrogation class always begin with 'cut the lady's shirt to shreds'? And what's with the chair? Why always a chair?"

Bravo gazed at Suzie with a scary smile. "What do you care anyway? You might as well have a little fun before it all ends, right?"

"It will end with one of Dylan's arrows in your butt if you don't let me go." Suzie tried not to sound scared, but she felt her chest tighten in terror. *Surely Dylan would find her.* He could find anything. This guy was really scaring her.

He paused for a moment. "I need to step outside for a moment. Don't go away," he chuckled.

Bravo pushed his head out the door and yelled across the clearing, "Hey Rookie! Watch her for a moment".

Rookie entered the cabin and immediately focused on Suzie: her bruised face, ripped shirt, tightly bound ankles and her hands bound behind the chair. He knew that Bravo would not be stopped. This would be Kin-shasa all over again.

"Please help me. Help me get away. He's going to hurt me."

Rookie poured a glass of water and brought it to her. She attempted to drink, spilling water down her front.

Just then, Bravo returned and instructed Rookie to guard the perimeter for the next two hours. Knowing it was a bogus job, Rookie left uneasily.

Suzie could feel her heart pumping adrenaline throughout her body. *Where was Dylan?* Suzie thought back to Dylan's breathing technique. How did he do that breathing thing? Behind her back, Suzie worked her hands in the bindings and found more slack. As she strained against the fabric, the pain focused her. She remembered: relax the shoulders, inhale, pause, exhale.

Bravo returned and looked longingly at Suzie. His eyes seemed to glaze. Her wet shirt accentuated her bra. "You're a little girl." Bravo recited the line like from a ritual. "And I'm your daddy." He unbuttoned another button and then put his face close to hers. Suzie recoiled from the sickening smell of alcohol, sweat and cigarettes.

Her skin beneath her bindings became slippery with blood and sweat, and her heart raced, as she felt more slack open around her wrists. *What will I do if I can get my hands free?* She eyed the arrow on the nearby table. *He's a monster.*

Inhale.

Pause.

Exhale.

40

. . . .

UPSTAIRS IN A DARK attic at the Senior Center, Ted flipped on a light to see his orderly arrangement of donated computers scattered about haphazardly. On a large table made up of a door lying atop two card tables sat an old Gateway computer set up with the monitor glowing and a green progress bar visible.

One thing Ted hated was to have people borrow things and not put them away. *Visitors seem to have no respect for the Senior Center!*

First thing he did was to unplug the laser printer and carry it downstairs to the main office. When he was setting it up, he noticed it was nearly out of paper and guessed it was also probably out of ink.

He checked the game room to scc two card tables were missing, so he had to go upstairs to fetch them. One thing Ted was good at was spotting rude people. This mess seemed even more egregious than what he typically found.

It was so impolite for Suzie and her odd friend to borrow SC resources and not put them away. It was a good thing they didn't use the kitchen.

He remembered last week when an Ultimate Frisbee team had a spaghetti dinner there and left much of the clean up to him. Everything had been carefully washed, but put away in the wrong places. Imagine, putting the salad plates near the coffee mugs! Ted hated disorder.

Peering at the Gateway's monitor, Ted could see it appeared that the progress bar was nearly all the way to the end. Always comfortable with order and having things put away, Ted watched as the progress bar seemed to be picking up speed as it moved to the right.

Instead of pulling the plug and stacking the components in their color-coded shelves, Ted waited until he heard a "ding" from the computer, as if an egg timer had sounded, then saw the message, "Upload complete. Return to DHS tip line?"

At that point, Ted unplugged the computer and started putting it away. He had no idea that over 4,000 miles away, Jill Griffith would receive the file. It was her first week on the job at DHS. They had her sifting the mostly garbage information that constantly came in on the tip line. It was her job to put the incoming tips into three virtual folders: crazy trash, regular trash, and someone-should-look-at-this-before-throwing-it-into-the-trash.

A week ago, Jill had brought a file to the attention of her supervisor and gotten chewed out for being gullible. Jill had been an easy mark for tricksters all through school at the University of Wisconsin. And when she had something serious to say, people seldom listened.

She was pretty sure her problems had to do with her appearance. Being 4 foot 11 inches and blond, even when she had something important to explain, her voice, which sounded like a Munchkin talking, made listeners smile and not pay attention to what she was saying.

After looking over the most recent files from a Seward, AK IPO address, she decided to run it through a Russian translator program. If this was yet another hoax, she decided it was pretty well done. Jill then cross-checked the dates and personnel records of the figures in the files.

She picked up the phone, called her boss and squeaked, "Larry, I think you should look at this."

41

· · · · · · · · · ·

DYLAN APPROACHED the hunting camp from the darkest woods. The original builders had arranged the cabins in a semicircle around a central campfire pit. Nearly all cabins were dark save the largest one. From the shadows, Dylan could see that two guards were lackadaisically patrolling the camp. No one appeared to be concerned about an attack.

As soon as the guards walked down the hill toward the road, Dylan moved close to the largest cabin's windowless wall to see if he could hear anything. The moment he put his ear to the wall, a loud ringing started with the cabin. Dylan dropped to his belly thinking he'd tripped an alarm. Then he realized the ringing was a phone.

Through the thin walls Dylan could clearly make out a cell phone on speaker and Zwart's voice.

"Zwart, it's me, Illya. We got a big problem." Dylan could hear Zwart stiffen as he came to attention right through the wall.

"Sir, what can I do?"

"For one thing you could have completed your mission. I just got word that some evidence against me, against us, came into our tip line. The director wants a meeting tomorrow, and I'm not sure how deep he'll dig into all this."

"That's too bad."

"Too bad? This could put me, put us, in jail if I can't convince them it's all phony."

"Sir?"

"Don't Sir me. You need to abort the mission. Pull back first thing tomorrow. Your new mission is to get the hell out of there and leave no trace. I'm sure as hell not going to jail."

"But Sir, we're nearly done here."

"I hired you because of your reputation. Your soldierly ethics are fixed onto your heart with rivets of steel. You follow orders. You get things done. Now, you need to abort. That's your mission. Get it done. Do it!"

Dylan heard the phone go dead followed immediately by the sound of the cell phone shattering against a wall.

"Fuck!" Zwart screamed.

DYLAN BACKED INTO the forest, noticed the guards were far down the hill, and then entered the hunting camp unarmed except for the broken wooden covers of the Bible with the CF card. He approached the dying campfire and stared at the smoke.

He bent down and carefully arranged wood on the fire and blew on the result. The fire came alive and flames began to burn in a lively, cheerful manner. Dylan put more wood on the fire, and it flamed vigorously throwing night shadows onto the walls of the cabins.

He walked the five yards to the largest cabin and knocked. As if waiting for the knock, Zwart opened the door wearing his spotless uniform, but with uncharacteristically messed up hair. Tango stood unashamedly naked in the background. Zwart, unarmed, stared at Dylan.

"Zwart, I want you to let Suzie go. I'm prepared to offer myself and this Bible as payment.

With an eerie calm, Zwart looked at Dylan. "I underestimated you again, Mr. Baker. I guessed you'd be long gone into the woods by now. You surprise me. Too bad I cannot hire you to work for me."

"OK, you've got me. Let Suzie go."

Zwart looked at the dog-chewed Bible Dylan held. "So I get to . . . debrief you?"

"You don't need me. You've been told your mission is aborted. You can give Suzie to me and leave unharmed. No more bloodshed."

If Zwart was surprised by Dylan's knowledge of the change in mission status, he didn't show it.

Zwart brought his sleeve up to his lips and spoke. "Bravo, we no longer need the girl. I have Dylan."

Dylan could hear Bravo's reply in the darkness. "Roger that."

"Looks like you lost. You lose the girl and your life."

Dylan stared coldly back at Zwart. "You don't need to do this. You can be true to yourself and follow orders—keep your honor."

"I'd rather have you."

42

. . . .

BRAVO'S ATTENTION was drawn away by a crackle on his radio. He picked it up, listened, and then spoke. "Roger that." Bravo set down the radio as he shifted his attention back to Suzie.

"Update from my captain. I'm afraid Dylan won't be killing me—Zwart has him in custody. Your backwoods boyfriend fell for our trap. I guess he's not such a hotshot woodsman after all, is he? Zwart used you as bait, and Dylan came running right into our camp. Zwart has Dylan."

Bravo examined the bow and arrow for a moment pondering the possibilities. "And I will take it from here." Bravo grinned. "The Captain says we don't need you anymore."

"No!" Suzie flinched at the thought that Zwart had trapped Dylan.

Inhale.

Pause.

Exhale.

The cabin door burst open as Rookie entered. "Hey, Bravo. I heard the Captain's update. So, what's next?"

Bravo's irritation was visible for only a moment.

Rookie moved toward Suzie. "We can take her back to base," Rookie's knife blade hovered as he prepared to cut her loose.

"Stop! I'll take care of the lady. Zwart's orders instructed me to 'clean up the situation' should Dylan return." Bravo paused and studied Rookie's reaction. "You walk back to base. The Captain may need some help. I'll tie up all of the loose ends here. I'll radio if I need you to return."

"Come on, Bravo. Let's take her back."

"I got this. You get going." Rookie tossed an ambivalent glance at Suzie and walked out the door. A moment later the sound of Rookie's footsteps faded into the forest.

Bravo roughly pushed the top of Suzie's chair backward so it balanced on two legs against the wall of the cabin. Next he moved the kitchen table closer to Suzie's chair, insuring that his tools were easily accessible. Undoing the final shirt button, Bravo paused to admire Suzie's athletic stomach. "Much better!"

As Suzie struggled, the bindings cut into her flesh making her wrists bleed and the fibers in her dishtowel bindings stretch.

Bravo set the arrow on the kitchen table then turned to close the thin yellow curtains. "Don't want anyone looking at us while we're having fun." He dropped his pants to his ankles and presented himself to her, his urgency clear. "I know what you can do for daddy."

Suzie's wrists were slippery with blood as she head-butted Bravo's groin and fell forward onto the floor. He grunted and doubled over looking surprised. Her hands flew out of the ties and she scrambled to her feet. Bravo, his pants down, awkwardly lunged at her.

All her fear and fury suddenly came to a sharp focus. Suzie screamed defiantly. A scream from deep within her released all her fear and anger. Before the scream died away, she grabbed the arrow from the table and jammed it deep into Bravo's eye.

He fell back like a wounded bear, hands flailing at his face. Suzie reached down and used both hands to pull the Desert Eagle from his holster and fired a .50 caliber round into his nose.

The heavy gun bucked up nearly hitting her face, and Bravo's head bounced from the floor, the arrow protruding oddly from his eye-socket.

Suzie attempted a second shot as a coppery-smelling red-black puddle of blood spread across the brain-splattered floor, but the gun jammed. She threw the gun at Bravo's chest.

"Dylan told me to strike a monster in the eye or nose. I'm Dylan's girl. No one fucks with me." She grabbed the pink bow and arrow with her bloody hands and ran toward the main hunting camp.

43

· · · · · · · · · · ·

IN THE DISTANCE, Suzie's fierce, defiant scream cut through the quiet night. After a beat, a single shot made Dylan wince. Silence enveloped the camp save for the soft smoky crackle of the fire.

Emotionless, Dylan stepped back. "I'm guessing I just lost Suzie. Now you don't get this Bible and you don't get me." Dylan turned away from Zwart and started walking out of the campsite—tossing the Bible covers into the fire.

Zwart yelled, "Intruder! Fall in. Fire at will." From behind him, Tango turned to get a weapon from the bedroom.

Lights came on in some of the cabins. A door opened and a skinny soldier burst out of his door naked save for his Sig 553. He blinked getting his bearings.

Gesturing toward Dylan, Zwart yelled, "Shoot him."

From near the campfire, Dylan had pulled the chrome hatchet from the log and focused all of his fury into the throw.

Like a twinkling bolt of lightning, the hatchet crossed the smoky space and embedded itself into the chest of the skinny soldier with a sickening crunching sound. The soldier gasped at the chrome handle protruding from his chest, then feel forward.

Dylan looked up at Zwart. "Leave now. If you stay, you and your men will die. These are my woods."

Like a wisp of smoke, Dylan vanished into some nearby bushes. Nearly instantly the bushes were raked with Sig automatic fire. After an absurd amount of ordnance was poured into the bushes, Zwart yelled, "Hold your fire!" The shooting stopped. Zwart looked over at a large blond body-builder type-soldier. "X-ray, verify the kill."

"I get the perp's wallet this time," X-ray dove into the bushes. A stunning silence ensued. A spidery-built soldier, wearing only smudged olive drab underwear, approached the bushes with his Sig ready. "How come X-ray gets the wallet? It's my turn." The spidery man poked his face into the bushes. Nearly instantly he pulled back screaming. His rifle dropped as Zwart noticed the red handle of a Swiss army knife protruding grotesquely from his throat.

As if linked by wire, the assembled soldiers poured magazine after magazine of deadly fire into the bushes. Not until their barrels were red hot could Zwart get their attention. "Hold your fire. X-ray is in there. I want Alpha patrol to assess the situation." Zwart commanded.

An obviously fearful soldier, Foxtrot, objected, "Why us? Why not Charlie patrol? They can have the wallet."

"Are you worried he'll have another Swiss army knife?" Zwart sneered. "Alpha Patrol, fall in."

Five soldiers lined up in various stages of dress, their weapons ready. "OK. I want you to suit up ready for battle in five. Full body armor and night vision gear."

Dylan rolled away from a pile of rocks that prevented any of the shots from harming him. He glanced at X-ray's body, full of his own team's lead. Dylan opened a jug labeled, Deer Blood: Bear Attractant, and dribbled a trail to a large rock 400 yards away. Here he paused and marked the rock with copious amounts of the deer blood.

His face smeared with the soothing smell of Alaskan mossy dirt, the nearly invisible Dylan picked up the automatic shotgun, verified a round was chambered and waited in a shadow with his infinite hunter's patience. He would mourn Suzie later.

The five well-equipped soldiers in Alpha Patrol appeared competent and professional in their appearance and technique. Their Sigs' barrel-mounted LED flashlights made an angry flash when they came up past waist high.

The patrol entered the woods carefully. No longer looking scared, Foxtrot spoke clearly into his sleeve mic, "Sir, he's wounded. We're following his trail. Judging by the amount of blood, he must be in bad shape."

The patrol members seemed to get a rush of confidence seeing all the blood on the trail. The flashlights winked as the soldiers disappeared into the woods. Soon from the hunting camp location, all traces of the flashlights were gone. The woods became silent and dark. Suddenly five rapid, concussive booms shattered the peace. A soldier screamed hysterically in the blackness. A sixth boom silenced the forest.

Putting his sleeve to his lips, Zwart said, "Alpha patrol, report."

A hiss was all that came back. "Alpha patrol, report now! What's happening?"

Once again only a hiss answered Zwart as the other soldiers stared uneasily into the black woods. Behind him the fire crackled and Zwart turned around to notice the Bible was nearly completely burned up. "Damn you, Baker!"

He gestured to Tango. Catlike, she entered the woods 90 degrees from where Alpha patrol entered. She would approach their last known position from an oblique angle.

A few minutes later, she appeared with Dylan's bloody shotgun. "He dropped it. He's injured, but all of Alpha Patrol is dead. He's moving south."

"South?" Zwart appeared pleased. "He'll be trapped on the peninsula. Let's get some rest, and we'll get him tomorrow."

Tango spoke up, "Sir, we have night vision goggles. We should go after him now, while he's hurt."

Zwart looked at her and smiled paternally, "We'll get him, but not tonight. In the morning he'll be cold and exhausted. We'll be warm and ready."

Dylan watched the soldiers move to their barracks, save for the guards and burial duty soldiers. Tomorrow would come soon.

44

· · · · · · · · · ·

THE REMAINS OF Zwart's little army, nine soldiers counting Tango and Zwart, were gathered around the cold campfire as the first rays of morning illuminated the forest mists. Zwart's gaze moved from the fire pit to his tattered and uneasy soldiers.

"Tango was out earlier. The target is wounded and was last seen heading south toward Cain Head. It couldn't be better for us since he's headed for the tip of a peninsula. He'll be trapped by noon with no place to go." A rare smile teased the edges of Zwart's mouth as a mote of ash from the campfire landed unnoticed on his sleeve.

"Tango found the shotgun he used to attack Alpha squad last night. He probably abandoned it due to its weight. He may have bled out, or he may still be armed, but none of the Sigs are missing. You should assume he has a civilian weapon. Every soldier here gets double combat pay upon mission completion." Zwart observed that the unease of the soldiers morphed to greed as they considered how well compensated they would be. "Any questions?"

There didn't appear to be any questions, so Zwart signaled MOVE OUT. "Stay in communication. Shoot to kill."

Tango led the squad out of the campsite past the place where Foxtrot and his squad were gunned down. The amazing amount of human-tissue-spattered trees, rocks and dirt testified to the carnage of the previous night. As the soldiers moved along the forest path, they spread out in a combat line.

Tango paused to show Zwart some abandoned shotgun shells and bloody rags. Zwart reached for his radio, "This confirms our target was severely wounded last night. This might be over before we planned, but maintain battle alertness"

As the soldiers moved deeper into the tangled dark woods, their unease returned. The same forest that granted energy and comfort to Dylan seemed to oppress Zwart's squad, and the captain could tell they were having second thoughts about this mission.

When a startled soldier fired at a crow, several other soldiers responded with fire. Hundreds of bullets ripped through the forest canopy sending showers of debris floating down on everyone.

Tango was not fooled into shooting. It was clear she was in control of her emotions.

"Hold your fire, god damn it! You guys are better than this. Don't shoot unless you have a target."

Zwart's red cheeks signaled his frustration and his uniform ap-peared peppered with shredded leaves. One leaf stuck out from his hat at a jaunty angle.

At a fork in the path, Tango lightly trotted down one pathway, returned, and then scouted the second one. "He's left a trail on both of these."

Zwart stepped to the head of the line. "We need to split up. Tango, you take Victor, Kilo and Romeo and scout the north trail. The rest of us will take the south. Meet up at the bridge by Tonsina Creek."

Tango's squad carefully explored the north trail. The woods again became eerie with sounds and movement that set the men on edge.

Near a stream, Victor called out, "Hey I found something!"

In the stream, a gold coin, about the size of a nickel sparkled in the clear water.

Tango's internal alarm rattled her consciousness. "Freeze. It could be a trap."

The three men gathered around the coin, Tango scoured the area visually.

Victor used his deadly looking combat knife to probe around the coin. Suddenly he reached into the stream, picked up the coin and polished it on his shirt. "I just got me a Chinese Panda!"

"Hey, you got to share, it's probably worth a thousand dollars!" Kilo eyed the coin.

"No way. You pussys could have picked it up—but you didn't."

"Listen, you're going to share, or we'll take it from you and divide up the value." Kilo assumed a defensive stance.

Romeo's voice broke the testosterone-laden tension. "Here's another one!" Without taking precautions, Romeo picked up the coin, flipped in the air and put it in his pocket. Instantly, the other men fanned out as their eyes scoured the forest floor.

Tango rolled her eyes. "I'm going to scout ahead. Keep your eyes open. The coins could be a trap."

Romeo, proud of his insight, "I think he's running through the woods with a hole in his money bag." Tango shook her head.

Kilo ran ahead of the group, stopping to pick up coins. The others tumbled after him. Tango remained still, explored the woods with her eyes while her internal alarms screamed. A hundred yards down the trail, the men came across an open area with a dozen coins scattered about.

The men laid their guns down before they dropped to their knees and started picking up coins. Leaves, needles and pinecones filled the air as the soldiers, like children searching for Easter eggs, frantically searched for gold.

From his perch in a tall tree, Dylan calmly watched as the men fell upon on their knees. The first arrow hit Romeo in the back of the neck, severed his spinal cord and exited his throat after opening his jugular vein. Romeo collapsed face down into the weeds, coins tumbling from his hands.

Victor's face glowed with the excitement of the moment. "Hey Romeo, let me see your knife, there's one stuck in this rock."

The second arrow hit Kilo also in the neck. Blood spurted in an amazing arch onto Victor who was confused by the spray. Gaining his wits, Victor dropped his coins, picked up his rifle and sprayed bullets into some nearby bushes. The third arrow ripped through Victor's back and out the front of his chest, a piece of his heart muscle dangling on the arrowhead's blades.

"That's for Shorty and Bergen," Dylan whispered as Victor dropped heavily onto the bodies of his companions: a semi-circle of gold coins surrounded them.

Tango reacted to the staccato burst from a silenced Sig Sauer 553. She brought up her sleeve to her mouth. "Romeo, report." A hissing radio answered her. "Victor, Kilo, Romeo report!" More hissing.

Zwart jumped onto the frequency. "What's going on, Tango?"

"Not sure, Sir. I've lost contact with my men."

Zwart checked a small tablet device and studied its map and the glowing dots. "We're about 800 yards south of your position. Your missing soldiers are just a few hundred yards up the trail from you, but hold your position until we get there." Zwart put the tablet into his belt pack and signaled his men to join Tango.

Dylan descended from his perch, removed a radio from Victor's head, rubbed his bow into the puddles of blood, and lightly jogged down the trail away from Tango's position. As he moved, Dylan disabled the GPS chip from Victor's radio. Partway down the trail, he dropped his bloody bow where it would be found.

Dylan came to a smooth, 30-foot-wall of rock and paused. He put the radio piece into his ear, and then expertly climbed the impossibly smooth rock face At the top, he peeled back several branches to reveal his Remington hunting rifle. He pulled the bolt back, chambered a round, and scoped out the forest below.

Zwart surveyed the killing area with the bodies of Victor, Kilo and Romeo. His gaze traveled around the forest. "That damned handyman. Who is he? I've never seen anything like this." Tango picked up the gold and handed it to Zwart. He put it into a cloth sack at his belt that held his binoculars. When his gaze traveled back to the bodies, he saw the missing radio and smiled. "He's made a mistake now."

He pulled out his tablet and showed it to Tango. She nodded and ran off into the woods. His eyes followed her as she silently disappeared. Looking at his men, "So who's going to lead?"

The remaining soldiers looked uneasily at each other. "So who wants all this gold?"

Echo stepped forward.

"Echo, you lead. I want the rest of you to cover him. Whoever gives the killing shot to Dylan gets this pouch of gold in addition to the pay of any dead soldiers."

Greed soon overcame fear. The party moved out with Zwart hanging back as he gazed at his tablet.

Again the forest seemed to take on a menacing feel. The sounds and movements all seemed malevolent to the soldiers. As Echo rounded a bend, he came into the sights of Dylan's rifle.

Echo spotted the bloody bow and signaled halt. "There's his bow. God it looks wicked."

"What are you waiting for?" Lima scanned the brush for clues. "Get him!"

"It could be a trap." Echo scanned the trees.

Zwart's voice commanded across the radio. "Men, standard assault positions. We need to check out the bow."

The men spread out and approached the bow in a semi-circle while Zwart continued to hang back staring at his tablet. Dylan put his cross hairs on Echo's head. He fired. Echo's head snapped forward and the back of his head splattered gore behind him followed quickly by the roar of the big Remington. From the POV of the soldiers, the shot seemed to come from everywhere. The report bounced off of trees and rocks. The remaining soldiers sprayed the woods with fire.

Tango, off to the side, saw something move atop a rock wall. Could it be Dylan?

Dylan coldly chambered another round and put the crosshairs on Lima. Dylan fired and Lima's head exploded in the same manner as Echo's. The remaining soldier, November, dropped his rifle and ran back the way he came. Zwart fired a burst into the man's back, "Failure is not permitted." November writhed on the forest floor as his life drained out.

Tango approached Dylan's perch from behind. She brought up her rifle and squeezed off a blast. Dylan dropped.

Trying to see where Dylan fell, Tango brought her sleeve to her lips. "Sir. He's down."

Zwart responded, "Cover him. I'll be right there." Zwart ran with a graceful lope to Tango's position. Brushing against trees and rocks, his once perfect uniform developed rips revealing padding where muscles were supposed to be.

Hyper vigilant, Tango and Zwart approached Dylan's shooting lair. Slowly they came closer and closer. As if mind readers, they both stood and aimed their guns where Dylan should be.

He was gone. He was gone and a massive amount of blood showed he was wounded. His Remington lay abandoned.

Zwart, his mangled uniform and disheveled hair looking odd, signaled that Tango should proceed.

Catlike, she followed the blood trail down a steep trail. She and Zwart observed Dylan, his stomach covered in blood, pick up his bow and disappear around a tree.

Tango made eye contact with Zwart. He signaled her that he's going left, and she should go right. Full of confidence, Tango and Zwart lightly jogged down the hill toward the tree that was hiding Dylan. At 100 yards, they poured fire into the tree and the area around it.

Dylan spun around when a 5.56 round grazed his shoulder. He twisted and went down heavily behind some foliage. Zwart and Tango poured more fire into the bushes where Dylan fell. Replacing their magazines with fresh, they crept toward Dylan's position.

Bursting from behind the tree, they saw that Dylan was gone. Tango gestured to the blood trail. Abandoning caution, the two walked upright after Dylan. Zwart, looking dirty and disheveled, commented, "You can have the gold." Zwart tossed the bag to her. "I want the kill shot."

They saw Dylan not far ahead near the bridge across Tonsina River. Dylan, bloody and weak, attempted to notch an arrow. Zwart fired. The bullet hit the top of his bow and smashed the upper cam. Now defenseless, Dylan looked flatly at Zwart.

Then Dylan's eyes rolled back in his head, and he fell back into the river with a muted plop.

45

· · · · · · · · · · ·

ZWART HEARD the splash. A splash that meant he had won. A body had fallen into the shallow river. He had defeated this handyman and hunting guide. He had fulfilled his mission.

Triumphantly, but cautiously he approached the bank and saw Dylan floating on his back. Movements told Zwart that Dylan was still alive. Zwart brought his rifle up to shoot.

A nasty ripping sound made Zwart's eyes dart to the right. A screaming arrow punched up Zwart's nose and five inches into his head knocking off his hat.

Zwart dropped to the ground and started spasming. His once perfect uniform was now torn, muddy, and covered in forest debris. His chiseled face now had one eye looking left, the other right while tremors in his back made his body flop like a halibut in a boat. The clown-like gaudy feathers of the flu-flu bobbing over his dirty face robbed him of his last bit of dignity.

Suzie approached Zwart from the woods. "You lost. A girl. An Alaska girl with a pink bow put an arrow up your nose, you bastard!"

Tango looked at Suzie then approached Zwart's body and stared dispassionately down. She looked into Zwart's functional eye, probably the only part of him not covered in mud. They exchanged looks. Tango's eyes asked, "Failure allowed this time?"

Zwart's eye desperately said, "Yes."

"Request denied." She brought up her rifle and put a single NATO 5.56 round into Zwart's chest.

Zwart's body twitched as his life flowed out onto the gooey banks of Tonsina Creek. She looked at Dylan floating in the pure waters, nearly unconscious among hundreds of huge salmon building and guarding their nests.

Tango turned around and gazed at Suzie standing disheveled with a pink compound bow in her hand and no arrows. The women made eye contact. Behind the single-minded determination, Suzie saw something else in Tango's eyes. Like a fleeting image formed by smoke curling above a flame; a sense of longing appeared and then faded.

Suzie dropped her bow and ran along the bank of the river. "Dylan? Dylan! Where are you?"

She climbed a mound and saw Dylan's pink socks as he painfully crawled up a gravel bar near where Tonsina Creek emptied into Resurrection Bay.

Cathedral-looking tall white columns, the trunks of a ghost forest, surrounded Dylan and provided perches for a choir of eagles eying the dying, spawned out salmon weakly splashing near Dylan's body.

Suzie could see Dylan had something in his hand, a yellow ribbon. She ran through the knee-deep shallow river creating a rhythmic splashing sound.

The river throbbed with life: thousands of salmon laying hundreds of thousands of eggs. All around the cacophony of hungry gulls warned her away from the feast of salmon eggs that awaited them. Higher in the eerie white trees, adult and juvenile bald eagles waited for the spawned-out salmon to die and offer their bodies to Alaska.

"Dylan, it's me, Suzie!" Dylan looked up, his eyes filled with tears, her yellow ribbon in his hand.

"You're a ghost?" Dylan's words sounded raspy and confused.

"Dylan, it's OK. It's me. I'm here. You don't need to cry."

Dylan smiled though the tears. "I do need to cry." his voice cracked, and he lay down on the wet gravel—tears flowing from his eyes: tears for his lost friends, tears for Bergen, his blown up cabin and tears for the kiss Suzie gave him.

Just outside his consciousness, he could hear gulls crying and salmon splashing in the crystal waters of Tonsina Creek. Alaska surrounded and sustained him.

Suzie took his head in her arms and rocked. "Dylan! Don't go! I need you! I want to eat weeds with you in the meadows."

AS SHE ROCKED Dylan, Suzie could hear boats approaching from Resurrection Bay. Above the natural din of Tonsina Creek, she then heard the sounds of a police boat pulling up on the sandy river mouth.

The beach quickly became crowded with rescue and police boats. Later Suzie would say that she didn't remember when the natural forest sounds faded into the background among all the hubbub of police and rescue personnel. She wouldn't remember that EMTs strapped a semi-conscious Dylan into a stretcher. The young EMT tenderly helped Suzie pull away from Dylan's stretcher. "Miss, you need to let us take him now."

Suzie's tears coated her face. "Stay with me, Dylan."

The young EMT murmured, "You can ride in the front. You don't need to leave him."

"I'm never going to leave him."

Across the river Officer Burl and two county deputies stood near Zwart's body. "She fired a flu-flu up his nose? Are you shitting me? I wouldn't think it's possible."

"Yeah, but it looks like he also took a bullet to the chest, Deputy. I'll bet the chest shot was meant as a mercy."

IN THE HOSPITAL emergency room, several layers of gauze covered Suzie's wrists. Her bruised face had reached maximum color. She refused to relax, even after a nurse gave her a shot to do just that. "I've got to see Dylan."

"Relax, Miss Alaneo. He's in surgery right now. Doctor Adeep will take good care of him.

Dylan's weak but steady breathing, was audible in the surgery. Dr. Adeep efficiently began the closing procedure on Dylan's abdomen. "That's that. I hope he recovers. Don't often see such nasty gunshot trauma."

"Think he'll make it, Doctor?" a surgical nurse said as she handed him a dressing.

"It's up to him now. I've done what I could. If he survives, he'll need some work done on that shoulder."

As Dylan lay on the table, hospital sounds faded. Despite the anesthesia, his mind seemed to clear as the oval breathing worked its magic. Steadily, his thoughts moved into a clear space, like a meadow on a mountainside. The next breath was extraordinarily relaxing. As he spent a few moments in the center of the meadow, a shape took form nearby.

Sid, what are you doing here?

I'm here to see you.

Sid! I wanted to tell you. I'm sorry! I'm sorry about Julie. I'm sorry I left you up there.

Hey, you did the right thing on Denali. Now you stopped Zwart. You survived for a reason. And I need to tell you; you're not looking so hot. Isn't this a little like Italy? You are hanging there on the wall of sheer cliff wondering whether you should let go or continue on? Do you remember? Dylan nodded.

Well, it is really a question of whether your story is over or if you have a few more mountains to climb. Sid paused as he stared into Dylan's eyes. *I'll tell you. It is time for me to move along. You have learned so much. It's also time for you to carry on and give back. Your story is not over.*

I can't do that. I'm not ready. The wounds are too deep.

Dylan, you are ready. Look, you have Suzie now. I can make your journey easier. I will take your ghosts with me when I go. May the rising winds ease your journey.

Wait! Wait!

Dr. Adeep looked up at the physiologic monitor and frowned at the waveform display. He shot a look at his nurse anesthetist, "The patient's BP is rising. He seems agitated. You sure you gave him enough juice to keep him under?"

She checked her monitors, "He's out, Doctor."

The surgeon put the finishing touches on the dressing. "Let's get him to recovery if his blood pressure stabilizes. There's someone waiting for him there."

Dr. Adeep walked out to the recovery room to report to any waiting family members. Meanwhile, the surgical team began to relax as Dylan's blood pressure, pulse and other vitals drifted into the normal range.

46

. . . .

STEVE EUBANK, THE PILOT of the pale green Gulfstream G650, and his co-pilot Dan Shimizu worked through their preflight checklists as their passenger loaded a large, heavy trunk and a simple black roller bag from the back of a government-licensed Chrysler 200.

Judging by the passenger's heavy clothes, Steve reckoned they would not be going to Honolulu as he was first told. Something about this guy said Moscow.

Steve could not believe how much he and Dan were being paid for this one-way trip. However, this wealthy passenger had demanded flexibility, speed and discretion. Steve had discussed it with Dan.

To avoid getting fired, they would need to come up with a really compelling reason for "forgetting" to file a flight plan change mid-flight. The passenger had said to include enough fuel to go 5,000 miles. With a range of

7,000 nautical miles and a top speed of mach .925, the Gulfstream 650 could get this man anywhere fast.

As the two-person flight crew went through the final checks, Steve thought about his boss. He would be pretty upset about the change in destination from a domestic flight to international. He liked everything about his executive jet service to be above board and completely compatible with international customs regulations.

Illya Ivanov shouted from the rear. "Let's go. Don't bother with serving me anything, I'm in a rush."

Dan hated being a waiter, so it was fine with him to get going. "Yes Sir. You need to buckle yourself into one of the big seats. They are for takeoff and landings."

As the engines spooled up for the final check, Ivanov sat back in his chair and smiled. "You guys know how to tell if God loves you? Check your bank account," he patted the large trunk. "*By this I know that thou favourest me, because mine enemy doth not triumph over me.*"

Steve tried to hide his perplexed expression as he slipped on his over-the-ear headphones, "Yes Sir. We'll get permission to taxi."

"Good. Let's go. I'm not going to relax until we are out of US airspace."

"Gulfstream 58 Juliet, requesting permission to taxi to runway one-niner charlie, over."

Ivanov watched as Steve put his hand up to his right headphone. "Repeat that please." He exchanged a nervous glance with Dan. Dan turned and looked back at Illya.

"What's wrong? Let's go." Illya slapped his knee in a gitty-up gesture.

"They are saying we need to wait. US Customs has put a hold on this flight."

Ivanov look furious. "What! You tell them that's bogus. We need to go. This is a Homeland Security priority one mission. No one's stopping me."

Steve made the call and turned around. "They are sending a car out here, and I'm ordered to shut down my engines."

Illya dug into his roller bag, pulled out a wicked-looking pistol, a Russian-made MP-443 Grach, and pointed it at Steve. "Listen you bastard, get this plane off the ground or you can eat some Russian lead."

"Sir, if you fire a round in this plane, it could compromise the hull. We won't be able to pressurize or go much faster than a single prop plane. Put the gun away please. We'll do as you ask."

Dan coolly reached down and locked the microphone to the ON position. "Yes Mr. Ivanov, put the pistol down, and we'll get this plane going. No one needs to get hurt."

Steve realized Dan was broadcasting this conversation to the tower. "That's right, Mr. Ivanov. Please put the gun down. I can taxi out to runway 19C, and just take off behind that black Lear Jet and that UPS turbo-prop."

Illya unbuckled his seatbelt and peered out of the left side window. "There's an airport security van coming. Get moving!" He moved over to the right side, put his face to the window and saw a fire truck and ambulance scrambling on the far side of the tarmac. He could hear the engine whine increasing as the engines reached taxiing power.

The jet turned into the queue and came to a dead stop. "Mr. Ivanov, you're seat belted in for take-off, correct?"

"Just a minute . . . yes, I am."

"Good. It will be another few minutes. We are number two for take-off."

Illya twisted in his seat. "Where the hell are those cars that were following us?"

"They're not allowed in the taxi way. Too dangerous." lied Steve as he opened the rear luggage hatch remotely.

"What was that? Bull shit!" thundered Illya. "I don't care about cabin integrity. Go around those two slow pokes or I'll shoot the co-pilot." Illya waved his Grach threateningly in the direction of the cockpit door.

Near the rear of the plane, a metal locking mechanism whirred. Like lightening, Illya swiveled his pistol back and fired four times in the direction of the noise. Somewhere a hissing sound erupted.

Heartbeat.

Illya reached for his seatbelt buckle. The belt seemed twisted, but his hand disengaged the latch. Illya pivoted on his left leg and stood facing two heavily-armored SWAT team members as they burst from the luggage compartment.

Heartbeat.

The Grach spat wildly.

The SWAT team's first bullet entered Illya's neck severing his spinal cord. Feeling on the right side of Illya's body stopped instantly and blood began rapidly flowing out his neck and down his white silk shirt.

No heartbeat.

Illya, his mind alert for a last instant, had only one thought: *I ran domestic security for the U.S. government, thousands of people looked up to me, and a fucking woodsman stopped me . . .*

Moments later a SWAT team member kicked away the Grach.

47

Epilogue
One Year Later

. . . .

TALL TEENAGERS and parents effectively blocked Suzie's view of the Mount Marathon Race finish line.

"Doolie, where's Dylan?" The old dog looked concerned as the contestants ran past the finish line.

"I wish I got taller as I grew older," Suzie remarked to Dylan's loyal dog.

The runners rounded the corner into view as Suzie and Doolie squirmed their way through the teenage wall. Booths and well-wishers channeled the runners down Main Street toward the finish line. *Where was Dylan?*

He had been practicing for months: up early, running and trying everyone's patience. Dylan was really focused on recovering his strength after getting shot.

"Suzie!" Nancy Pierce parted the layers of teenagers and ambled to a stop, next to Suzie. "Seen Dylan?"

"Nancy, it's good to see you out and about. Hey, I saw the Knitting Barn booth across the street. Extraordinarily artsy this year." Suzie grinned at the unusual fabric bunny adorning Nancy's collar.

"Thanks, dear."

Suzie glanced up Main Street, "No sign of him yet. I hope he's OK."

Nancy sighed. "You know Dylan. He's shy, but not timid."

"Don't let him hear you say he's shy." Suzie smiled

"OK, I'll say he's a survivor. Speaking of surviving, how is the newest USA Today field reporter? Yearning for the more peaceful life yet?"

Suzie smiled. "Nancy, I love it! I'm able to keep a home base here in Seward, but I'm covering stories all over the Pacific Northwest. They are flying me to Portland next week.

"Being here for our 4th of July extravaganza is doubly wonderful: home and friends. This is my favorite Seward event. I'm so happy."

"Well you deserve your dream. You and Dylan really went through the wringer. At least your article in the *The Atlantic* had repercussions all the way back to Homeland Security in Washington. And, I think your story even helped Peter begin to understand how Illya manipulated him."

"Dylan plans to visit Peter next week. He's uneasy about Peter's upcoming release date, but he wants to do something." Suzie struggled to get a clear view through the small space between two teenagers.

"How did your granddaughter do in the Children's Mount Marathon Race?"

"Don't know." said Nancy looking over the crowd. "Age five is the first year she can participate, and it was so important to her. She and her mom should be here any minute.

"Suzie, look! It's Dylan! What is he carrying?"

"Nancy, is that your grandchild?"

Suzie squirmed to a clear view as Dylan rounded the corner and approached the finish line. The bundle in his arms was clearly a child. "It's Krissy!"

Both Suzie and Nancy plowed through the lively crowds as Dylan and Krissy crossed the finish line. Krissy's face was a blend of tears, dirt and joy."

"Krissy, what happened?" Nancy came to a complete stop in front of Dylan.

"Grandma Nancy! I fell and hurt my ankle. I was sitting there when Dylan asked me if I wanted to finish the race. I said, 'Yes'."

"Oh, Krissy. I'm so proud of you! You are the youngest person in our family to finish the Mount Marathon Race. We will need to get you a sticker!"

LATER, DOOLIE SLEPT at Dylan's feet as he and Suzie watched the annual spectacular midnight fireworks flare over the nearly dark waters of Resurrection Bay.

Suzie looked up at Dylan and gave him a long hug. "Getting psyched for the cabin to be finished? I can hardly wait to spend the night in it, with you and Doolie."

"How about tonight? We can camp on the floor. I got a big sleeping bag." Dylan smiled down at his pretty fiancée.

Dylan put his arm around Suzie as she leaned against him. He played with the yellow ribbon in her hair, and they gazed at the celebration in the sky.

Who is Tyler Blackthorne?

• Black belt in Shotokan Karate
• Kayak guide for two summers in Seward, AK
• Honored by the National Teachers' Hall of Fame
• Has a US patent on a microbiological test method
• Has traveled the world writing and photographing for motorcycle magazines
• Published dozens of articles in mainstream print magazines and professional journals, under a different name
• Has a total of 5 graduate and postgraduate degrees.
• Plays on an elite Ultimate Frisbee team
• Is author of 4 other books under different names
• Speaks fluent Spanish and German
• Currently has three screenplays available from Mt. Hood Press

. . . .

Tyler Blackthorne can be the father/daughter writing team of Bruce and Kelly Hansen. Tyler can also be Bob Young and Bruce Hansen. Or just Bruce.

Denali was written by Bruce Hansen, Kelly Hansen and Bob Young.

Arctic Forces was written by Bruce Hansen and Bob Young.

Arctic Protocol was written by Bruce Hansen

Bob Young, a writer/scientist, lives in Savage, Minnesota with his family and two cats.

Kelly Hansen writes and works in application performance monitoring technology in Portland, Oregon.

Bruce Hansen is an adjunct college professor, writer and fine-arts photographer in Portland, Oregon. brucehansenphoto.com

Dear Reader,

If you enjoyed this story, please review Denali at Amazon.com or your favorite review site.

Turn the pages to see the previews of some other Dylan Baker thrillers.

Best wishes,

Tyler Blackthore

Preview of the Dylan Baker Thriller:

Arctic Forces

. . . .

PROLOGUE

PROFESSOR NEIL CARLYLE examined the settings on his tripod-mounted-camera using his red-light headlamp. He checked for the constellation Aquarius rising over Mt. Hood. This was the perfect night for star photography: no moon, Eta Aquarids meteor shower at full blast, and crystal clear skies at the snowy six thousand foot level.

He opened the shutter for a 20-second exposure, and then marveled at silver-gold meteor streaks over the cold beauty of Mt. Hood. Perfect!

Somewhere behind him, he heard a twig snap. Part of Professor Carlyle's mind wondered what would cause a stick to snap on a black, cold night illuminated by only star shine on snow. He had hiked for hours to get away from any light pollution and set up his winter campsite just at dusk.

As his camera shutter clicked, he heard a snow-laden branch give up its load with a deep thump. If someone else was up here, the professor hoped they'd have enough sense not to turn on any lights while his camera's shutter was open.

Dr. Carlyle moved his camera to capture the southern night sky. It seemed more of the meteor trails were appearing over there.

From out of the blackness, a strong female voice filled the silence, "Dr. Carlyle?"

Starting, Dr. Carlyle bumped his tripod sending the camera lens-down into a pile of rocks. "Damn! I nearly peed my pants. Look at my camera!" Carlyle reached to his forehead and switched on his dim red light. In the eerie red glow, he could see two soldiers in Arctic combat gear standing right next to him. They were regarding him like robots through night-vision goggles.

"What's going on?" Dr. Carlyle asked as he picked up his tripod and examined the camera's lens. With only the faint red glow from his headlamp, he couldn't tell if the lens was scratched or just dirty.

"Dr. Carlyle? Dr. Neil Carlyle?" the female soldier's voice indicated she meant business.

"Yes. What's going on? Why are you here in the night asking for me? Is it Jennie?" Dr. Carlyle thought of his ailing wife at home with family in Eugene.

"Sir, you need to come with us." The female soldier took his arm and started to lead him out of the camp.

Pulling his arm out of her grip, Dr. Carlyle turned his headlamp to full white light flooding the area with brilliant LED-powered illumination. The two soldiers flinched in the light. Carlyle could see four other well-armed soldiers back in the woods.

"What's going on? Why are you here?" Carlyle was obviously frightened and confused.

Snapping their NV goggles up, the soldiers raised their rifles towards him. "Dr. Carlyle, you are interfering with a military exercise. You need to come with us." This time the soldier's painful grip on his arm made it clear, he wouldn't be able to just pull free.

"Military exercise? On National Recreational Land? I don't think so. You guys are not allowed to train up here." From behind, a large male soldier with long blond-red hair cascading from under his helmet, cuffed Dr. Carlyle's hands behind his back.

"What the . . .?" Carlyle struggled.

The female soldier shoved a large roll of gauze into his mouth and taped his face so he couldn't talk.

They led the bewildered professor, not back to the parking lot, but up the mountain to a steep hillside. Here the cuffs and gag came off. Carlyle looked around to see soldiers near the hillside were arranging his tent and other camping gear.

"Reno, get him into the tent," the female solder ordered.

Anyone observing could tell the professor was on the verge of panic. Matter-of-factly, Delta slammed a chunk of ice into the side of Carlyle's head. Groaning, Carlyle went down to his knees. Two soldiers shoved the semi-conscious man into his tent, and then ran back the way they came.

At a signal, a powerful blast exploded up the mountain, followed by the roar of heavy snow and rock sliding downwards. Moments later, the tent containing Carlyle, vanished under 30 feet of avalanche debris.

"Tango, what about our footprints?" Reno asked.

"He told everyone not to expect him for two or so days. Snow showers are forecast for the morning. We're done here."

1

DYLAN COULDN'T REMEMBER EVER being so uneasy as he gazed out the windows of his hand-built log home. Even the deep in woods, the surrounding Kenai Fjords of Alaska couldn't seem to calm him. In minutes, he would meet his daughter for the first time, and he ached for it to go well.

The cloudless skies offered a false promise of a perfect dry day but Dylan, highly attuned to the outdoors, knew it would rain in a few hours. He hoped his daughter would bring rain gear and boots. If she had asked him how he knew it would rain, he would have been unable to explain what he knew about the section of woods bordering Resurrection Bay on one side and the great Harding Ice Fields on the other.

When he received a terse email a week earlier, it was nearly impossible for him to comprehend. According to the sender, a former lover and fiancée had had a baby during the year they had been apart. Painfully, Dylan thought back to his last conversation with Heather. She had been trying to tell him something when an icefall ended her life near the summit of Denali. Maybe she had been trying to tell him about Anja.

A daughter! The idea excited Dylan. He could form a deep relationship with her, show her important places, have conversations about life and go on dad-daughter outings. Anja would get to know Dylan's wife, Suzie, and love her like the mother who had perished on Denali. How Dylan longed for this daughter, even if she was in her twenties! Anja could be the child Dylan and Suzie never had.

In the email, Anja had explained that she was taking an administrative job in Anchorage with the Mountain

Club regional offices. She'd be just a couple of hours from Dylan and Suzie.

Dylan was impressed by his daughter's job. The Mountain Club had started as a local climbing group in Seattle, and grown into the nation's largest pro-environment group. It was probably most famous for its political lobbying, but it also organized outdoor events, published pro-environment books and raised public awareness of important issues. To get an administrative job with the big office in Anchorage meant she had talcnt.

Dylan had been in the library checking his email when he first heard from Anja. He'd looked her up and learned that her name was Anja Hart. Hart was her grandmother's maiden name and what her mother had gone by. He found out that she was only 28 but very successful in the non-profit environmental activist community.

What if she hated him? What if she blamed him for her mother's death and for not being a dad to her? What if she thought Dylan knew about her but didn't care to find her? What if she was coming to see him, not to form a relationship, but to unleash bitter resentment about a dad who never calmed her fears, kissed her goodnight or coached her soccer team?

As Dylan fretted about what could go wrong with the meeting, he let his eyes wander around the cabin. On two walls, large windows let in the soft greeny light from the Sitka spruce forest and ushered in stunning views of Resurrection Bay and the range of snow-capped mountains surrounding it.

Another wall held Dylan's tools for guiding outdoor adventures: large gun safes, racks of bow-hunting apparatus and climbing gear. Near the ceilings, rusted and banned, antique leg-hold bear traps decorated the walls.

Dylan's eyes paused on a photograph of him and his journalist-wife Suzie. She looked so much younger than he. His salt-and-pepper beard and craggy lined face made him look like a mature movie action hero. At nearly 50, Dylan's outdoor lifestyle had maintained his lean, athletic build.

Outside, some crows started making a ruckus. From their fuss, Dylan figured a hiker or hikers were probably coming through. Maybe it was Anja. Dylan felt awkward with people sometimes. He wished Suzie were home and not in Africa on a month-long assignment for Wild Outdoors. He didn't want to start off his relationship with Anja poorly.

A loud rapping at the door startled Dylan. It was probably Anja. *Should I hug her? Shake her hand? What if she cries? What if I cry?* Dylan decided to let Anja set the tone of their meeting.

When Dylan opened the door, he saw his daughter, looking like a blond Jennifer Lawrence. Her short hairstyle and androgynous outdoor clothes made Dylan wonder momentarily if she were gay. She had the athletic poise of her mother, but not the overt sweetness.

If he had planned it better, he wouldn't have been so stunned. His heart filled with affection for this beautiful person who would be his loving daughter.

"You Dylan?" the voice was deeper than her mother's and more confident.

Dylan gazed, speechless.

"Are you going to answer me?" the voice had a note of command in it. She was a top administrator for the Mountain Club. She definitely could command.

No hug. No handshake. Dylan found his voice. "Yes. Come in."

If Suzie had been at home, she would have noted that Anja jumped right into the purpose of her visit. She would have watched Anja coldly interview Dylan about her mother and any property her mother had left behind.

Suzie would have noticed that Dylan stumbled over his words as emotional pain slowly welled up inside of him. It was obvious that Anja was not the warm and fuzzy person Dylan hoped for. Not at all like her mother. Dylan wanted to ask her about her childhood, youth and college days. This wasn't going to happen.

"So you are an Alaskan now," Dylan found himself saying.

"Yes, imagine my surprise to learn my biological father is also here."

Dylan could not detect any warmth in her choice of words. "So you are a big shot in Mountain Club?" Dylan tried to make conversation.

"I'm the chief fundraiser for all the Pacific Northwest. It's a good job."

While she talked, Dylan tried not to smile. He could see so much of Heather in this beautiful, competent young woman. He blurted out what he had wanted to say since she arrived.

"Anja, what kind of relationship do you see us having? I was hoping to attempt to make up some of the lost years."

"Lost years? They are gone. Right now I don't need anything from you, my absentee father." Dylan felt a sting in her cold words. He steered the conversation to her mother, which is why she probably came to visit. When Dylan's stories started to peter out, Anja stood up.

"I'm holding open the possibility of continuing contact between us. You don't have a phone. I checked. Here's a smart phone." Anja placed a phone on the table. "Maybe we can be helpful to each other."

"You're giving me a cell phone? There's no reception up here."

Anja stood up abruptly. "Keep it anyway. I'll call you sometime."

Dylan looked at the cell phone like he had never seen one before.

"Once I get settled in Anchorage, I'll invite you up. Take the phone with you when you are town. We can have another conversation."

As Anja strode toward the door, it was obvious that there would be no physical contact between her and Dylan. It was likely that she had some healing to do before she would ever call him *Dad. But, at least she took the time to take the first step.*

2

ANCHORAGE IS A DOWN TO EARTH TOWN with little tolerance for glitzy or incongruous luxury. A good meal is a good meal. It doesn't need to have crystal and silver to taste good. Given this attitude, the Netsvetov Hotel stands out as an Alaskan anomaly. Taking up an entire city block, the Netsvetov shines like a polished diamond cast onto coarse black leather.

Built by oil-rich investors to rival the extravagant opulence of a Dubai palace hotel, the people of Anchorage accept the existence of the Netsvetov with an uneasy tolerance that would be offered to a mad aunt living in an attic. Given Alaska's enormous oil industry wealth, the 500-room hotel is frequently booked up.

If the hotel is as brilliant as a diamond, the penthouse is more so. Designed to appeal to the taste of a vain Saudi prince, with gold toilets, art museum paintings and flamboyant furnishings, only someone with an absurd amount of money to burn would ever rent the place. Colonel William Bolton had it booked for three months.

Sitting at an expansive Italian antique desk, wearing jeans and looking like a balding Clint Eastwood, business tycoon William Bolton made a call. About 150 miles away and seventy feet up a formation called High Rocks, the phone in Dylan's pack rang.

Dylan was placing a spring-loaded cam into a crack between two rocks. He was scouting a climbing route he'd take his more advanced climbers. This climb featured a lower ledge big enough to park a minivan and a protected view of Resurrection Bay.

The High Rocks formation started with an intrusion of silica-rich magma, which cooled and hardened deep below the earth's surface. If Dylan had been a geologist, he would have known that High Rocks was an intrusive dike formed millions of years ago when quartz-dense magma filled a crack in the weak sedimentary rocks and hardened into a wall of stunning rigidity. Dylan loved to climb it for the same reason shore birds nested in it: inherent stability. His hands on the rough, sparkling stone gave Dylan a feeling of confidence. He didn't know how he knew it, but somehow he could tell this formation's roots penetrated deep inside into the earth

High Rocks may have been a climber's dream, but it was surrounded by graywacky, or crumbly rotten rocks. No birds nested in the fragile, sandy area on either side of the sparkly gray High Rocks.

The phone ringing in his pack astonished Dylan; at first he didn't realize that the ring was coming from his pack. Dangling on a rope high above the big ledge and working the phone out of his pack; the screen glowed with a number Dylan did not recognize.

"Hello."

"Dylan Baker? Is this Dylan?" the voice crackled.

What the hell? Colonel Bolton? Dylan hadn't heard from Bolton since he took a beating from some thugs who warned him to stay away from Heather, the rich man's daughter. Now, 25 years later, the old man's scratchy voice pulled Dylan back into the past.

"This is Dylan. How did you get this number?" Dylan eased the cam out of the rock. He needed to get down and concentrate on this call.

"Dylan, you need to come to Anchorage. We have to talk." Dylan could picture Bolton expecting everyone to instantly jump to his bidding.

"What's this about, Colonel Bolton? Is it Anja? Did she give you this number?" Dylan pushed the speakerphone button, shoved the phone into the neck of his climbing shirt and hoped it would stay there.

"Anja hates my guts. She thinks I treated her mother poorly, raised her wrong and throw too much carbon dioxide into the atmosphere. I got this number because I'm good at getting information."

"So that gives Anja and me another common interest: hating you." Dylan stood on a ledge and shook the rope to clear it from an outcropping.

"It doesn't matter what you think of me. You took my daughter away from me, and for that you owe me a few minutes." Bolton's words stung Dylan. Long ago he had started to shed his guilty feelings about Heather's death. Now this asshole was bringing it up again.

"I don't owe you anything. I rescued Heather from your sick family. Her death was an accident. Tell me why I should talk to you?"

"I don't want to talk about blame or any of your past mistakes. I want to talk about your carbon scrubber."

Dylan spun slowly on his rope. *My college senior project? How did he know about that?*

Years ago, Dylan was studying biology at University of Oregon when he wasn't climbing mountains. Inspired by a desire to reduce greenhouse gases, Dylan stumbled upon and then later patented a process to convert carbon dioxide into alcohol.

The process would have made him a millionaire, but it had some problems that prevented it from going anywhere. The biggest obstacle was that the alcohol produced by the bacteria built up to the point where it was toxic to the culture. All the bacteria died in gelatinous goo before a significant amount of the CO_2 could be removed.

"My carbon scrubber? Why are you interested in that?" Dylan was curious as he slowly repelled downward.

"Why am I hearing there's interest in your carbon dioxide removal procedure, you ask? Did you not hear the rumors about a technology breakthrough?"

"I have no idea about rumors or why anyone would be interested in my old patent. That patent is expired now. Anyone can use that process. I have no interest in getting millions if it means I must leave my home and friends. Now you tell me, what are you doing in Alaska? Are you on vacation, or have you purchased the North Slope oil fields?"

"I'm here because a friend of mine, Greg Yeung, is running for governor, and he asked me to help. My interest in your carbon scrubber is private."

"That carbon scrubber was just an extra credit lab assignment. It will never be of any use because it doesn't work. The same biochemical reaction that removed CO_2 from a mixture of gases produces an alcohol that kills the bacteria responsible for the reaction

"My professor, who speculated that the culture produced the alcohol, also told me there's no simple way to effectively remove the alcohol. I think you are just trying to annoy me because you found out Anja has come into my life." Dylan's feet touched the ground under the rock wall.

"So rumors about a breakthrough are news to you?" Bolton said.

"I've heard no rumors. I've heard nothing. The system is a curiosity, not a process to save the world. You can't make money on it. And I see no reason why we should meet. And now that I know you support Yeung, I'm voting for the other guy." Dylan closed his phone and wondered who Yeung's opponent might be.

3

THE MERCEDES-BENZ ZETROS is about the size of a large motor home and designed for military use with a 7.2-liter inline six-cylinder diesel engine that pumps out 960 lb-ft of torque through all six wheels. This monster off-road vehicle can go just about anywhere it wants and can be equipped with a state of the art communication center, ATV/snowmobile storage, weapons locker and luxury furnishings. This particular Zetros had been built for a Mongolian millionaire who later changed his mind about the mansion-sized price tag.

The vehicle was parked out of sight near a newly renovated research station called Alaska Remote Climate Station or ARCS. ARCS looked like an old log-constructed national park building, but it was designed and built to study climate phenomena. The state of Alaska had repurposed the aging facility to study carbon dioxide and global warming. Tango thought about the terrible road into ARCS and wondered how the state could keep it supplied. No wonder the ARCS was in such bad shape! Her Zetros had no problems with the snow and mud, slushy journey from paved highway to ARCS.

The Zetros had just two semi-permanent occupants, the unit commander and a communications sergeant. However five additional guests were seated around a gorgeous teak dining table whose polished surface reflected the chandelier's light with a pleasing buttery glow. The guests appeared to be assembled from a major hotel chain, dressed in cook's white uniforms, custodian khakis, and building-engineer greens.

The leader of the group, and the only one dressed in winter combat camo was a dark-haired, cold-eyed woman in her mid forties who went by "Tango". She spoke with such confidence, that the others had no problems following her orders.

"Theta, has the ARCS security team finished their sweeps of the facility?" Tango's gaze fastened on a wiry, fit man wearing a green uniform. His nametag identified him as *Chuck* and his job as *Maintenance*.

"Yes, Ma'am. They are using cheap security equipment, like they don't expect any actual surveillance or attack."

"Good, then we can activate our micro cameras and mics." Tango turned her attention to a wide man in a cook's uniform. With his round head and big teeth, he looked to her something like a jack-o-lantern. "Omicron, see that everything's up and working by tonight."

"Yes, Captain." Omicron bobbed his large head.

"Reno, is the exterior surveillance set up as we planned?" Tango directed her comment to another man in a cook's uniform with *Josh* on his nametag. He looked like he belonged on a romance novel cover with his big chest and long reddish-blond hair.

"Yes, but it's hardly necessary. Everyone in there seems so intent on their lab and instruments, it's unlikely they'll want to come out in this weather." Outside a fierce gust of wind futilely attempted to rock the sturdy RV.

"Keep it on anyway. I know it's a pain to replace the batteries in this weather, but we want to know what they are up to when they are outside."

Tango glanced up at a clock on the wall. "When you go back to your quarters at the ARCS, remember you are to act like a contract support staff just doing your jobs. Show no overt curiosity about the work of the scientists. Unless they bring it up, don't discuss their work. Our surveillance should get us all the information we need." Tango gestured to a soldier sitting at a monitoring station, "Sergeant Denver will collect what we need."

Tango stood up, followed by a near simultaneous standing by the rest of the group. Tango smiled to herself, *These people are fanatics. They obey like no others I've ever worked with.* She delivered her last orders for the meeting.

"We have about an hour before any of you are back on duty in the ARCS, I want you to clean and check your weapons.

"Don't form emotional ties to any of the occupants of the ARCS. They are not enemies, but they are pawns that will probably need to be sacrificed for the greater cause. You need to be ready to kill, and soon." The fierce nods of her soldiers told her they would obey.

Arctic Forces is available as a paperback or ebook at Amazon.com or other booksellers.

Preview of the most recent
Dylan Baker Thriller:
Arctic Protocol

Prologue

. . . .

FOR THE LAST WEEK, it had been visible in the daytime sky, similar to a daytime moon. Unlike a moon, this daystar grew larger each day.

The asteroid was over twenty miles wide and moving at several thousand miles per second. In its wake were smaller asteroids keeping pace as the collection hurled toward an unsuspecting vibrant blue planet.

As the space-flung objects entered the atmosphere, they rapidly heated and edges began to vaporize. Nearly instantly, the softer elements burst into flame. Then the intense heat began to burn off various minerals and rocky parts. Gold, nickel, iron, palladium, platinum, magnesium—all changed to flaming gases under the intense heat.

There was one eerie component of the asteroid that seemed unaffected by the ever-rising temperatures—iridium. This otherworldly, super-dense mineral appeared unaltered by the thousands of degrees of heat destroying the rest of the asteroid.

At the point when the main asteroid struck the unsuspecting Earth near Central America, the atmosphere had managed to burn away over half of its mass, concentrating the iridium.

When the impact came, it released a colossal explosion over a billion times the energy of all the atomic bombs ever exploded, turning even the iridium into a vapor. An intense, hours-long heat pulse and a powerful compression wave destroyed living tissue on distant continents.

The impact also transformed thousands of tons of earth into a sulfuric vapor that would spread out over the entire planet and rain down as sulfuric acid for the next three years. The ash turned nearly all the sweet, breathable air on Earth to a toxic mix of harsh particulates and caustic gases.

The vaporized iridium and rock erupted into the atmosphere where it spread and changed into a dense cloud of ashy dust. The tiniest ash particles remained suspended in the air, turning day to night—nearly ending all photosynthesis for years. The iridium, heavier than the other particles, rapidly precipitated. The collision terminated the reign of dinosaurs, giant sea creatures and vast forests.

Today, at nearly any place on Earth, sediment located and dated at 66 million years ago, reveals a fine dusting of iridium to mark the change between the Cretaceous and Paleogene periods. Despite the many tons of iridium brought to Earth by the devastating collision, it remains one of the rarest minerals on Earth.

As that huge asteroid fell to Earth, some of the trailing, iridium-rich pieces struck Earth in present day South Africa, Russia, Canada and central Alaska. The smallish piece that landed in Alaska formed a deep crater that would be uplifted to over 5,000 feet above sea level. Later, massive continental tectonic plates folded the iridium-rich impact zone into an eerie mountain that the natives called Kila Ikpic and the whites called Shaman Mountain.

1

. . . .

RETTIEF SEME WAITED OUTSIDE the elegant doors of the Johannesburg corner office and planned how he would kill his white, African boss.

Nearly unconsciously, he scanned the waiting area looking for objects that could be improvised for defensive or offensive weapons.

A rolled up magazine could turn away a knife, one of the framed mineral samples on the wall could be thrown frisbee-style to unbalance an opponent, and a pen from a nearby secretary's desk could be thrust into the neck of the white executive.

He saw the black secretary look at a tablet screen and knew she would soon tell him to go on into the opulent office. Rettief could tell from her clan name, that she was Zulu, like his mother.

He wondered if his mother looked like her. Surely his mother would not have had the money for the stylish business attire and subdued make-up of the secretary.

His mother: black. His father: white. Himself: neither, and besides not belonging to any one culture, his existence was actually illegal during apartheid South Africa. When Rettief was a child, according to the state, he had no right to exist.

"Mr. Seme, Mr. Meijer will see you now," the secretary spoke to him in English, not Zulu. Maybe it was his Zulu last name, his Afrikaans first name, or perhaps his well-groomed and stylishly dressed appearance, but she appeared completely at ease with him. People who knew him well were not.

People told Rhett that he was so fine-featured and smooth-skinned, he appeared feminine, while his lean, well-muscled body spoke clearly of his masculine gender and high degree of physical fitness.

Anyone watching Rhett enter the office would not suspect he was ready for a fight. He moved with a relaxed confidence that reminded Pieter Meijer of a jungle cat. But Rettief Seme was always preparing for a fight. This constant state of preparation was involuntary and not specific to Mr. Meijer.

"Mr. Seme, I've got an important job for you." Pieter Meijer stood up from behind his desk. Rhett looked intensely at Meijer's facial muscles and posture. He determined that Meijer was not preparing an attack. Some wire-tight muscles inside Rhett relaxed a bit. He wondered why he always seemed ready to kill.

Meijer opened a drawer, Rhett tensed unconsciously as he watched Meijer's pupils dilate a fraction. He saw Meijer pull out a small, elegant box that looked like it contained a high-end men's wristwatch and handed it over. "Rhett, do you know what this is?"

Rhett noticed Mr. Meijer smelled like he had eaten Asian food for lunch as he opened the unusually heavy box. Judging by the weight, he expected to see a gold ingot. What he saw was a wickedly beautiful, silvery nugget vaguely in the shape of a melted transformer toy with a macadamia nut-sized chunk of quartz occluded in it.

Rhett knew this was a test as he hefted and examined the shiny metal. This white man was going to attempt to humiliate him. Rhett said nothing, but inwardly guessed it was a piece of raw platinum that had crystallized into an odd shape.

"Stumped? So was I. At first I thought it was platinum, but it's nearly pure iridium. Can you believe it?" Meijer took the nugget from Rhett.

Rhett was surprised. Meijer seemed to show no unease when his white hand touched Rhett's lighter, latte-colored skin. Rhett was certain that Meijer viewed dark-skinned people as something to be avoided, but hid his feelings remarkably well.

"I had the lab go over it. They'd never seen anything like it either, but it's the real thing. That piece of quartz has been shocked by heat and pressure. Can't fake shocked quartz. I think it's the biggest raw iridium nugget I've ever seen. Nearly a kilo."

Meijer held it up to a light and gazed at it. By the pulse in Meijer's neck Rhett noticed his boss's heart rate rose. The object fascinated him.

Rhett himself had never seen anything like Meijer's nugget. He'd been to Meijer's iridium mines. The most productive mine processed 100,000 tons of material to get one pound of iridium dust. A poppy seed-sized nugget would be a rare find.

"Mr. Meijer," Rhett switched the conversation from English to perfect Afrikaans, the Dutch-based language of the elite whites. "This is truly an amazing nugget. Did it come from your mines?"

If Meijer was surprised at Rhett's linguistic abilities, his pale blue eyes didn't show it. Few blacks used Afrikaans as fluently as Rhett.

"No. I'm not sure where it came from. That's why I called you. I need you to find the origin of this nugget, and do whatever is necessary to make sure no more of this comes onto the market." As he spoke, Mr. Meijer looked significantly at Rhett. The message was clear—"whatever is necessary".

2

. . . .

SLADE FELT COLD. He had folded his large, husky body into the small blind for more than four hours, and still no wolves.

Shivering behind the camouflaged netting, Slade wondered if his hairspray was tipping off the wildlife he was hunting. His last girlfriend teased him about looking like a 50s teen idol with his narrow face, strong jaw and extravagant pompadour hairstyle.

Now that perfectly groomed hair, which proved handy at getting dates, might be thwarting his mission. Slade pulled his down aviator hat lower over his ears as if to hide any hairspray odor. So what if it ruined his hair, he was deep in Central Alaska.

He could hear wolf howls in the clear, cold Alaska woods high on Shaman Mountain. The snow revealed the route the wolf pack had taken to the caribou carcass the day before. Bright yellow urine marks in the snow showed Slade the wolves considered the carcass theirs. Maybe they had eaten so much, they didn't want any more. Slade had spent considerable effort to kill a small caribou this high up the mountain. He did not want to go home empty-handed.

At a disturbance, Slade readied his rifle, but it was only the magpies and ravens fighting over the open rib cage. Earlier, several red foxes had visited the carcass and eaten their fill and left their obnoxious scent marks nearby. Now a lone vixen stood guard about ten feet away from the grinning face of the dead caribou, watching for anyone who might try to take over the hundreds of pounds of fresh meat.

Slade rubbed his eyes and again scanned the area. The red fox had vanished, and the ravens had flown up into some nearby tree branches. Silently, a smallish white wolf approached the carcass. Slade quietly reached over to a tripod and activated the silent Sony A7 rIII camera, which started shooting 4K UHD video. Any of the video frames could be processed as a high quality still. Nearby, Slade could see a mostly black wolf and two more white ones. He wanted a white one. They seemed to be different from any wolves he had read about or seen pictures of.

Silently gripping his rifle and holding the stock to his cheek, Slade sighted through the built-in iron sights on his Browning BLR 30.06. At 20 yards, he didn't need a scope.

The first rifle shot threw the small white wolf up into the air and down a snow bank. The other wolves vanished as if made of smoke. The ravens took to the air with harsh cries as snow, fine as flour, floated down from nearby trees. The bold magpies continued quarreling over the carcass undisturbed by the rifle blast.

Taking out a black Springfield .45 caliber pistol, Slade grabbed his pack, unfolded himself from the blind, and cautiously approached the place where he expected to find the dead wolf. Instead, he saw a blood trail leading to some bushes.

Pistol ready and on high alert, Slade approached the bushes where he could see the semi-conscious wolf panting heavily as it lay on its side. Once again, a gunshot disturbed the peace of the woods as Slade fired into the already bloody chest of the wolf.

One more headshot assured Slade the wolf was not faking its condition. For a moment, the shocking contrast of red blood on white snow made Slade pause. Then opening his pack, he took out two vials and filled them with the wolf's blood, labeled them, and shoved them back into his pack.

He was done for now and could leave while the magpies examined the new carcass steaming in the frozen air.

3

· · · · · · · · · ·

DYLAN BAKER DREW BACK the arrow on his high-tech, compound-hunting bow aiming it toward the path. He fiercely wanted to kill these men, but the hunter in him kept his heart rate and respiration steady.

At any moment the butchers who had killed his girlfriend and hunted him throughout these woods, would step out into the clearing. They carried military-grade automatic M16s selected to full automatic fire, but these were Dylan's woods, and he was an expert with the bow.

Dylan's pale gray eyes coldly swept the clearing. He felt the arrow's fletching soft on his cheek and noticed the metal smell of the arrow. He used a high-tech hunting arrow with an aircraft aluminum inner body, surgical stainless steel blades and a titanium tip that would rip into the killers' bodies at over 320 feet per second. Six more of these arrows lay positioned to fire. He could fire all them with uncanny accuracy within four seconds.

He didn't understand why these men were shooting at him, or why they had killed Suzie. He was just a simple forest recluse. His principle asset was his expertise as a hunting guide and woodsman.

"Why are they hunting me?"

Ten years ago, he had guided a winter ascent of Denali that resulted in the loss of his fiancé and all his clients. The guilt and grief had propelled Dylan into a reclusive life in the wilds of Alaska. Just now he felt he had begun to heal and reemerge into society as a professional wilderness guide. But now this.

The first man stepped into the clearing. Dylan remained still on his rocky perch. He could fire, but wanted to kill at least three of them.

Just then a rifle shot rang out jarring Dylan from his reverie.

Dylan realized he was having a vivid flashback. This meant that soon his nightmares might return. He hoped this did not mean his other PTSD symptoms would also return: anxiety, daymares, difficulty focusing, and depression.

Since the traumatic events several years ago, he and his counselor met regularly, and he took a daily, low-dose anti-depressant to treat his PTSD— post traumatic stress disorder.

The combination of the counseling and drugs had worked well. He found himself able to control his negative feelings and form positive relation-ships with others. He had fewer vivid, recurring memories about the attacks on him and his loved ones.

On this Shaman Mountain scouting trip, he had accidentally left behind his meds, and the flashback to the carnage in the woods was a reminder that he needed to continue his therapy regimen.

Other gunshots rang out, this time pistol shots. Somewhere up the mountain, Dylan guessed that someone was hunting. The second shots were likely used to euthanize severely wounded game. He'd been on the mountain a week and not seen any sign of humans, despite a small zinc mine operating just a few miles up the mountain.

Dylan emerged from his tent, stretched his 50 year-old body and looked down at his legs as he touched his toes. Some people might call him skinny, but Dylan kept himself fit so he could fully enjoy his hobby of rock climbing.

The difference between holding 165 or 175 pounds with just fingertips, could ruin a climb. He trimmed his beard short and left his still-brown hair long enough for a ponytail. A friend told him he could have leading-man good looks if his skin were not so craggy and weathered.

Shaman Mountain, which the Natives called Kila Ikpic, would become a great place to take clients on a wilderness experience. The area had the reputation of being haunted, but was actually a perfect place to take tourists.

Tourists generally loved the idea of a haunted place, and several articles in major magazines and a website mentioned ghosts. Dylan didn't believe in ghosts, but he was comfortable using the idea to promote a new wilderness excursion he was planning.

Besides the thrill of ghosts, Kila Ikpic had much to offer visitors. Dylan had noted a milky-green lake for a floatplane to land, a massive glacier fed by distant mountains, and a forest, full of springs, meadows, flowers, animals and even a hot spring for bathing.

Dylan also noted some strange wolf prints: too small for mature adults. If the small wolves were adults, then they might be a sub-species of the gray wolf. He decided to file a report with fish and game. If he had discovered a new wolf, he would be guiding trips to Shaman Mountain all summer.

What a beautiful place to guide trips! Despite the nearly perfect attributes of Shaman Mountain, Dylan felt uneasy about the place. Dylan attributed a vague sense of foreboding to his missing PTSD meds.

Arctic Protocol is available as a paperback or ebook at Amazon.com or other booksellers.

**Special Thanks to our readers who
were instrumental in strengthening
Denali.**

Sharon Hansen, Susan Mace, Anita Bendickson, Roger Hansen, Susan Edmonson, Seamus O'Kirwan, Brent Lossing, Bryan Young, Sig Anderson, Deborah Robillard, Erin Young, Jeff Bloom, Lindsey Hansen, Louise Young, Mary Brandl, Richard Mace, and Sam Zordich